To My Good Friend Irv
Enjoy
William Keats

The Young Millionaire From Breakwater

William C. Keats

D1713248

Tellwell Talent
www.tellwell.ca

ISBN
978-1-77370-569-9 (Hardcover)
978-1-77370-570-5 (Paperback)
978-1-77370-571-2 (eBook)

Dedication

Thanks to my wife Mary for encouraging me
to continue writing, and for her ideas.

Thanks to:

Anne and Michelle for their technical support.

Bert and Marcel for their much-appreciated help.

TABLE OF CONTENTS

CHAPTER 1

A SMALL TOWN IN EASTERN ONTARIO, CANADA, IS WHERE Ben was born. Breakwater, it was called. It was 40 miles west of Ottawa, the nation's capital. Its first name was Waterfalls, because of the lovely ten-foot waterfall in the North-West corner of the town. The name was changed to honour Ben's father, Willie Breakwater. The name was changed on Willie's 59th birthday. He died three days later on the 4th of June 1964, in a car accident.

Ben was an exceptional child. Brilliant mind and a strong body. He was always full of energy and seldom sick. He was seventeen years old when his Dad died. He had been only five years old when he lost his mom, Selina, who lost her battle with cancer at age thirty-six.

All through his childhood Ben spent many hours walking through the forest around Breakwater with his dad. Many nights they spent in the forest and his dad taught him to live off the land and to be truly a part of nature.

Ben's school days were also happy days. He wanted to know everything about everything. One of his teachers, Mr. Robert Pebble, was amazed at many of Ben's questions. Robert spent many hours finding the answers to Ben's questions.

In his last year of high school Ben was bored. He knew more than the teachers and would often take over the class and share with his classmates his knowledge of Mother Nature and the wonderful planet on which we live.

At a very young age, he learned a few facts that amazed him. Like the earth spinning at one thousand miles per hour and at the same time travelling at approximately 67,000 miles per hour in orbit around the sun. Also, our planet was 5 billion years old.

The saddest day of his young life was the day his dad died. He missed him so much. He cried himself to sleep many nights, in spite of what his dad had told him one evening while they were sitting around a campfire. His dad had said, "Everything living will die someday, and we should celebrate the life and not mourn so much the dead". He also said, "However, son, dying ain't on my list of things to do".

Ben planned to live life to the fullest. He wanted to travel and see the world. His dad had told him that very same thing, but unfortunately, he did not have the time or the money to fulfill his dreams.

After finishing high school, Ben took a job in Breakwater at the local hardware store. He wanted to save the money his dad had left him, which was a few thousand dollars. He knew he did not want to stay in Breakwater for too much longer. He planned to sell his house and start travelling.

Ben was to become a lucky young man. He was hiking in the forest one sunny day, a Saturday, when he heard a man moaning in pain. He soon located the man, who had been bitten by a snake. His name was John Dillon. He said he was 59 years old. He was in very bad shape, and knew he didn't have long to live. Ben did all he could to comfort the man and offered to carry him to Breakwater. John refused, and Ben could see the man was near death. Then John began to speak. He said, "Young man, I have no children and no relative that I care much about". He then put his hand in his pocket and handed Ben a key. "Young man", he said, "this is the key to my safety deposit box in my bank in Toronto. The address is on the little tag attached to the key. I have instructed the bank Manager that whomever has that key, has access to the safety deposit box. I had no idea who would end up with that key, young man, but I guess it's your lucky day." He then reached out his shaking hand which Ben held until the man died.

Ben cried for about ten minutes, then, gathered himself so that he could figure out what he would do next. Without thinking, he picked up the deceased man and carried him to the edge of town. He placed the body at the back of the first building he saw. He then went to the police station and told his story. Luck was on Ben's side. The policeman knew John Dillon. He had once been on their Wanted List, many years ago. He had been wrongfully convicted and spent many years in jail. Upon gaining his freedom, he had sued and received a large sum of money. The policeman told Ben to stay in town until the autopsy was completed, and the cause of death was confirmed.

Ben went about his daily work until he was cleared by the police. He then decided to head to Toronto to check out the safety deposit box of which he now had the key. He went by cab to Ottawa and then by bus to Toronto. Again, he took a cab to the address on the key tag. It was a TD Bank on Yonge Street. He walked into the bank. There was no one in the line-up so he walked up to the first wicket and told the lady he wanted to see the manager. He held up the key and said, "Safety deposit box". The lady said, "Have a seat, I will get you the manager". Ben walked to the nearest chair and sat down. The manager, a tall man with gray hair, soon arrived and greeted Ben. "Follow me, young man", he said, and Ben did.

Ben found himself in a chair in the manager's office. He asked Ben his name and where he was from. Ben told him. The bank manager said his name was Malcolm and then said, "I understand you have a key to a safety deposit box in this bank". Ben said he did, and held out the key. Malcolm took the key and noted the small number on it. He then went to a filing cabinet and pulled out a file with the name John Dillon. He opened it and read the note on the first page, and put the file back in the cabinet. Back at his desk, he asked Ben how he obtained the key. Ben told him the story. Ben also told him he could call the police in Breakwater to confirm that John was dead and what caused his death. The bank manager made the call using the phone number Ben had given him. After hanging up the phone, he looked at Ben and said, "My instructions are clear, the person holding the key to John's safety deposit box has access to its holdings. Follow me." In a matter of a few seconds, Ben was holding the box. The bank manager had walked out of the room so that Ben was alone to check the box. Ben looked inside, and could not believe his eyes, Canada Savings Bonds. He counted and as the amount increased, tears rolled down his cheeks. He was now a millionaire - one million dollars in Canada Savings Bonds.

No one knew he had such a large sum of money. Nobody. The only man who knew was dead. This was now a secret. He then remembered what his dad had once said, "If more than one person knows about something, it's no longer a secret". Thoughts kept running through his mind – 'who should I tell, can I keep this a secret? I need someone with whom I can celebrate my good fortune. I can't tell my friends in Breakwater because everyone will want a piece of my pie, and my friends will then become my enemies and I don't want that to happen. Who can I trust?' The answer came in a flash, Mr. Pebble, his best teacher and a very respected man in Breakwater. Robert Pebble would keep his secret.

Ben took a room at a hotel in Toronto that night. Lying on the bed, he had so much to think about. He wanted to travel, further his education, choose a career, get married and raise a family. He had lots of time. He had just turned eighteen the day before he found Mr. Dillon in the forest. Many times, his dad had said, "Planning ahead leads to productivity". He had always planned his activities. Ben thought about his next move. He would go back to Breakwater, celebrate with Mr. Pebble, sell his house, move to Toronto and start a new life.

CHAPTER 2

UPON HIS ARRIVAL BACK IN BREAKWATER, BEN CONTACTED a real estate agent. A sign was on his lawn in just a few days. He did not spend much time at his house the next few weeks. He loaded his camping gear in his old pick-up truck and headed into the forest to some of his favourite camping spots. He would drive by his house every third day to see if his house had been sold. He had instructed the real estate agent to accept the first offer within 5,000 dollars of the asking price.

It was on a Monday afternoon Ben drove by his house and saw the SOLD sign on his lawn. He then drove to the real estate agent's location to see him. His house had sold for the asking price. Ben was happy.

He then drove to the school to see Mr. Pebble, who was very happy to see him. Ben told him about Mr. Dillon and the safety deposit box. Mr. Pebble shook his hand and said, "I am so happy for you, Ben". He then asked Ben to meet him at Bob's Diner at 6 pm that evening and he would buy him the best steak the restaurant had to offer. Ben accepted.

Mr. Pebble was seated at a table in the far corner of the restaurant when Ben arrived at 6 pm. They ordered a steak dinner and a bottle of fine wine. The waiter did not question Ben's age because Mr. Pebble was one of their best customers. Ben had tasted wine only a few times. His Dad had given him a glass of wine on his sixteenth birthday, and two other times to celebrate a good hunt, when they hunted deer.

Again, Mr. Pebble congratulated Ben on his good fortune. They talked about school days and many other things that happened in Breakwater over the years. They talked about the time Ben rode his bicycle across the small pond in early November and the ice could not support him. He found himself in icy water. He would have died if not for two of his school friends who found a long pole on shore and laying on their bellies, pushed the pole out to him. He had been in the water about five minutes before they heard him call for help. The ice could not support his weight and his fingers were going numb. However, he held onto the pole and managed to roll out onto the ice. These two friends had saved his life. Ben walked home, happy to be alive, even though his fingers and toes were numb. It felt like he was walking on sponge. When he arrived home, his Dad had to pour hot water on his boots to thaw the laces. The next day, Ben was back in school as if nothing had happened, minus his bicycle of course! Later, he went back to the pond and saw that his bicycle frozen in the new ice that had formed where he had fallen in. He waited until the ice was safe to walk on, and using an axe, he carefully chopped away the ice and retrieved his bicycle. He has never ridden his bicycle on ice again. He is grateful to his two friends, Tom and Billy, for saving his life. They now live in Toronto, but he did not know where. Oh well, there were more pressing things to discuss now…

Mr. Pebble continued talking about the good ole days when he was a kid. The house they lived in was not insulated, no running water, no indoor toilet, no furnace. The only heat was from a kitchen stove, and no wood was added after everyone went to bed. It would get very cold during those cold winter nights. The water in the steel bucket on the counter would freeze over, and you would have to break the ice in the morning to get a drink of water. Also, they kept pee pots under each bed. In winter, they would be frozen over. Mr. Pebble told Ben that many times he would make holes in the ice in the pee pot when he had to pee. Sometimes, he would compete with his younger brother to see who could make the most holes in the pee pot. They both laughed.

They talked for about two hours. Mr. Pebble asked Ben what his plans were and what he was going to do with his life. Ben then told him that his house had been sold and that he was moving to Toronto. It was then that Ben asked Mr. Pebble to keep his good fortune a secret. Mr. Pebble agreed and said Ben could come visit him anytime he wanted to. He also told Ben he should attend the University of Toronto and get a degree. Ben said he would think about it and thanked him for his advice.

Three days later, on the 10th of August 1964, Ben was in a hotel room in Toronto with all his possessions in the back of his old pick-up truck. He was reading the newspaper he had picked up in the hotel lobby. From the Apartments for Rent section, he wrote down several addresses. Finding an apartment was his next objective.

A week later Ben found a one-bedroom apartment on Dundas Street, west of Yonge Street, in Toronto. He would move in on the first of September.

On one of his outings looking for an apartment, he had passed a Ford dealership. He saw new shining pick-ups all in line. They looked mighty nice and he made a U-turn and pulled into the Ford lot. His truck was ten years old and he knew he would have to spend money on it soon. Why not buy a new one? He had the money. He was living off the interest of his new found million dollars anyway.

On the 21st of August, Ben transferred his possessions from his old truck to a new shiny red Ford. He took the long way home and he felt good driving these new wheels. He was happy. He did not have a care in the world until he noticed an old black pick-up following him. He made a few turns and it seemed like he lost the apparent follower. So he drove on to his hotel, parked his new truck and reached into the glove compartment to retrieve the information booklet on his new Ford. He was planning to take it with him to his room to learn about the features of the truck.

As he stepped down from his truck he heard the sound of screeching brakes and saw that the black pick-up truck had stopped behind him. He could see the driver, who was looking straight ahead. Then a voice behind him said, "I'll take that truck key you're holding young man. I want to take your shiny new truck for a spin." Ben then saw the knife in the man's right hand. He quickly glanced over at the black truck that had stopped behind his and saw that the driver was now looking at him, and he heard the man say, "Let's go Jimmy, take the key and let's go". Ben then slowly stretched out his arm toward the man called Jimmy, as if he was giving him the key to his truck. Jimmy smiled and reached out his left hand to take the key Ben was now offering.

Just before Jimmy's fingers reached the key, Ben dropped the key to the pavement. For a second, Jimmy's eyes followed the key to the pavement and Ben moved swiftly, seized Jimmy's wrist that held the knife and twisted. At the same time, Ben moved his shoulder and with his back now toward Jimmy he suddenly bent forward and threw Jimmy over his head and onto the ground. The knife skidded across the pavement and lay under Ben's truck. Jimmy did not move. Ben then heard the squeal of tires and the pick-up that Jimmy came in now roared off and disappeared out of the parking lot. Ben did not get the license plate number, it all happened so fast. He did, however, notice as the truck sped away, that the tailgate was white, the truck was black.

Jimmy lay still. Ben hoped he had not killed him, but he was not going to let him take his new truck. He had reacted the only way he knew how. His dad had taught him many things. He knew how to fight. He then reached into the back of his truck and retrieved a ten-foot-long piece of rope. He tied Jimmy's hands behind his back and tied the other end to the door handle of his truck. As he turned toward the hotel he heard a moan. He looked back at Jimmy and saw him move. He smiled and walked in the back door of the hotel and to the main lobby, at the front. There he located a pay phone and a phone book. He noted the number for police, slipped in a dime, and dialed the number.

Ben was sitting in his truck when the police arrived. Jimmy could be heard saying, "Fuck, fuck, fuck". Ben laughed out loud so that Jimmy could hear him. Jimmy just kept repeating the same three words.

Two policemen got out of the police car and walked over to Ben's truck. Ben had told the dispatcher he would be waiting in a red truck at the back of the hotel. Jimmy was now silent sitting in the fetal position.

Ben met the two policemen near the back of his truck. He told them what had happened, to the very last detail. One of the policemen walked over to check on Jimmy. When he came back he said, "He seems to be okay, but he won't say anything. We will take him to the hospital and have him checked out." The other policeman told Ben he was very brave to have done what he did. He then asked Ben if he wanted to press charges against Jimmy. Ben said, "I don't know if I want to, all that court stuff and when he gets out he will come after me. I don't want to be looking over my shoulder all the time. Maybe he has learned his lesson."

The police retrieved the knife that was under Ben's truck and placed it in a plastic bag. They took Ben's full name and the address of his apartment he was moving into in September. They then handcuffed Jimmy and placed him in the police car. They told Ben they would be in touch and drove away. Ben noticed another car as it was parking in the hotel lot at the rear. He had not seen anyone else around during his ordeal.

In a hot bath Ben did some thinking and planning. Toronto was a much different place than Breakwater. He would have to be on his toes and learn to be street wise, quickly. He had always loved a challenge and to survive and thrive in a big city would be a challenge. He planned to succeed at it.

The hotel phone rang as he walked out of the bathroom. The police had called him as they said they would. He was asked to come to the police station the next morning.

Ten-thirty the next morning Ben walked into the police building on Eglinton Avenue in Toronto. At ten-forty-five Ben was in the office of Sergeant Downing, who read the police report on the attempted armed robbery of Ben's truck. Ben confirmed that the report was accurate. Sergeant Downing asked Ben to please change his mind and press charges against Mr. Jimmy Falls. He told Ben that Jimmy should do time and it would make the streets of Toronto safer. He then told Ben that Jimmy's finger prints were found on the knife picked up at the scene. He said he was 99% sure he would plead guilty. Ben agreed to press charges. Jimmy pled guilty at his trial and was sentenced to six months in jail and one-year probation.

Tomorrow he would purchase furniture for his apartment. Joining a fitness club was also a priority. He was now six feet tall and weighed 200 pounds. He was naturally muscular like his dad. He had handled Jimmy easily, who was tall and skinny and only about one hundred and fifty pounds. If he had been two hundred or more, could he have taken him out? Here in Toronto he knew he could find people who could help him become whatever he wanted to become.

Three days later Ben joined a fitness club that was only a five-minute walk from his apartment. A man named Leon would be his trainer. Leon was very fit and could bench press four hundred pounds. Ben would set his goal at four hundred. Two twenty-five was his best, so far. He had a lot of work to do.

On the first of September Ben was in his apartment. His furniture arrived in the afternoon. After everything was in place, he made his bed and decided to go out for dinner. He would pick up groceries on the way home.

After dinner, Ben picked up groceries at the Dominion store on Dundas Street. At that time, it was not very busy.

There was only one person ahead of him at cash number five. The young lady checking groceries at number five was very friendly and Ben could not keep his eyes off her. She was absolutely beautiful. The name Anna was on her name tag. They made small talk and Ben left the store. Sitting in his truck, Anna was on his mind and he was still visualizing her. He had feelings that he had never felt before. He reached down and pulled the key from the ignition and walked back into the store. He picked up a couple of items and slowly walked to cash number five. It was closed. He looked around, but could not see Anna. He felt sad and a little foolish. He paid for the items at number four and left the store. Back in his truck he just sat there and contemplated the situation. He did not look to see if Anna had a ring on her left hand. There was a good chance she had a boyfriend. He would check her hand for a ring the next time he saw her. If there was no ring, he would think of a good line to find out if she had a boyfriend. He started the engine and headed home.

CHAPTER 3

ANNA SHARED AN APARTMENT WITH HER CLOSE FRIEND CORA. Anna arrived home to find Cora reading, as she often did. She took a quick shower and joined Cora on the sofa. It had been Cora's day off.

Cora asked Anna how her day went. Anna answered, "Fine, same ole, same ole". Cora also worked at the same store as Anna. Cora then said, "All I see coming through the line are middle age people or older. I wish some good looking young men would get in the line-up sometime."

"Well", said Anna, "you should have been on number five cash today".

"Why", said Cora, "what happened?"

Anna said, "I was about to put the CASH CLOSED sign up when a handsome young man came along with a cart full of groceries. He was very polite, but I caught him looking at me a couple of times. He noticed my name tag because he called me by my name. When I had all his groceries checked I put up the CASH CLOSED sign. He sure took his time putting his bags in his cart, and he looked good walking away. He sure was handsome."

"You lucky girl", said Cora. "Tell me more. Was he tall?"

"Yes, he was", said Anna. "He must have been six feet tall, and he looked like an athlete. I sure hope he comes back for more groceries sometime. Then again, I may never see him again."

"Think positive," said Cora. "It seems he took great interest in you. He will be back. However, if he comes to my cash I might just slip him our phone number and may the best girl win." Cora laughed and said, "Just kidding, but I would give him our phone number. He would be confused when you answer."

Anna laughed. "That would be fun", she said. "You sure are fast on your feet. I guess you are the rabbit and I am the turtle." They both laughed.

After putting his groceries away, Ben decided to do a load of laundry. However, even though he had made a list before going to the grocery store, he had not added laundry soap. He had not planned to go back to the grocery store so soon, but he had to get laundry soap. Tomorrow he would pick up soap and maybe see Anna. He could not get her off his mind.

At three the next afternoon Ben walked into the Dominion grocery store. He quickly surveyed each cash line-up. Anna was at number three. He picked up a box of laundry detergent and proceeded to number three. The lady in front of him had a mountain of groceries. This made Ben happy. He would have lots of time to observe Anna. And he did so with great pleasure. He tried not to be vividly conspicuous, but it was hard. She was stunning. When their eyes met he just said, "Hi Anna, how are you?"

"Fine," she said, "back so soon".

"Yes," said Ben, "I forgot to pick-up laundry detergent." He then noticed there was no ring on her left hand. He also noticed the elderly gentleman next in line was in no hurry and was talking to the man behind him. Ben leaned over and said, "Anna, I would love to talk to you on your break. Just tell me when and I will meet you outside the entrance door."

Anna thought for a second and said, "Okay, four o'clock. That's about half an hour from now. But I won't have much time because I am meeting a friend on my break."

"See you outside at four", said Ben. He smiled, thanked her and left.

Ben sat in his truck and thought of his best approach. He did not want to come on too strong. He started to day-dream. He had been alone since his Dad died. How nice it would be if Anna was to be his friend or girlfriend. He could accept whatever her decision would be. He would show her that he was mature for his age and would show her respect above all else.

Ben glanced at his watch, three fifty-five. He stepped out of his truck and proceeded to the front door of the grocery store. People were going and coming. He stood to one side and waited. Glancing at his watch – four minutes after four. Thinking to himself – she is making me wait, maybe she won't show, could be lots of reasons she was a little late… Then there she was standing and smiling right beside him.

"Sorry I am a bit late", Anna said. "Usually I am very punctual."

"Don't be sorry," Ben said. "Waiting to see you has been a pleasure. My name is Ben – Ben Breakwater. I am new in town. I really don't know anybody around here except my personal trainer at the fitness club I joined. I don't want to take up much of your break. I just wanted to ask if you would like to go out for dinner sometime. I could meet you at the restaurant of your choosing. Here is my telephone number. I will be looking forward to your call. Thanks again for meeting me."

Anna took the piece of paper. She looked Ben in the eye and said, "You seem like a very nice guy and I will consider your offer."

Ben said, "That's all I am asking. Hope to see you soon. Bye for now."

Anna stood there and watched Ben walk away. She saw him get into a shiny red pick-up, it looked new. He drove away. She opened the piece of paper Ben had given her. It read – *Thanks again, you won't regret calling me, Ben.*

She folded the paper and headed for the lunch room in the back of the store. Cora would be waiting for her. Anna entered the lunch room with a smile on her face. Cora said, "He asked you out, am I right?"

"Yes," said Anna. "He wants to take me out for dinner."

"Did you say yes?" asked Cora.

"No," said Anna. "He gave me his phone number and I told him I would consider his offer. I don't want him to think I am starving for affection or that I am quick to accept a date."

"Don't wait too long," said Cora. "I would have said yes on the spot, if he is as good-looking as you say he is."

"Well," said Anna, "we are different. You have more experience than I do. I take things slow."

"That's okay, Anna," said Cora. "He will respect you if you go slow."

Anna looked at the big clock on the wall. It was time to go back to work.

Seven P.M. on Thursday evening Ben's phone rang. Ben thought it could be but two people - Leon or Anna. He hoped it was Anna.

Ben said, "Hello."

A female voice said, "Hi Ben, this is Anna. I have decided to accept your offer to take me out for dinner. I am free tomorrow evening."

"Tomorrow evening is fine," said Ben. "Where?"

Anna said, "How about the quaint little Italian place at the corner of Dundas and Dufferin Streets. Six thirty okay?"

"Six thirty it is," said Ben. "See you there."

"See you there," said Anna, and she hung up the phone.

Ben was very happy. His first date in the big city. He had only a few dates in his whole life, and none that he cared to remember. He hoped this one would be different.

Anna would be the most beautiful girl he had ever dated. Ben thought she was about five-foot seven, brunette, with lovely complexion and dark eyes. He hoped she was not over twenty and therefore think he was too young at eighteen. Other thoughts crossed his mind – was she dating other men, would he tell her he was rich? No, he could not. Only if they fell in love, would he tell her.

For the next couple of days Ben tried to stay busy. He spent extra time at the fitness club. He went for walks and read. He was fascinated by the events of the American Civil War 1861 – 1865. A war between the Union States and the Confederate States of the South. More than 600,000 lives were lost. Slavery was abolished in 1863, two years before the war ended. In school he had read about the Spanish Civil War – a war in which a million (1,000,000) lives were lost. Ben often thought there had to be a better way to solve differences than people in the same country killing each other. It made him sad.

Friday afternoon, Ben was a happy young man. At six twenty-five he entered the little Italian restaurant. He sat on a chair just inside the door and waited for Anna. He was hoping she would show up. This would be his first real date.

Sharp at six thirty Anna walked in. She smiled upon seeing Ben. He arose quickly and greeted her.

Seated at a table, Ben once again thanked her for accepting his offer to dinner. Anna replied that she was happy that she did. They reminisced about how they met and that relaxed them. The waitress took their order and a much-anticipated conversation began.

Anna simply said, "Tell me about Ben Breakwater. Who is this young man who has asked me to dine with him?"

Ben told her his life story up to meeting her at the grocery store. However, he did not tell her about Mr. John Dillon and the safety deposit box. Ben then said, "Tell me about Anna."

Anna was two years older than Ben. She was born and educated in Toronto. Her parents had moved to Hamilton and she was sharing an apartment with a girlfriend. She was working at the grocery store to help pay for a dental assistant course even though her parents would pay for most of it. She had an older brother, Bobby, who lived in Vancouver, B.C.

Ben then asked her if she was dating anyone at present. She said she was not. She had dumped her last boyfriend about a month ago. It had not been a serious relationship. She also told Ben that she had never been in love but was hoping to, some day. Right now, she was looking forward to the dental assistant course and then getting a decent paying job. She was hoping her '57 Chevy would last a few more years. Her parents had given it to her on her sixteenth birthday, as they had bought a new one.

Ben was impressed, and he told her so. They talked about the activities they liked to do. They had some common ground. They both liked camping, swimming and cross-country skiing, as well as, cycling. For a first date, they had covered a lot more than usual. Ben asked her if she would like to go to a movie sometime. Anna answered she would and she would call him.

They left the restaurant. Outside, Ben leaned over and kissed Anna on the cheek. Anna said, "Thank you for a lovely evening." Ben replied, "See you later beautiful one." They parted.

The next day, Saturday, Ben decided to do some shopping. He needed new clothes. If he was going to continue to date Anna he wanted to look good. He spent nearly three-hundred dollars in clothes, including a leather jacket. He always wanted a leather jacket.

Sunday evening, he decided to go to a movie. He located a theatre on Yonge Street. *Doctor Zhivago* was playing. He parked his truck at the far end of the parking lot. He backed it in near the bushes. He always tried to park his truck where at least one side would not get hit by other car doors opening and hitting the side of his truck.

Ben enjoyed the movie. It was the longest movie he had ever seen. As he walked through the parking lot to his truck, he noticed the parking lot was not very well lit. Another truck, much bigger than his, was parked beside his truck. He unlocked the driver's side door and was about to step up into his truck when a voice said, "Don't step up, don't turn around, just remove that nice leather jacket, nice and slow. Do what I say and you won't have to bleed."

Ben was thinking – was he bluffing, did he really have a knife? He began to shuck his new leather jacket – the first time he had worn it. He didn't think that this low-life had a gun, or he would have said so. His truck door was still open. Just inside the door Ben had placed a baseball bat, just in case he needed a weapon to defend himself. He wasn't sure how far away the man was. He thought he was rather close. Ben was now holding his jacket in his right hand, holding it by the collar. He turned slightly to the right and extended his right arm. He then said, "Go ahead, take it. I have another one anyway. It's all yours."

The jacket was now hiding his left arm, as he was now holding the jacket at eye level. He reached in and grasped the baseball bat with his left hand. Quickly, he turned his head and at the same time pitched the jacket at the man's face. The man did not see the baseball bat, but he sure as hell felt it as Ben brought it down upon the hand holding a knife. He looked at the man who was now crying and on his knees. Ben could not really see his face. He stepped forward to pick-up his jacket and the man looked up and Ben saw his face.

"Tommy Seal, is that really you?" said Ben. "What the hell are you doing?" Tommy had helped save Ben's life when he had fallen through the ice.

"Ben," said Tommy, through his sobs. "Ben, I didn't know it was you. I am so sorry. I'm so messed up, Ben. I should have stayed in Breakwater."

"What's going on here?" said a voice. It was the driver of the truck parked beside Ben.

"It's okay," said Ben. "My friend has been hurt. I am going to take him to the hospital." The man drove away.

THE YOUNG MILLIONAIRE FROM BREAKWATER

"Tommy," said Ben, "what has happened to you? You were a good kid. You helped save my life when I fell through the ice back in Breakwater, you and Billy."

"I wish now I had stayed in Breakwater", said Tommy. "Billy and I decided to come here because there was no excitement in Breakwater. We lived on the street and got into drugs. We became thieves. I guess I'm the lucky one. Billy got stabbed and died a few months ago."

"Well," said Ben, "I wouldn't say you are lucky. You are a drug addict and you need help. Get in the truck, I am taking you to the hospital."

Tommy gave Ben directions to the hospital. Ben told him to get help, and if he became drug-free they could become friends again. Ben gave him his phone number and asked Tommy to call him when he got his life in order.

Tommy promised him he would seek help and would call him. Ben dropped Tommy at the hospital and went back to his apartment. He felt sorry for Tommy. He had hoped to meet him again under much different circumstances than they had met tonight. The same thought would have applied to Billy. They had both crossed his mind many times since he had arrived in Toronto. Upon meeting them, he had planned to tell them a rich uncle living in the United States had died and left him money. He would share the money with them for saving his life. Now, that had all changed. Billy was dead, and Tommy was a drug addict. Money was the last thing Ben would be giving him.

CHAPTER 4

BEN ATTENDED THE FITNESS CLUB FIVE DAYS A WEEK. HE
was now seeing Anna three times a week. They went
out for dinner, went to movies, or watched T.V. in each
other's apartment.

Anna had been really impressed when she first saw Ben's
apartment. She knew expensive furniture when she saw it. The
clothes he wore, a new truck, taking her out so often, it made
her wonder where he got the money to do this. She knew he
had sold his house in Breakwater, but he didn't say for how
much. She also knew he was not working. She planned to
choose an optimum time tell him about her concern and to ask
him how he could spend so much money and not have a job.

It was a Saturday night and they were watching T.V. at
Anna's apartment. The show they were watching ended. Ben
suggested they turn off the T.V. and talk. They sat facing each
other on the sofa. Ben held both of Anna's hands and said,
"I think I am falling in love with you, Anna." Tears ran down
her cheeks. She leaned toward Ben and kissed him. She then

said, "You know I think the world of you Ben Breakwater. You may be stuck with me for the rest of your life." Ben replied, "What more could I wish for." They kissed and hugged, then lay in each other's arms on the sofa. Anna felt secure and very happy in Ben's arms. Then the money thing crossed her mind. "Ben," she said, "I have to ask you a question." "Shoot," said Ben. Anna said, "Ben, I've been thinking about all the money you have been spending since you came to Toronto. It's probably none of my business, but I am curious."

"Well," said Ben, "as you know, I sold my house in Breakwater. That would account for some of money, but there is more. I did not want to tell you yet, because I thought it may have influenced your feelings toward me."

Anna interrupted and said, "Ben, I hope you are not involved in some nefarious activity."

"No," said Ben, "nothing like that." He then kissed her and said, "Anna, you are falling in love with a millionaire."

Anna gasped. "You are not kidding me, are you?" asked Anna.

"You are eighteen years old and you are a millionaire. How did that happen? Don't tell me a rich uncle," said Anna.

Ben laughed. "No," he said, "not a rich uncle." He then told Anna about his good fortune of finding John Dillon, and the amazing inheritance that made him a millionaire.

Anna was speechless, and that didn't happen very often. Finally, she said, "How lucky can one be? You meet a stranger and he makes you rich."

"Yes," said Ben, "I became a rich teenager, then I met a beautiful young woman named Anna, and I became a very happy, rich teenager."

Once again, tears ran down Anna's cheeks. She held Ben close as she thought about the events that led to her meeting Ben. For a while she had second thoughts about meeting him. It was Cora who convinced her to go and meet him. She had said, "What do you have to lose?" Anna had said, "My virginity, that's what." They both laughed. Cora said, "Yes, and it's about time, virginity is overrated anyway." More laughter.

Anna wiped away her tears of joy. "Pinch me, Ben, so that I know I am not dreaming," said Anna. Ben pinched her nose and said, "Wake up, Anna, it's time for me to go home." Anna punched him lightly, then, kissed him. A few minutes later he was gone.

Anna lay there on the sofa and her mind was racing. What did the future hold for her? If she married Ben she could have just about anything she wanted. Would she work? What would she do all day? Did she want kids? Maybe two, but not more. Maybe Ben would buy her that sports car she wanted since she was sixteen. Maybe they could live in Niagara Falls. She loved to watch the falls. She had been there five times. Ben was so young, although he acted much older than his age. She really believed he cared for her deeply. He treated her with great respect. He was not your ordinary eighteen-year-old guy. The few she had dated always tried to get into her panties. Ben had not. Soon she would tell him she was a virgin, maybe on their next date.

The first time Ben came to her apartment, Anna had introduced him to Cora. Later that evening, when Cora came home, Anna asked her what she thought of Ben. Cora said, "He is a real hunk, Anna, and if he were my boyfriend, my panties would sure look good on his bedroom floor."

Anna just said, "Cora, you are just too much."

Cora said, "Life is short, Anna, I live each day like I don't have many left. However, as long as one is happy, it really doesn't matter."

"I guess you are right," said Anna.

It was Friday evening. Ben cooked one of his favourite meals – spaghetti and a thick meat sauce and garlic bread. Anna arrived as planned at six-thirty. She loved Ben's spacious apartment. She noticed he had done a good job in hanging the pictures and paintings she had helped him choose. She told him so.

Ben said, "Thank you. A lovely lady who lives down the hall helped me hang them."

"Are you kidding me, Ben Breakwater? You better be," said Anna.

"Just kidding," said Ben, "but it was worth it to see the look on your face."

Anna chased him around the dinner table, but she could not catch him. They laughed, hugged and kissed, then ate dinner. She complimented Ben on his cooking, and told him it was the best spaghetti dinner she had ever eaten.

Ben said, "My dad taught me. This was one of his favourite meals."

After dinner, the dishes done, they each slipped into the bathroom to freshen-up and slip into night clothes. Anna had told him she was going to sleep over.

There was no space between them as they lay on the large leather sofa. They kissed, talked, tickled each other and laughed.

Ben placed his hand on Anna's leg and slowly moved it up her inner thigh. Anna reached down and held his hand. She then began to cry. She wept uncontrollably. She held his hand and would not let go.

Ben started to apologize, and Anna just shook her head, still holding his hand against her leg.

"No, Ben," she said, and when she stopped crying. "It's, not you, it's me. Please listen to me, Ben. I have something to tell you that I have never told anyone, not even my mother or father. Let us sit facing each other and hold hands like we do many times." And they did.

"I was eleven years old. It was New Year's Eve. My mom and dad went out to celebrate. My uncle George came to babysit me. He is my mom's brother. He let me stay up until around ten, then, I went to bed. He tucked me in, kissed my forehead and said, 'Sleep tight, sweet little girl.' He turned out the light and closed my bedroom door. I was tired and fell into a deep sleep."

"I woke up. Something was touching me. It was in my panties. I reached down and felt a hand. I screamed. It was dark and I could not see anything. Then the hand was gone. The light came on and Uncle George was standing there, by the door.

" He said, 'What is wrong, Anna? Are you having a nightmare? I heard you screaming.'"

"I was confused for a few seconds. Then, I realized what had happened. I really did feel a hand in my panties. It had to be Uncle George's hand."

"I sat up in my bed. I said, 'Don't you come near me. You are a bad man.' I remember I was mad. I was screaming at him. 'You touched me, and you are in trouble when I tell my mom and dad.' "

"He spoke softly. 'No Anna, you will not tell your mom or dad. Listen to me very carefully. If you tell your dad, he will kill me and then he will go to jail and you won't see him ever again. If you tell your mom, she won't believe you. If she does believe you, she will tell your dad, and as I said, he will go to jail. So you see, Anna, it will be much better for you if you keep it a secret. No one will get hurt. You don't have to worry about me cause I am going away and you will never see me again. You will keep it a secret, right Anna? You know it will be your fault if your dad goes to jail.' He closed the door and he was gone. I jumped out of my bed and locked my bedroom door. I left the light on and lay on my bed. I thought about what Uncle George said. He didn't hurt me, and I made up my mind right then. I had to keep it a secret. I did not want my dad to go to jail."

Ben just shook his head.

Anna continued, "I've kept it a secret for nine years, Ben. No one has ever touched me, I am still a virgin."

They hugged each other and they both cried. Ben was much like his mother. She was a very emotional person. His dad had told him, "If your mother saw someone crying, she would cry as well."

After wiping away each other's tears, Ben said, "I love you Anna, nothing will ever change that. I will do all I can to help you. I hope you agree with me that you need professional help to deal with the fact that you were violated by your uncle."

"Yes," said Anna, "you are right."

"Just remember Anna, you were an innocent child, you did nothing wrong," said Ben.

Anna's eyes filled with tears once more.

"I have the money," said Ben. "I would be happy to pay for all the help you need."

"Thank you," said Anna. "I will pay you back, but you may have to wait a while."

"You don't need to pay me back," said Ben, "remember, I am a millionaire, end of story."

"It's time for bed," said Ben. "I will tuck you in, in my bed and I will sleep on the sofa."

"No," said Anna, "we will both sleep in your bed. I have never been held 'til I fell asleep since I was a baby."

"If that is what you want, that is what we will do," said Ben.

The next day, they looked through the yellow pages of the phone book. Anna chose a lady psychiatrist whose name was Lynn Miller. The office was closed. Anna said she would call Monday morning before she went to work. She left Ben's place before noon because she wanted to clean her apartment and do laundry.

After Anna left, Ben decided to go for a walk. He liked to walk when he had to do some thinking. Anna's Uncle George was on his mind. Anna did not mention his last name or where he lived. He planned to find out when he saw Anna again. As he walked he considered the situation. When he located George, what would he do? He felt he had to do something. First things first – he would hire a detective to find George, a private detective.

When he arrived back at his apartment, he was back into the Yellow Pages of the phone book. As Anna did, he just chose a name – Joseph Blackmore, Private Detective.

Ben made himself a sandwich and a cup of tea. It was one thirty when he called Joseph's office number. Three rings and a voice answered. "J. Blackmore, how can I help you?"

Ben said, "My name is Ben Breakwater. I would like to talk to you in person. Could we meet next week? I got your phone number in the Yellow Pages."

"Yes, I think we could do that," came the answer. "I am out of town until Thursday. Let's make it two PM on Thursday, in my office."

"Fine," said Ben. He then repeated the address to make sure it was correct.

"Yes," said Joseph, "that is correct, see you on Thursday, Ben."

Ben hung up the phone. "That was easy," he said.

Then his phone rang, it was Anna. She asked Ben if he wanted to come for dinner. Cora was bringing home chicken from Scott's Chicken Villa. She told Ben he could come anytime and that Cora would be home at six. Ben accepted the invitation and said he would be there at five. He then sat on the sofa, he had some thinking to do. He had to find out from Anna where her Uncle George was living, what city or town. Also, what his last name was. He knew Anna's mother's name was now Wood, but what was her maiden name. George was her brother. He did not want to arouse any suspicion that he was trying to locate George. He now planned his approach.

At five he arrived at Anna's place. They sat and talked. Ben asked her how her mom and dad were. Anna said they were fine. He then asked her where her parents were from, and where were they born. Anna replied that they were born in Ottawa, met each other in Ottawa and had moved to Toronto. Ben told her that he had relatives in Ottawa. "What was your mother's maiden name?" asked Ben.

"It was Jacobs", said Anna.

"I don't recall my dad mentioning that name," said Ben. "Anna," said Ben, "did your Uncle George really go away?"

"Yes, he did," said Anna, "he is living in Halifax, Nova Scotia. My mom said he works on the docks. I wish he would fall into the water and drown."

"I hope your wish comes true," said Ben.

The chicken was delicious. Ben had never tasted chicken like that before. Cora told him where Scott's Chicken Villa was located. Ben said he planned to be a frequent customer.

Anna said, "Maybe too much of this chicken may not be good for you Ben. You may have to go to the Fitness Club twice a day, or your clothes may not fit you."

All three of them laughed.

Ben chatted with them for a while, thanked Cora for the chicken, kissed Anna and went home.

On the way home, he repeated a few times – George Jacobs, Halifax docks. It would be a long wait 'til Thursday.

After parking his truck, Ben just sat there, and stared out the windshield. His mind started to work overtime. He now knew where George Jacobs lived and worked – why not just go to Halifax and find him – why bother to hire a private investigator. But after more serious thought, he decided a private investigator was required. It was not a wise idea for him to be seen around the Halifax docks. He did not want anyone to know he was in Halifax, period.

CHAPTER 5

THE CLOCK SEEMED TO SLOW DOWN, FOR BEN. FINALLY, Thursday came. Two PM found Ben in a large leather chair in Joseph Blackmore's office.

"What can I do for you, young man?" said Joseph.

"Well sir," said Ben, I need to know the address of a man who lives in Halifax, Nova Scotia. The man's name is George Jacobs and he works on the docks in Halifax." Joseph wrote down the information.

"What other info can you tell me about George?" said Joseph.

"Nothing, sir, except he is around fifty years old," said Ben.

"Why do you want to locate this man?" said Joseph.

"I am doing this as a favour for a friend of my dad. George and my dad's friend were in business in Ottawa. George ripped him off, took the money and ran. My dad's friend had to declare bankruptcy. He is broke. My dad died and left me some money, so I told my dad's friend I would find out where George went. He can take it from there."

"I see," said Joseph.

"What would you charge to find George's address?" asked Ben.

"I charge twenty-five dollars an hour, plus expenses," said Joseph. "I am good at what I do, and George will never know I obtained his address."

"Then you will take the job?" asked Ben.

"Yes, young man, I will take the job. However, I require expense money up-front." (Ben, being a smart young man, had brought cash with him.)

"How much?" asked Ben.

"Three hundred should do it," said Joseph.

Ben pulled out his wallet and placed fifteen twenty-dollar bills on the desk. "A receipt, please," said Ben.

"Of course," said Joseph. He wrote out the receipt. "One more thing," said Joseph, "your phone number, I will call you as soon as I arrive back in town."

Ben gave him his phone number. They shook hands and Ben left.

Back at his apartment, Ben had a couple of hours to kill before Anna would arrive. He was making fish cakes for dinner. He hoped she would like his fish cakes as much as she liked the spaghetti dinner he had made.

He was a very happy young man when Anna came to his place. He also realized his life had become a little more complicated since the day he went shopping and met Anna. However, he would never regret having her in his life, no matter the outcome.

He was flipping the fish cakes when Anna knocked on his door. After a hug and a kiss, she said, "Sure smells good".

"Well, I hope they will taste as good as they smell," said Ben.

"I am sure they will," said Anna.

After dinner, they sat and watched T.V. It was only a half hour program, and when it finished, Ben asked Anna if she would like to talk about her appointments with Lynn Miller – the psychiatrist. He knew she had gone to see her twice.

Anna said they were going fine. Lynn had told her the same thing that Ben had. That she was an innocent girl at eleven years old, and she had done nothing wrong. What had happened was not her fault. Lynn said she could help her as she had helped others.

Anna thanked Ben for his suggestion for her to seek help. She was quite confident that Lynn could help her deal with her memories.

Ben was pleased, and reassured her that everything would work out fine.

They watched T.V. for an hour or so and Anna went home.

Ben took a shower, went to bed and read.

Sunday afternoon, Joseph Blackmore, private investigator, arrived in Halifax, Nova Scotia. He took a cab to a hotel near the Halifax docks.

Monday morning, he went to the hotel restaurant and had breakfast. Nine A.M. he was back in his room. He undressed and opened up his suitcase. From the suitcase he took out a plaid shirt, it was dirty and full of holes. He put it on. Next, he took out a pair of trousers that were in the same condition as the shirt and he put them on. For a belt, he used a piece of rope, tied at the front. Then he reached into the suitcase and took out a pair of boots that looked like they had been through a war. He put them on. Next out, a jacket, well-worn and dirty, one sleeve was torn, threads hanging down. Last was a New York Yankee's baseball cap. It was old enough to have been used by Babe Ruth. He slipped it on his head. All dressed up, he went to the bathroom and looked in the mirror. "Perfect," he said. With the hotel key in his pocket, he slipped out the back door. He headed for the dockyard. With a seven-day growth and his shabby clothes, who would guess that he was a private investigator.

Upon reaching the dock area, he walked very slowly. There on a bench seat near one of the wharves sat a man whose appearance was much like his own. He thought, my lucky day. When the man saw him, Joseph gave him a wave. He walked slowly toward him.

Joseph said, "Hi there."

The man nodded his head.

As Joseph got near him, the man said, "Haven't seen you here before."

"No, I..."

"Never mind, stranger, have a seat," he said. "I could use some company."

"Thank you," said Joseph. "Whom do I have the pleasure of sharing this bench with?"

"Joe's the name," said the man.

"My name is Rob," said Joseph. "Kind-a quiet around here this morning."

"Oh," said Joe, "that won't last long. These cargo ships out there will be here soon, lots of goings on then."

Joseph nodded his head. "You live around here, Joe?" said Joseph.

"Only in the summer time," said Joe. "The Boss man, Jimmy, lets me sleep in that little shack over yonder."

"Well," said Joseph, "that's very nice of him."

"Yes," said Joe, "it is. However, when Jimmy is away, George is the boss and he is a prick. He says if he was the Big Boss he would take my key, and I wouldn't get to sleep in the shack. He is a son-of-a-b."

"Sounds like it, Joe," said Joseph. (George, the name was music to his ears. Could he be George Jacobs?) "I think I'll stay away from him."

"Yea, he's a mean one alright," said Joe.

"How would I know him if I saw him?" asked Joseph.

"Oh, he's just a little man with a big mouth," said Joe. "You can't miss him. He wears a straw hat on sunny days and rides here on an old bicycle. Guess he lives rather close to the docks here."

"I'll make sure I stay out of his way for sure," said Joseph. "I guess he's not working today."

"He's here alright. They all takin' a break," said Joe.

Joseph stood up and thanked Joe for his hospitality and said he was going to find something to eat. Joe just raised his right hand and said, "See you around".

Joseph let himself in the back door of the hotel. Back in his room, he shed his hobo clothes, then, to the bathroom for a shave. Back into his suitcase for some average clothes – slacks, shirt and a jacket. He would wear the shoes he wore when he arrived.

This time he went out the front door and headed back to the Halifax dockyard.

As he approached the area where Joe had been sitting, two other men (they looked like dock workers) were occupying the bench. They looked like they were quite relaxed with their legs stretched out and they were chatting and laughing.

Joseph walked straight toward them. "Hello gentlemen," he said. "I am looking for work. I was told to ask for George or Jimmy. I don't know their last names."

"It's Jimmy Conners, he is the real boss, and George Jacobs, he thinks he's the boss," said the man nearest Joseph.

The other man laughed and said, "Jimmy won't be here til about one P.M. George is out on the dock there (pointing), supervising the unloading of that freighter. He is the little man wearing the white hard hat. Our little Napoleon. He's always uptight cause he never gets laid."

They both laughed.

"Thank you, gentlemen," said Joseph. "I'll be on my way."

He was in no hurry. He was paid by the hour and it looked like this was one of his easiest jobs. He slowly walked toward the little man in the white hat. Everything seemed to be going smoothly, very little conversation taking place. As Joseph got closer, George saw him and said, "Stop right there, this area is out of bounds. Only workers with hard hats are allowed here."

Joseph stopped. Then he said, "I was told you were the boss man here, George Jacobs I was told. I am looking for work. Are you hiring any time soon?"

"You were told correctly," said George, "but no, we are not hiring at the moment. We may next week, I don't know. We do have a turn-over of men here. Some men don't want to do much and get paid as if they worked hard. They don't last around here. Move along now, come back next week."

Joseph turned and quickened his pace. He passed the bench where the two men had been sitting, and soon he was on the street to his hotel. As he walked along the sidewalk he thought about the morning's activities: He had met George Jacobs, and knew he wore a straw hat on sunny days while he rode a bicycle to work. How could he miss?

Lunch at the hotel restaurant was next. After lunch he went to the hotel lobby and called a cab on the direct line.

He asked the cab driver to take him to the nearest bicycle shop. Twenty minutes later he was cycling back to his hotel. He parked it in the back and locked it to a post.

Back in his room, he relaxed on the bed for a few minutes. His day's work was not completed. Time to change back into his hobo clothes. Once again, out the back door, unlocked the bicycle and rode down to the dockyard. It was now two fifty in the afternoon. He did not know when George would get off work. Surely, he would not finish work before three. He selected a tree, a large tree near the main road leading to the dockyard, and parked himself underneath it. He was prepared to wait until seven in the evening, but hoped he would not have to wait that long.

He had chosen a very good spot underneath the big tree. There were some low-lying bushes in front of him but he could easily see over them. He felt he was rather inconspicuous. Lady luck was on his side, it was a nice sunny day. He doubted George would be riding his bicycle in the rain.

He glanced at his watch every ten minutes or so. It seemed as though time had slowed, the second hand on his watch was moving slower. Then he remembered a line he once heard – waiting for a bus, ten minutes feels like twenty.

Joseph kept his eyes on the main road leading from the dockyard. A few vehicles went in and a few came out. Three P.M. – no sign of a man on a bicycle. Four P.M. – no bicycle. The last time he checked his watch was four fifty-five. He watched as three large trucks drove by rather slowly. They were obscuring his view of the dockyard road. After they passed by, he just happened to look left. The first thing he saw was a straw hat. He immediately stood up – a man on a bicycle wearing a straw hat – George...

Joseph quickly pushed his bicycle out onto the street and ran across the street pushing the bicycle. He then mounted the seat and pedalled hard. He had to keep George in his sight. He was two hundred yards behind him, but he was gaining.

A black and white pick-up truck passed him. He was now about fifty yards behind George. He smiled as he pedalled. His smile quickly turned to a frown. The pick-up truck stopped near George. The driver got out and helped George put his bicycle in the truck bed. They hopped into the cab and drove away.

Joseph stopped pedalling and alighted from the bicycle seat. He just stood there for a moment. Then he said, "Son-of-a-bitch, close but no cigar, but failure is not an option. Tomorrow is another day."

Back at the hotel he changed his clothes once again. He watched the news and weather. He was happy to learn tomorrow would be mainly sunny with a few clouds. A good day to ride a bicycle.

After supper he watched T.V., then, he read. There was no reason to get up early. His work would not start until two-thirty P.M. He called his wife in Toronto, read until midnight and turned out the bedside lamp.

Joseph often dreamed about his work. His snooping around was sometimes dangerous. In some of his dreams he had been shot at. Tonight's dream would be a little different, not dangerous for him, but very tragic.

In his dream, he was back under the tree waiting for George to appear. The weatherman had been right, sunny with cloudy periods. As he had done the afternoon before, he checked his watch periodically. He reached into his jacket pocket for his little canteen of water. He took a drink, then, as he looked across the street, there was George wearing a straw hat and riding his bicycle. He turned right as he had done yesterday. Again, as he had done before, he hurried across the street. George was now about the correct distance ahead of him. Suddenly, a loud crashing sound. A vehicle flipped over and hit George's bicycle. Joseph watched as George was thrown up in the air and landed on the sidewalk. He walked toward the scene of the accident. Many vehicles were now stopped near the scene. People started to gather. Joseph was now only twenty feet from where George lay. A man was kneeling beside him checking for a pulse. There was blood on the sidewalk. Joseph heard the man say, "I am a medical doctor. This man is dead, his skull has a major fracture."

Joseph woke and shook his head. He heard himself say, "George is dead." He sat up and rubbed his eyes, then realized he had been dreaming. He turned on the bedside lamp, went to the washroom for a glass of water. He checked his watch – four a.m. He turned out the light and hoped if he were to dream again it would be a pleasant one.

He slept 'til ten a.m. and decided to skip breakfast. He ate lunch at twelve noon and went for a walk to stretch his legs. At two-forty-five he was riding the rented bicycle, dressed in his hobo clothes once again. Ten minutes later he was sitting under the same tree as he did yesterday. He repeated the activities of yesterday, waiting and watching. Clouds kept obscuring the sun from time to time. Today the wait would be shorter.

Just after four p.m. George made that right turn as he had done yesterday. Joseph once again followed him. George turned left on the first street, then, right on the next street. Joseph followed. After about five minutes George turned right into a driveway. Joseph got off his bicycle and slowly walked past the driveway pushing the bicycle. He noted the number on the house (1774). The street he was on was Barrington Street. George was putting his bicycle in a shed at the end of the driveway. Joseph kept walking. He did not think George saw him at any time. After passing a few more houses he crossed the street and cycled back. As he passed number 1774, he saw George watering plants in front of his house. He thought to himself – mission accomplished.

Back at the hotel he changed clothes, cycled to the bicycle shop, took a cab back to the hotel. He then called and booked a flight back to Toronto

CHAPTER 6

IT WAS NOON ON WEDNESDAY, BEN WAS MAKING HIMSELF A sandwich. The phone rang. He thought it might be Anna on her lunch break. She often called him on her break. This time it was not Anna, it was Joseph Blackmore, the private investigator. He asked Ben if he could meet him in his office at two p.m. "Bring $600.00 cash," he said. Ben said he would be there and hung up the phone.

He stopped at his bank on his way to Joseph's office. He hoped he was not wasting his money. He knew he would have to pay Joseph for his effort, even if he had bad news. Like George was dead, or moved to another city or country.

Sharp at two p.m., Ben was seated in the same leather chair in Joseph's office.

Joseph said, "Young man, I have good news and not so good news. The good news is, I found the address of one George Jacobs in Halifax, Nova Scotia. The not so good news is, (Ben thought he was going to say, but he's dead) you owe me $590.00 cash."

Ben said, "The address you found, is George living there now?"

"Yes, he is," said Joseph. He then flipped over a sheet of paper that was on the desk, and handed it to Ben. It was a summary of his hours and expenses. Total owing was $590.00. At the bottom of the page Ben read: 1774 Barrington Street, Halifax, Nova Scotia. Good luck.

Ben stood, and pulling out his wallet he counted out $600.00 cash. He then threw three more twenties and said, "Tip".

Joseph said, "Thank you, young man, it's been a pleasure doing business with you." He then proceeded to tell Ben that George did in fact work at the Halifax docks. And that he cycled when the weather was good and wore a straw hat. He also told Ben that George was a small man and was referred to as "Our Napoleon" by the dock workers. "I guess he is a fiery guy," said Joseph. "I think he lives alone."

Ben picked up the summary sheet, thanked Joseph for the information, shook his hand and left.

Ben drove back to his apartment. He had some thinking to do. He now had George's address – what did he plan to do, when would he do it, how would he handle the situation? He just couldn't let George get away with what he had done to Anna. He didn't think he could kill him, but whatever he did, Anna must never know. He would go to Halifax as soon as possible. He did more thinking about what he would do.

He booked a flight to Halifax for Monday morning. Friday evening he was taking Anna out for dinner. He would tell her that he was going to his home town, Breakwater, for a few days. He wanted to visit a few friends and also pick up some camping gear that he had lent one of his friends. He would leave Monday. Sunday afternoon he would take Anna to a movie.

A cab to the airport and Ben was on his way to Halifax. He arrived at noon. Another cab to a hotel near the Halifax dockyard. In the main lobby of the hotel he located a map of the area. He found Barrington Street; it was not very far from the hotel.

He ate lunch in the hotel restaurant. He wondered if this was the same hotel that Joseph had stayed in. After lunch he took a walk to see how far it was to 1774 Barrington. It only took him fifteen minutes.

Back at the hotel, he made his plan. He would go back to 1774 Barrington Street just before four p.m. He would take his briefcase with him.

Ben left the hotel at three forty p.m. Just before reaching 1774 Barrington, he started to hum and whistle. He saw that there was no activity in the driveway. He proceeded in the driveway to the back of the house. There was a shed at the end of the driveway. The backyard was small and quite private. He was now behind the shed. He reached into his briefcase and retrieved a ski mask, and put it on. Next, he took out a small toy pistol (it looked real) and placed it in his jacket pocket. He quickly glanced up the driveway but did not see anyone. He walked to the back door and knocked. He knocked again, much harder. No answer. Another quick look up the driveway then back to the back of the shed.

Once more he opened the briefcase. He took out a small mirror and a little stand. He placed the mirror on the stand, then, positioned it so that he could see up the driveway. He sat and waited for George to come home.

Ben kept his eye on the mirror. He thought George would be home either at five or six p.m. He hoped it was five. He got his wish.

Suddenly, a bicycle appeared in the little mirror. It was ten past five. Then the bicycle disappeared, and Ben heard the shed door squeak. (Ben thought – Thank you George for not oiling the hinges, I know right where you are). Quickly Ben moved to the corner of the shed near the front. He heard the shed door squeak again as George closed it, and locked the door. Ben stepped out behind George. As he placed his left hand on his shoulder, he put the pistol to George's head, and said, "Don't make a sound Mr. Jacobs. Let's go inside your house and talk. With his left hand, Ben directed him to the back door. As he fumbled with the key, his hands shaking, he said, "Please don't kill me. Take anything you want."

They were now inside the house. Ben closed and locked the door, pushed George into the living room. "On your stomach, little man," said Ben. "Do as I say little man, and I won't make a hole in your brain. You see, George, if you had used your brain some years ago, about 9, I wouldn't be here."

George was now on his stomach on the floor, shaking his head, and said, "I don't understand."

Ben said, "I will explain, now put your hands behind your back." George complied. Ben had two pieces of rope around his body inside his jacket. One was about two feet long, the other about 10 feet long. He used the shorter piece to tie George's hands. He used the other piece to tie his feet together. He then said, "Now don't you go anywhere George, I am going to have a look around your house. Is that okay with you?"

"Go ahead," said George. "I already told you to take anything you want, you don't have to hurt me."

"I'll think about that George," said Ben.

He found the door to the basement and went down. "An unfinished basement, just my good luck," said Ben. He looked around the ceiling and located what he would use. Time to go back up and see what George was doing.

As he approached George, he said, "Nothing better to do than lie around on the floor George?"

George replied, "How do you know my name?"

"Oh," said Ben. "That is a long story, and I don't have the time to tell you or the inclination to do so." He reached down and untied George's feet. He doubled the rope and hung it on his left shoulder. He pulled George to his feet and pushed him to the basement stairs. George did not resist, for he knew this man was so much bigger and stronger than he was, and therefore, resistance was futile. Down the stairs they went. Ben stopped him in the middle of the basement. Once more George was on his knees. Ben said, "You see George, when you cooperate there is less pain. Know what I mean?" George did not say a word. Ben threaded one end of the rope that was on his shoulder through the top of two supports between the beams. The other end he made into a crude noose, but it would do. (His dad taught him to tie many knots, but never a noose.)

Quickly, Ben put the noose over George's head and with both hands on the other end, pulled George to his feet, then up on his toes.

George started to cry.

Ben tied off the rope so that George was kept on his toes. He would have no problem breathing. He then went to face George, face to face. He began speaking: "George, do you feel frightened?"

George nodded as best he could and said, "Yes."

Ben continued: "George I want you to listen to every word I am about to say. George Jacobs, I'll bet you are not as frightened as an eleven-year-old girl was nine years ago, in her own bedroom, in the dark. She woke up because a son-of-a-bitch named George Jacobs had his filthy little hand in her panties. You see, George, it's no longer a secret."

George cried louder.

Ben slapped his face with one hand, then the other. Suddenly, George stopped crying and said, "That night was the worst night of my life. I don't know why I did it. I was so sorry after the fact. I wanted to tell Anna, but I couldn't face her. I told her I would leave and I did. My sister would have banished me if she knew."

"How many other little girls have you fondled George?" asked Ben.

"None," said George, "and that's the truth, so help me God."

"Well," said Ben, "I could make sure you won't fondle any young girl. All I have to do is pull you up so that your feet cannot touch the floor. Then I would bring a chair from the kitchen and tip it on its side a few feet away. Print a suicide note and Bob's your uncle. They find you and conclude – death by suicide."

George then started to plead for his life.

Ben surmised that George had been through enough. He thought he had inflicted enough psychological stress on George Jacobs.

Ben reached up and untied the rope. He took the noose off George's neck. Then he commanded George to lie once again on his stomach, and he tied his feet together. Ben took his pocket knife out of his pocket. He pretended to be tightening the rope that was binding George's hands and while doing so cut the rope leaving a tiny strand still holding. He knew George could easily break that tiny strand and free himself. George remained silent.

"Good-bye George," said Ben. "I guess when you don't show up for work you will be found. I will let myself out. Don't get too thirsty."

Ben left the house, picked up his briefcase and fifteen minutes later he was back at the hotel. He then called and booked a flight back to Toronto.

CHAPTER 7

BEN WAS BACK IN HIS APARTMENT JUST AFTER NOON ON Tuesday. He had told Anna he would be gone a few days, so he waited until Wednesday evening to call her. She asked him to come to her apartment because she wanted to talk to him.

On the way to Anna's place Ben wondered what Anna wanted to talk to him about. Surely, she did not know that he had gone to Halifax. He was raised not to tell lies but in this case, he felt he had to.

He knocked on her door. Anna opened the door and said, "Come in Ben". Her usual greeting was to throw her arms around him and kiss him. This time she did not. She walked to the living room and said, "Have a seat Ben."

Ben sat down on the sofa and Anna sat beside him but not really close. (Ben was thinking – She is going to dump me.)

Anna looked Ben in the eye and said, "Ben, I think you lied to me." Ben thought – how the hell did she know that? I remember my dad telling me – never lie to your woman cause she will know. "Cora and I went shopping Monday after dinner and we happened to drive by your apartment. Your truck was parked in the usual place. I thought maybe you changed your mind or you would leave Tuesday instead. You told me you were leaving Monday. We stopped and knocked on your door. There was no answer. I was puzzled. After we got back I called your number, no answer. I checked on Tuesday, you truck was still there. Explain Ben, where were you?"

"Well," said Ben, "I left town, but I didn't drive my truck. I took a plane. I left Monday morning. I took a cab to the airport. I did not want you to know where I went or why. However, I guess now I will have to tell you. You see, Anna, I didn't think you would approve of what I planned to do, so I tried to do it without you knowing. Anna, I hired a private detective to find out where your Uncle George lived, in Halifax. He found the address and that is where I went."

Anna said, "Why did you... Oh, Ben, what did you do to him?"

"I didn't kill him Anna," said Ben. "I could only kill in self defense, but I sure as hell scared him. I reminded him of what he did nine years ago. I had a rope around his neck in his basement. He said he was sorry and that he wanted to tell you, but he just couldn't face you. He said he never molested any other girls. He thought I was going to hang him Anna, so I think he was telling the truth. I left him on his basement floor with his hands tied behind his back. I cut the rope so that he could easily break free. I covered my face with a ski mask. He never saw my face. I had to do something Anna. I just couldn't let him get away with what he did to you. He cried like a baby Anna. I guess I did it for you, cause I love you."

Anna hugged him and then began to cry.

Ben waited for her reaction to what he had just told her.

She said, "I guess it's a small consolation that he admitted to what he had done, and said he was sorry. I would have kicked him where it hurts if I had been there. Ben, would you have told me about this if I had not found out that you had misled me?"

"I don't know," said Ben. "At first, I thought I would not, then, I considered the fact that it might help you knowing what you know now."

"Thank you for telling me," said Anna. "I am sure Lynn, my psychiatrist, would agree that this can only help me."

"I think it will, Anna, I really do," said Ben.

"Enough talk," said Anna. "If we want some snuggle time, we better get started. Cora will be home soon."

About a half hour later, Cora did come home. Cora was all smiles, as usual. Anna excused herself and went to the bathroom. Ben got up from the sofa to look out the living room window to see the view. As he passed close to Cora she reached out her hand and slapped his behind. Ben stopped and whispered, "You're lucky Anna didn't see you do that, you naughty girl."

Cora just laughed. Ben proceeded to the window and then back to the sofa.

Anna came back and sat beside Ben. All three chatted for a while, then, Ben went home.

The very next day, as Ben was putting on a clean shirt, someone knocked on his door. He was rather surprised and wondered who it might be. Not taking the time to button up his shirt, he answered the door. To his great surprise it was Cora, all smiles.

"Hello sexy," said Cora, as she walked on by.

"What are you doing here," asked Ben, "and how did you know where I lived?"

"Well," said Cora, "I came here with Anna one time to check to see if you were home."

"I see," said Ben. "What brings you here today?"

"I came to see you," said Cora. "I know you are not getting any nookie from Anna, so I thought you might like to get laid. Since the first time I saw you I wanted to jump your bones. I'm just a bundle of fun, Ben."

"You may be a bundle of fun Cora," said Ben, "and if I was not dating Anna, I might let you prove that. Then again, maybe you are checking on me to see if I would cheat on Anna. I love Anna, so I am turning down your offer. Sorry. However, if Anna and I break up, you can come and knock on my door again."

"I guess I've made a fool of myself. My lust overcame my common sense," said Cora. "Please don't tell Anna, she is my best friend. I should never have come here."

"It's okay Cora," said Ben. "Nothing happened, so there is nothing to tell Anna."

"Anna is lucky to have you," said Cora, as she turned and walked to the door.

Ben followed her to the door. As Cora reached for the doorknob, he tapped her on the behind and said, "Now we are even." Cora turned to look at Ben and her usual smile returned. "Does this mean we are friends?" said Cora.

"Just friends," said Ben. He then opened the door and said, "See you later."

Cora just smiled and walked away.

Ben closed the door and locked it. He then said out loud, "Ben Breakwater, some would say you are a fool. Here you are in the Big City, living alone, single and a beautiful woman wants to take you to bed and you turn her down." Anna crossed his mind. She was the one he wanted, and he would not do anything to jeopardize that.

There were days when Ben did not do much of anything. Other than when he had gone to Halifax, he never missed a day at the fitness club. He could now bench press two hundred and forty pounds. He was happy with his progress. He went for long walks at a good pace. He did crossword puzzles, and he had books with puzzles and mental games that challenged the brain.

His dad had taught him so much about life, mostly as they sat around the campfire. Ben would never forget what he said about boredom — if one can see and think, one should never be bored — it's a state of mind you don't need to be in. Ben never forgot and promised himself he would never be bored.

Among the many books his Dad had left him, the one Ben cherished the most was a book of poems, written by his dad*[1]. Many times, he would read them. In a way it kept his dad alive in Ben's mind. Many times, Ben would reminisce about the love and camaraderie he shared with his dad. However, now he hoped to share his life with Anna. She was the love of his life. He wanted to meet her parents. He had heard it said that the mother at forty-five or so, is what the daughter will look like at the same age. He was intrigued by that, even though he knew that it wasn't necessarily so.

Anna had been seeing Lynn, her psychiatrist, for about two months. Lynn had given her a tip on how she could overcome

---

1   * Some poems are included in the last pages of this book.

the body memory of her uncle touching her. Anna was eager to try out Lynn's suggestions.

It was on a Friday evening, Anna and Ben had gone to a movie. Anna was planning to stay overnight at Ben's place. They had both slipped into comfortable clothes. They were in each other's arms on the sofa. Their kisses were passionate. Anna began massaging Ben's right hand. Then slowly she moved his hand underneath her loose-fitting top and placed it on one of her breasts. She held it there, it felt good. She kissed him and said, "Now the other one", as she removed her hand. She felt elated. This was the first time anyone had touched her bare breast. She could now feel Ben's manhood as he pressed against her. She then took his hand and moved it down between her legs. She kept her hand on top of his. Lynn had told her that, because she was in control using her hand, it would be fine. Lynn was right. Anna thought – now the biggest test. She moved Ben's hand underneath her panties and once again held it there. Her body accepted that which her mind wanted. She removed her hand, and told Ben to keep his hand right where it was. They kissed, and tears of joy flowed down her cheeks. Anna now knew she could enjoy all the pleasures of being a woman. She wanted Ben to be her first lover, and she told him so. They moved to the bedroom and soon, no longer a virgin, she lay happily in the arms of her lover. This was not the first time for Ben. However, it was the first time he made love with someone that he truly loved.

CHAPTER 8

AS A BOY, BEN WOULD TELL HIS DAD THAT WHEN HE GREW up he would be a fireman or a policeman. When he decided to move to Toronto, he thought he might go to university and get a degree. Now he didn't think he wanted to attend classes for four years. Maybe he would join the Toronto Police Force. He would talk to Anna and get her reaction.

Anna sat waiting for Ben's phone call. The phone rang. She picked up the receiver and said, "Hello," and almost said lover-boy, when she heard her mom's voice say, "Hi, Anna'. They exchanged pleasantries, then, Anna told her that she had met a very nice young man, and that they were going steady. Anna told her she would write her and tell her all about Ben. Her mom then told her the reason for her call. She was inviting her to come to Hamilton for Christmas. She now extended the invitation to Ben as well. Anna thanked her and said she would get back to her. She said bye and hung up the phone.

In a few minutes Anna's phone rang again. It was Ben. He would pick her up in fifteen minutes. They were going out for dinner. It was Saturday evening and a few snowflakes were falling.

On the way to the restaurant Anna told Ben that her mother had called and that they were invited to Hamilton to visit with her parents for Christmas. Ben said he would be thrilled to meet her parents. Anna said she didn't know if they would go on Christmas Eve and stay overnight or not. She would check with her mom.

Ben then asked her if they were staying overnight if they would sleep together. Anna said no, her mom was very strict about unmarried young people sleeping together under her roof.

"I think I would feel better anyway if we didn't," said Ben.

"Well," said Anna, "they only have two bedrooms, but the basement is finished and there are two big sofas where two could sleep. I slept there a few months ago. That's where the T.V. is."

"I am looking forward to meeting your parents," said Ben.

"I'm sure you will like them," said Anna.

After dinner they went to Ben's place. Anna usually spent Saturday evening and Sunday at Ben's place. She would make breakfast and they would eat in bed. Later, they would make love in the shower.

After a light lunch they played two handed Whist (a card game) and Scrabble. Ben taught her the finer points about Scrabble and sometimes she would win.

Together they would make dinner, watch T.V. and Ben would drive her home around ten P.M.

Anna and Cora had a one-bedroom apartment. The only time Ben would stay overnight there is when Cora stayed overnight at her boyfriend's place. Many times, the three of them would play Scrabble.

On Christmas Eve it was snowing. Ben and Anna decided to wait until Christmas morning. They placed the gifts in the back seat and set out for Hamilton. They were planning to be at Anna's parents by nine a.m., and have breakfast with them. Then they would open the gifts. Turkey dinner was planned for five-thirty, after which they would drive back to Toronto.

They arrived on time. Audrey, Anna's mom, had told her the door would be unlocked and they could just walk in. Anna opened the door and yelled, "We're here". Ben followed her in carrying the Christmas gifts. Audrey, and Andrew her dad, rushed out to greet them. They hugged Anna and shook hands with Ben.

"Have a seat in the living room," said Audrey. "Breakfast will be ready soon."

Audrey disappeared into the kitchen. The smell of bacon permeated the house.

Anna was sitting beside Ben on the sofa. Andrew was in his leather chair. Anna and Ben were looking at Andrew as he spoke about how he liked Hamilton, when they heard Audrey say, "Surprise Anna, look who is here."

There beside her stood her brother George. Audrey had not told George that Anna would be coming for Christmas. Neither had she told Anna that George would be visiting them at Christmas time.

Anna froze. She felt like the blood was draining from her face.

Ben tried to act nonchalant, but inside he was churning.

George just stood there. Then he said, "My, my, Anna, you're all grown up. How beautiful you are."

"Anna," said Audrey, "Come here and give your Uncle George a big hug. You haven't seen him for many years."

Anna's mind was now racing. She was trapped. If she didn't do as her mother asked, she would have to explain why she didn't.

George knew why Anna was slow to react. He knew he was the only one who could get her off the hook. "That's okay, Anna," said George, "I have a bit of a cold and I don't want to pass it on. Nice to see you."

Anna felt as if a heavy load had been lifted off her shoulders. She just said, "Hi Uncle George."

Ben quickly came to his feet as Audrey was introducing him to George. He walked over to George and shook his hand and said, "Pleased to meet you George." He was hoping George would not recognize his voice. But after sitting back down and thinking about it, he knew George would not say anything even if he did. There was nothing he would gain; therefore, he would keep his mouth shut.

Audrey and George went back into the kitchen. Audrey shouted that breakfast would be served in ten minutes. Andrew, Anna and Ben made a short visit to the washroom and sat back down in the living room.

After a few minutes, Audrey asked them to please be seated at the dining room table. Anna waited until her dad was seated at the end. She sat on his left and Ben sat on her left. She wanted to be as far away from George as possible.

Audrey and George served scrambled eggs, ham, fried potatoes and rye toast. Tea and coffee were already on the table when they sat down, as well as apple juice.

Andrew, Audrey and Anna did most of the talking during breakfast. George said very little, and Ben only spoke when he was spoken to. Andrew did ask Ben what kind of work or job that he might like. Ben replied that he was thinking about joining the Toronto Police Force. Audrey said that would be a noble profession. They seemed to be impressed.

After breakfast they sat around the living room. Andrew handed out the Christmas presents. Soon after the presents were unwrapped, George said he wasn't feeling well and that he was going to his room and rest. Anna was happy to see him depart.

As George lay on the bed in the spare bedroom a few things crossed his mind. He was feeling fine. He knew that Anna was very uncomfortable with him in the room. He could understand that. He knew that Anna had still not told her Mom what he had done to her. He was thankful for that. Then he thought about Ben, Anna's boyfriend. He thought he had heard that voice before – when they had shook hands and Ben had said "Pleased to meet you George." Could he be the one who tied him up and almost hung him in his own basement? He certainly was of the same stature. It had to be him. Who else would know? Anna told him, and he decided to do some payback. He wondered if Anna knew. He may never know. All he knew was that if this young man, Ben, was the one, he sure handled the situation this morning very well. Maybe he was a young cop.

George knew Anna and Ben would be going back to Toronto soon. It looked like he was in the clear. He picked up his book that he had been reading and once again found himself immersed in its pages.

While the turkey was cooking they talked and played a card game called Hearts. Anna and Ben played against Audrey and Andrew, who won every game. Ben was more gracious than Anna in their losses. Anna was a serious player in any game. That was her nature. That was her dad's nature.

Dinner was at five p.m. They adopted the same seating arrangement. Anna was a little more relaxed at dinner than at breakfast. She thought about how George had really saved the day when he said he had a cold and a hug was not a good idea. If he had not said that, she would have had to give him a hug which would have made her skin crawl. Maybe with the rope around his neck he had told Ben the truth, that he was genuinely sorry for what he had done. She did not think she could ever forgive George. She hoped he would never visit her mother ever again for Christmas, not as long as she was invited.

After dinner, Anna helped her Mother clean up and wash the dishes. George had said his good-byes and was back in his room. Anna thought maybe he was developing some common sense. He was staying out of her way.

Ben thanked them for their hospitality and after hugs and a hand shake, Anna and Ben were on their way back to Toronto.

They talked about the big surprise that was George. Ben said, "He had never thought of that possibility." Anna said, "It never crossed her mind. If she had known, she would have declined, and said she was not feeling well." Ben then asked her, "What would she have done if George had not said he had a cold, would she have crossed the floor and given him a hug?" Anna said, "I guess so, but it wouldn't have been much of a hug. I would have done it because otherwise my Mother would be losing her only brother. I couldn't do that to her."

Ben told Anna that he could hardly believe his eyes when he looked up and saw George standing beside her Mom. He said he felt a little weird, as his memory flashed back to that basement in George's house in Halifax. He knew George but George didn't know him. Also he thought about the ski mask he wore on his face. It would have been a very awkward occasion for him and for George, if he had not covered his face that day in Halifax. Ben just shook his head and said, "Son-of-a-B".

Anna said, "Yes, I guess we both had flashbacks when we saw Uncle George standing there beside my Mom. I really wanted to walk over and slap his face, and then kick him where it hurts. But I couldn't, because of my mom."

"Well," said Ben, "it's over now. It didn't turn out as bad as I expected."

"I guess you're right," said Anna, "I'm thinking he felt uncomfortable. He had a place to go and hide. I didn't."

"Another thing just crossed my mind," said Ben, "I wonder if George thought that I was the man in the ski mask who nearly hung him in his own house."

"He may have," said Anna, "another good reason for him to go and hide. Let's talk about something else. What did you think about my mom and dad?"

"They are very warm people," said Ben. "I like them. I think your mom is in control of things. She would be an alpha female. Your dad is easy going and a very intelligent man."

"I think you got it right," said Anna, "except when it comes to the big things, my dad usually makes the decisions."

"We are almost back to my place," said Ben. "You know Anna, if we become a couple, like married, I will always let you think you are the boss."

Anna punched him in the shoulder and he laughed. "One thing is for certain Anna, you will always be the boss when we are naked," said Ben.

"Promise?" said Anna.

CHAPTER 9

BEN AND ANNA CELEBRATED THE DAWN OF 1965 IN FRONT of the T.V., sipping wine. They ate cheese and crackers and talked about the past, the present and the future. Anna talked about starting the dental assistant course soon. Ben told her, "Why not take the dentistry course and become a dentist? It will take longer but you will earn a lot more money." Anna said she did not have the funds to do that. Plus, she would have to work part time and it would be just too much. Ben told her he would pay for any course she wanted to take. But she said no. She wanted to do it on her own, with the help from her parents. Ben did not push the issue. He knew she was a proud young woman and he respected that.

Ben told Anna he had given it some serious thought about joining the Toronto Police Force. He planned to walk into a police station and find out the procedures he would have to follow in order to join the Force. His high school teacher, Mr. Pebbles, had told him he could choose any profession he wanted to, and he would excel. He had been an honour student all through school.

Ben asked Anna if she would like to take a vacation. They could go and relax on a nice sandy beach in Mexico or in the Bahamas. Anna said she would love to. She had never been on the beach in winter. They decided to make plans in the next couple of weeks.

Meanwhile, someone else had plans for Anna. She was being watched while she worked in the grocery store, and while walking to her car. Unbeknownst to her, the man watched her get into her car. He already knew where she lived and what number was her apartment because his accomplice was now waiting inside the main door of her apartment building.

As she drove, Anna did not notice a car following her. Anna parked her car and entered her apartment building. She lived on the second floor and she always took the stairs. The bearded man at the top of the stairs heard her footsteps so he quickly moved to a door that was two doors before Anna's apartment, on the opposite side. He pretended to be inserting a key in the door as Anna walked by. She unlocked her door. As the door swung inward, the bearded man quickly stepped in behind her and placed his left hand over her mouth and said, "Don't make a sound or I will cut your pretty face." He turned, locked the door, and holding a knife in front of Anna's face, walked her into the living room. He then told her to lie on the floor. Anna started to cry. He tied her hands behind her back and blindfolded her. Next, he proceeded to tie her feet together and gag her so she could not scream. He picked up the key that Anna had dropped, unlocked the door and glanced up and down the hallway. His lucky day, no one to be seen. Closing the door, he headed for the stairs. Quickly, down he went. His partner in crime was waiting for him to let him in. Thirty seconds later they were both in Anna's apartment.

Anna knew she was now at their mercy. There was nothing she could do. She hoped that Cora would not come, and that she would go to her boyfriend's place. Other than to be sexually assaulted, she wondered why she was being forcefully confined. She thought about Ben. He would be absolutely furious. Another thing crossed her mind. Was she being kidnapped and held for ransom? Ben was a rich young man. But she was sure he had told her that only two people, her and his high school teacher, Mr. Pebbles, knew that he was rich. She hoped that Mr. Pebbles had not betrayed his trust. However, she thought that if she was being held for ransom, who else could be responsible but Mr. Pebbles. She knew that money can cause nice people to be greedy. She knew Ben would pay to have her back.

The two men never spoke, they whispered. She never did see a face. She could never recognize them. Suddenly, she felt her feet being untied. Tears from her eyes were absorbed by the blindfold. She was ushered out, down the hallway, down the stairs and into a car. She was placed in the back seat.

They drove for miles. Anna could not tell how far, but she could tell that they made a lot of turns. Then the car came to a stop. She was taken into a building. Her feet were again tied and they sat her in what felt like a kitchen chair. Her hands were then untied, the gag was removed and so was the blindfold.

Once her eyes became accustomed to the light, she realized that she was in a kitchen of a house. They pushed the chair she was tied to so that she could see that she was sitting at a table. Both men had long black beards, and they wore Lone Ranger like masks. When they spoke, they used guttural sounds to disguise their voices.

One of the men said to Anna, "You don't have to be afraid, we are not going to harm you in any way."

Anna started to cry. Could she believe them? Should she question them as to why she was being held hostage? How long before this was over?

They were both sitting at the table across from her. It was a large table. The same one that spoke before said, "I am going to untie your feet. There is nowhere you can run. The door can be locked with a padlock on the inside and the outside. The windows, as you can see, have steel bars on them." He came around to Anna's side, pulled her chair out and untied her feet. He then went back and sat down.

Anna arose and moved her chair back to the table and sat back down. The two men seemed mesmerized as they just sat there and stared at her. She wanted to use the washroom, but she could wait. One of the men left the table. A little while later she heard the toilet flush. When he came back, he told Anna there was cold meat and bread in the fridge. Would she make them sandwiches? Anna nodded her head and said, "Yes." She went to the sink, washed her hands, wiped them on one of the tea towels on the oven door.

"How many sandwiches do you want?" asked Anna. The reply came. "Make a bunch, you can help us eat them. There's pop in the bottom of the fridge."

Soon they were eating and drinking pop. Anna started to feel a little better. Maybe these men were not going to hurt her. Maybe now was a good time to ask them why they had abducted her. One of them must have read her mind. He said, "I guess you have been wondering why we kidnapped you. Well, we really don't know. We were paid to do this, and we were told not to harm you. We don't even know for how long we have to keep you here. The man did not say."

Anna started thinking again. If it was Mr. Pebbles, then indeed she was being held for ransom. If no ransom was demanded, then that would eliminate Mr. Pebbles. What then? She would have to just wait it out. She was hoping these men would leave, at least for the night. She did not relish the thought of sleeping in this house with these two men. Then again, what if they left, locked her in, and never came back. At first Anna did not partake of the sandwiches. The two men encouraged her to eat, so she did. After the sandwiches were eaten, the two men said they were leaving and would return in the morning. They were gone, Anna was alone. She had mixed feelings. But if they were true to their word, and so far they had been, she would at least get some sleep. She then went to explore the house.

It was a small house, only one bedroom, with a double bed. The sheets did not look clean. She checked for bed bugs but did not see any. She wasn't sure she could sleep in the bed. She looked in the chest of drawers and found two warm blankets. She would use these and sleep on the chesterfield. Next, she tried opening the door. She could not, it was locked on the outside, as they had told her. She looked at her watch, it was eight forty p.m. Mother Nature was now calling her to the washroom. On her way back to the small living room she noticed a little book shelf containing several books. She looked through them and selected one. Maybe she could get lost in the book for a while to take her mind off her dilemma.

She started to read the book. It was difficult to concentrate. She thought of her mom and dad. She hoped this would be over before they found out she had been kidnapped. Then there was Cora. Was she at their apartment now? If she was, she would know that something was amiss – she had dropped her purse on the floor and Cora would have found it. She would call Ben to see if I was there. If she stayed at her boyfriend's place, then she would be oblivious to what had happened. Back to the book.

After the two men left Anna, they stopped at a pay phone and made a local call. The man spoke into the receiver and said, "Phase one completed," and hung up the phone. He got back in the car and they drove away.

The next morning the two bearded men arrived at the hotel to see the man who had received yesterday's phone call. One of them slipped in the back door behind a man who had a key. He went to Room 107 and tapped on the door. The door opened and a man handed him three envelopes. Without delay, the man went out the back door and back into the car. The two smaller envelopes contained their second payment. On the other envelope Anna's address was printed. They then set out to deliver the envelope. They parked in a visitor space in the apartment lot. One of the men got out, lit a cigarette and walked over to one of the pillars near the door. He was waiting for someone to go in or come out. After about five minutes a lady carrying two bags pushed the door open. The man quickly moved to the door and held it open for her to exit. She said thank you, and walked away and didn't look back. The man then entered the apartment building, went up the stairs and walked to door 202 and slipped the envelope under the door. Back out to the car and as he closed the car door he said, "That was easy". They drove away.

Cora was scheduled to start work at ten a.m. She had stayed overnight at her boyfriend's place. She arrived at the Dominion grocery store at nine forty-five. Anna was also to start at ten a.m. Usually Anna would be there before her if she stayed at her boyfriend's place. Ten minutes to ten, still no sign of Anna. Cora then called their apartment, no answer. This was not like Anna, something happened, thought Cora. Shen went to the office and asked to be replaced, because Anna was missing. She would go to their apartment and check.

When Cora opened their apartment door she almost stepped on the envelope that was on the floor. She picked it up. Then she saw Anna's purse on the floor. She called her name, no answer. Carrying the envelope, she searched the apartment, no Anna. She looked at the envelope, no name, just their apartment number. She opened it. Another smaller envelope was inside, written on it was "For Ben". Ben's phone number was on the fridge, Anna had placed it there. Cora checked the number and made the call to Ben's apartment. No answer. Her mind started racing. Why was Anna's purse on the floor? What was written inside the envelope with Ben's name on it? Should she call the police? No, she would wait a few minutes and call Ben again. He may have been in the washroom. She dialed his number again, one ring, two rings, three rings, four rings. "Hello," said Ben. Cora identified herself and told him what she had found in their apartment, and that Anna was missing. Ben told her he was on his way.

Ben fought his emotions as he drove to Anna's apartment. He wanted to go faster but he did not want to get stopped by the police or get in an accident. Her apartment seemed much farther away from his, this time. He kept repeating, "Anna please be safe," as he drove.

He parked in the visitor lot, and ran to the apartment door. Cora was there to let him in. She handed him the envelope. He ripped it open and unfolded the sheet of paper, and began to read: *Anna is waiting for you at 2429 Tenth Line West, Mississauga. She is there alone.*

Cora knew where Tenth Line Road was and gave Ben directions. He ran to his truck and burnt rubber as he pulled out of the parking lot. He didn't know he was being followed by two bearded men in a black car.

Anna awoke at seven forty-five a.m. She was disoriented. She had slept well, as the chesterfield was quite comfortable. She sat up, looked around and then realized where she was. She had slept in her clothes. It was very quiet. The memories of yesterday quickly came back to her. She went to the washroom. Once more she tried to open the door, no success. She looked out each window, and saw nothing but trees, and wondered how much longer she would be locked in this house. She was supposed to work today, so was Cora. She knew that Cora and Ben would be looking for her after ten a.m. Cora would surely call Ben and tell him that she had not showed up for work. How could they ever find her? She felt like a prisoner when she saw the bars on the windows. She must stay strong. She must eat. Walking to the fridge she knew there was more meat and bread. Then she saw the toaster, and wondered if it worked. She plugged it in and pushed down on the handle – it worked. She made herself a toasted ham sandwich, it tasted good.

As she ate, she wondered if the two bearded men would return. Maybe if they did, this time she might not be so lucky. She made up her mind, she would fight them with every ounce of strength in her body. She needed a weapon. She searched the kitchen drawers and found a sharp knife, about eight inches long. Where would she hide it so that it would be available if she needed it? Then she remembered a western movie, where the good guy had placed a knife in his boot. She could do that. After putting on her boots, she picked up the knife and looked at it. It was sharp. It might cut her leg. Think, think, she said to herself. Then she had an idea. Wrap the blade in paper and then place it in her boot. After doing so, she felt proud of herself.

Once more, Anna looked out each window. Trees, everywhere she looked. She folded the blankets and put them back in the drawer in the bedroom. She decided to continue reading the book she had started to read yesterday. It was a good book.

She read. Checked her watch – ten twenty. Read, checked her watch – ten fifty. Read about one more page and suddenly she heard a noise, but could not identify what it was. Closing the book, she looked out each window. Again, only to see trees. She listened at the door, all quiet. Then she heard another sound, it seemed further away. She stood at the door for about five minutes, listening intensively. Then, sounds she immediately recognized. A vehicle engine, the sound of tires skidding on gravel, the slamming of a vehicle door, then a gun shot. She ran to each window but could not see anything. There was no window facing the lane leading up to the house. There once was a window in the door, however, it was now boarded up. She asked herself the question, who was shooting at what?

Ben had come speeding up the gravel laneway to the house. He saw two cars parked in the laneway, but there was nobody in them. He stepped out and slammed the truck door. He held his baseball bat in one hand. Then a gun shot. Two bearded men appeared from behind one of the cars. One held a pistol, and he said, "Stay where you are and drop the bat." Both men were wearing Lone Ranger type masks. Ben froze, dropped the bat and said, "What is this all about, where is Anna?" The man holding the pistol said, "Just turn around and put your hands behind your back or the next bullet will come much closer. Tie his hands, Jim Bob." The other man stepped forward and tied Ben's hands. Ben was tempted to turn around and smash the man's face as he began to tie his hands. However, he knew he had too much to lose, with a pistol pointed at him. After his hands were tied the man stepped back. Ben turned to face them. The man with the pistol said, "It's payback time". As he said the word "time", the other bearded one stepped toward Ben and landed a hard punch to his stomach. Ben doubled over, he had never been hit so hard, but he stayed on his feet. As he was bent over he saw an upper-cut coming, he moved his head and the punch missed its mark. However, a kick to the side of his knee did not miss. The kick to his leg was worse than the punch in the stomach. He almost went down. The man holding the pistol spoke again. "The pain inflicted upon you is revenge for our friend in Halifax, Nova Scotia. Do you remember? Of course you remember." Two quick punches to Ben's face as his head snapped back. Ben thought his nose was broken, for sure. He was wondering when this would end. Then he saw the man pick up his baseball bat, and he thought he would be killed. But the man walked away. He stopped and said, "Nice truck", then proceeded to the front of Ben's truck. He swung the bat, it smashed the headlights on one side, then the other. Another swing left a large depression in the hood of the truck. Ben could not believe this was happening to him and his new truck. Another swing and the driver's side door was a lot thinner. "That's good," said the man holding the pistol as he moved closer to Ben. "Where are the keys," he asked Ben. Ben said, "In my left pocket." "Jim Bob," said the man, "get his keys". The keys were fetched from Ben's pocket, and passed to the pistol holder, who then said, "Now I don't want you chasing us in that beat-up truck." He tossed the keys into the trees. "Untie him, Jim Bob," he said.

Ben's hands were untied, and the pistol was pointed at him. He was told to stay right where he was until they drove away. As they walked to their car, Ben asked where Anna was. Nothing was said. The two men got into the car, started the engine and started to drive away. Then it stopped. The driver's window came down a few inches and the man shouted, "Try the house," and they sped away.

Anna heard voices, and loud noise like something crashing. She was scared. She felt hopeless, and started to weep.

Suddenly, a loud noise right at the door. Someone was breaking the door down. The door swung open. It was Ben. He looked and saw Anna. They ran to each other, as tears of joy began to flow.

Ben was looking at his battered truck before his hands were untied and he did not notice that one of the cars had driven away. The little man driving that car was now en-route to the Toronto airport for a flight back to Halifax.

Ben asked Anna is she was okay, and she nodded and said, "Yes, let's get out of here. I will tell you everything that happened as we drive home." She put on her coat and they left the house.

As they approached Ben's truck, Anna said, "Ben, look at your truck. It's been smashed." Ben said, "I know, I watched as it was being done. There was a gun pointed at me. They used my own baseball bat. I guess I should have left it in the truck. No big deal, it can be fixed. Let's go find my keys. They were tossed in the trees over there" (pointing in the direction the keys were tossed).

They found the keys and drove down the laneway and headed for home. Anna told Ben everything that had happened. Ben did the same. Anna then asked Ben who these men were and why all this took place. Ben told her it was revenge. Her Uncle George was responsible. He got his revenge by hiring these two men to kidnap her and get him out to nowhere to beat him him up, and smash his truck. Ben continued, "I didn't realize it at first, but there were two cars parked at the house when I arrived. One of them drove off and I didn't notice. I'm guessing George was sitting in that second car and watched the whole thing as I got punched. I guess he feels better now, he got his revenge."

Anna told Ben they would have to stop at the grocery store. She wanted to explain to the manager what had happened, why she did not show up for work. Also, they would have to pick up Cora's keys. She had no key to the building nor to her apartment. Her kidnappers had taken the key to her apartment. She was happy now that she kept her car keys and the building key separate from her apartment key.

As they entered Anna's apartment, Ben told her she would have to see the building manager and have her apartment door lock changed. If her kidnappers still had her key, they would have access to her apartment.

After picking up her purse on the kitchen table, they went to the manager's office. Anna explained what had happened. She was told to go back to her apartment and a man would be there to replace the lock and provide them with two new keys.

While they waited for the man to come and replace the lock, Ben made lunch and Anna took a shower. They ate lunch.

After the lock was replaced, they went back to the grocery store and gave Cora her building key and the new apartment key.

Back to Anna's place where they talked, hugged, kissed, got naked and made love.

CHAPTER 10

BEN WOKE UP THE NEXT MORNING WITH A SHINER. BLACK and blue around his left eye, and it was swollen. His left leg was bruised around the knee area, and it caused him to limp a little. That bearded Lone Ranger had kicked him 'pretty hard'. Ben thought he would recognize him if he saw him again, but not without the beard. His partner called him Jim Bob. Ben wondered if that was his name or was it a nickname. He thought it probably was the latter. He wished he had been able to read the licence plate of the car the two men were in as they drove away, but the plate was deteriorated, and the numbers could not be discerned. Upon looking in the mirror at his shiner, he wished he could meet these two men separately in a back alley. He would make them cry uncle, and leave them with shiners. Then he thought about Anna, in that house with these two men. George must have instructed them that Anna was not to be touched. In doing so, he was protecting himself from the wrath of his sister. Ben thought that maybe he should just let sleeping dogs lie and move on.

As he was eating breakfast, he thought about his truck. He was forced to leave Anna's place yesterday before dark, because the truck had no headlights. After eating, he would drive to the Ford dealership where he bought the truck. They would know where he could take his truck to get it repaired. He wanted his truck to look new again, and therefore, he wanted a reputable body shop.

At ten a.m. he parked his truck at the Ford dealership. As he opened the door the salesman who sold him the truck was about to exit. Ben held the door and said, "Good timing." The man's name was John. They exchanged pleasantries. John asked Ben if he could be of assistance. Ben said, "Yes, come with me, I have something to show you."

"How did you get that shiner?" asked John.

"I will tell you, come along," said Ben.

When John saw Ben's truck he said, "What the hell happened, did you piss someone off or what? Looks like it got whacked by a club of some sort."

Ben said, "Yes, a baseball bat, the one I keep in the cab".

"You smashed your own truck?" said John as he laughed.

"No," said Ben, "it's a long story, however, I did piss someone off. Both me and the truck paid the price. I received a black eye and my truck, well, lights out."

John chuckled again.

Ben said, "Might as well laugh as cry. It was payback, so I guess it's time to forget it and move on. Can you recommend a good body shop, John?"

"Sure can," said John. "Go west down the street here, turn right at the first lights. The body shop is on the left. It's called Jim Bob's Auto Body Shop."

"Jim Bob's, you say," said Ben. (The name shocked him a little.) However, he did not want to show any emotion, although he was churning inside. Then he thought about the irony of the whole situation. If he was the same Jim Bob who had smashed his truck, he was now being directed to take it there to get it repaired. Suddenly, he started to laugh. He couldn't stop himself. But now he would have to explain himself.

"Sorry John," said Ben, "that's a real funny name."

"Yea it is," said John, "but they do really good work. His name is Jim. Rumour has it he got the name Bob when he was a young lad learning to swim. He kept bobbing up and down in the water almost drowning. One of his friends said, "Look at Jim bobbing again." So, they called him Jim Bob. The name stuck."

They looked at each other and laughed.

Ben didn't have to think about it very long before he decided not to take his truck to Jim Bob's shop. He asked John where else he could recommend so that Ben could get a second opinion. John gave him directions to Rob's Auto about a ten-minute drive from the Ford dealership. Ben thanked him and was soon on his way to Rob's Auto.

After they gave him a price, Ben told them he had another appraisal that was one hundred less, and if they would match that price, he would give them his truck to repair. Business was slow. They dropped the price by one hundred and Ben handed over the truck key. The shop boss called Ben a cab. While he waited for the cab, he thought they might cut a few corners because he had them drop the price, so he decided to tell them if the work they did was good, he would pay the original price and maybe more.

While riding in the taxi to his apartment, Ben wondered if he should rent a car for a week or not. He could easily manage without a vehicle. Anna could pick up groceries for him or he could take a taxi as he was doing now. Before reaching his apartment, he decided he would not rent a car.

After lunch Ben walked to the fitness centre. His limp was not as pronounced as it had been. However, he would give it more time to heal before subjecting it to strenuous exercises. Nonetheless, he could still give his upper body a good workout, and he did so vigorously. Today would be the first time he would bench press over two-hundred and forty pounds, that being two forty-five. He was very happy with his progress.

On his way home Ben thought of many things. He hoped Anna would still be his girlfriend come summer. She had said she liked camping, and if she was being truthful, he knew they would have a lot of fun. He wondered if he should buy a house or stay in his apartment. Would Anna move in with him if he were to ask her? Then he thought about Cora. If Anna moved in with him, Cora would have a problem. She couldn't afford the apartment by herself. Maybe he could help her, but would she accept? He would talk to Anna about it.

Jim Bob's Auto shop crossed his mind. Once again, he pondered whether or not it was the same man who beat him up. He did not want any further dealings with Jim Bob. However, he knew it would bug him until he knew the truth. An idea crossed his mind. Maybe Cora was the answer. Did her car need any bodywork? If so, she could take it to Jim Bob's place for an estimate. She may not see Jim Bob, but then again, she might. Nothing ventured, nothing gained. He would talk to Cora the next time he saw her.

After her abduction, Anna became very much aware of her surroundings. At work she would park as close to the building as she could, and if possible, near small vehicles. People could hide much easier around large ones. Also, she never walked directly to her car. She'd walk pass and circle back, always checking for unusual sights. In her apartment building she would never go to her apartment door if she saw anyone she didn't know. Cora would sometimes bug her and tell her she was becoming a little paranoid. But Anna insisted that it took very little effort to be vigilant, and she felt much safer. After a while it would all be done automatically, she told Cora. Cora agreed that Anna was doing the right thing, better safe than sorry. What she didn't tell Anna (but it crossed her mind) was the fact that if she was as beautiful as Anna, she would probably be more aware of her surroundings as well.

It was Saturday night and Anna was sleeping over at Ben's place. They were asleep. Suddenly, loud screams woke Ben. Anna was sitting up screaming. Ben suspected she had had a bad dream. He said her name, told her who he was, and then he held her and told her she was safe. Her screaming stopped, and she began sobbing. She then relayed her dream to Ben.

She was back in the house where the two bearded men had taken her. She had finished the toasted ham sandwich. She had placed the knife in her boot. She looked out each window only to see trees. As she sat on the chesterfield reading a book, there was a noise at the door. The door swung open and a bearded man stood there. He closed the door and locked it. As he walked toward Anna he had a smile on his face. Anna placed the book on the chesterfield and stood up. Inside she was scared. She must think fast. She must outsmart this big man walking toward her.

He said he had changed his mind. He had never had such a beautiful woman. Anna backed away. He followed her. Before she got to the far wall, she crouched down on her right knee. She then pulled the knife from her boot with her right hand and stood with her shoulders perpendicular to the bearded man. As he reached for her, Anna quickly turned and in an upward motion plunged the knife into the man's chest. She ran to the door, frantically she tried to unlock it. Success, the door swung open. She made only one step when an arm went around her waist and another bearded man said, "Where do you think you are going?" Anna woke up and started to scream.

Sunday after breakfast, Ben asked Anna what she thought about the idea that Cora take her car to Jim Bob's. Anna thought it was a good idea. She too wanted to know if in fact the owner was the same man, along with his accomplice, that had kidnapped her. She hoped she would never see them again, and that they lived in Halifax, Nova Scotia. She had surmised that they were from Halifax, after finding out her Uncle George was responsible for everything that had happened.

Anna went home after lunch. She had housework to do. Ben asked Anna to call him when Cora came home if it wasn't late. He would pay them a short visit and talk to Cora.

The phone rang at Ben's place at eight thirty p.m. It was Anna. Cora had just walked in. Anna told Ben that Cora said tell him to come on over, we can have a threesome. Ben laughed and said, "See you in a few minutes," and hung up the phone.

Cora was receptive to the idea. She would take her boyfriend along with her. The three of them agreed that Cora's boyfriend would be oblivious as to the real reason they were going to Jim Bob's Auto Shop. Ben and Anna gave Cora a good description of Jim Bob. But what if Cora didn't see him? What then? They would be no wiser. The trip to the auto shop would be for naught.

Ben, of a sharp mind, had the answers. If Cora did not see the man in question, and not to sound too inquisitive, she would say: "Jim Bob is a funny name. Does he own this place? My friend Jenny has an Uncle Jim who used to work on cars. He was a little bald-headed guy Jenny had told me."

Ben and Anna were hoping that Cora would get a description of Jim Bob, to compare it to the bearded man named Jim Bob.

The Saturday following the conversation with Ben and Anna, Cora and her boyfriend Sammy parked Cora's car at Jim Bob's Auto. The time was ten forty-five. Inside at the counter they were greeted by a clean-cut man. Cora thought he looked around thirty years old, and that he was handsome. Cora could fall for any man that was handsome. His name was Mike. She told Mike she wanted an estimate to fix the rust spot on her car. She said she was thinking about trading it and she wanted to get the rust spot fixed.

Mike and Cora left to check out the car. Sammy sat in one of the four chairs and waited. On the way Cora mentioned to Mike that she thought Jim Bob's was a funny name for an auto shop. Mike explained that the owner whose name was Barry, had a son named Jim. Barry gave him the nickname Jim Bob and it stuck. Cora asked him how old was Jim Bob now, and Mike replied around ten years old. Cora just smiled as she walked around her car to show Mike the rust spot. After examining the rust spot, he walked around the car and suggested she should get a new paint job. Cora said she could not afford that, and asked him how much to fix the rust spot. Mike gave her an estimate of one hundred dollars. Cora asked him if that was the best he could do, and he said yes. Cora winked at him and said, "I can make it worth your while if you were to drop your estimate," as she winked at him again.

Mike said, "Sorry lady, I can't do that. This is not my shop, and I am engaged. I don't fool around on my fiancée."

"You're a good man Mike," said Cora, "I hope she is deserving of you. I will consider your estimate. Thanks for your time. When you go back in, tell Sammy I'm ready to go."

Cora was delighted with the news she had to tell Anna and Ben. She had a big smile on her face. Sammy noticed and asked her why she was so happy.

"Well," said Cora, "he wanted a hundred to fix the rust spot. I offered my body for one night and he dropped it to seventy-five." She laughed.

Sammy said, "No you didn't, you're not that cheap, and you're not that good at lying either. Mike told me you drive a hard bargain." (Cora said God bless Mike, to herself.)

Ben and Anna were elated with the news. Jim Bob was ten years old. Ben told Anna that she probably had it right. The two bearded men were from Halifax. It was time to really forget the past, and move on with their lives.

CHAPTER 11

SEVEN DAYS AFTER BEN TOOK HIS TRUCK TO ROB'S AUTO, HE got a phone call saying his truck was ready for pick-up. Anna was not working that day. Ben called her, and she drove him to the autobody shop to pick it up.

After a thorough inspection Ben was very happy to see his truck looking like new. He paid the bill with cash. He then placed a fifty-dollar bill on the counter, and thanked the man for a job well done. The man smiled and thanked Ben, as he handed him the truck key.

Anna followed Ben to his place, as they had planned.

Ben made tea and they ate a few tea biscuits. Anna told Ben she had talked to her mom who had invited them to come to Hamilton for a weekend visit. Ben said he would love to go. Anna said she was off this coming Saturday but was scheduled to work Friday. However, Cora was off Friday. She would ask her if she would take her shift on Friday. They had changed shifts many times before.

Ben asked Anna if she would like to take a vacation. They could fly to New York City and from there take a Caribbean cruise. Anna said she would love to see New York, and especially Times Square. A Caribbean cruise would be wonderful. She would ask the manager at her work for the time off. They would make plans for a vacation in February.

Anna called Ben later that evening to tell him Cora would work for her Friday. They decided they would leave Toronto Friday morning at 10 a.m. There would be less traffic at that time.

After hanging up the phone, Ben decided to do some reading. It was time to read his dad's book of poems. He picked up the little book. A picture of his dad was taped to the inside of the front cover. He stared at the picture. He would forever miss him. Tears rolled down his cheeks as he began reading. It happened this way every time. It was his way of connecting with his dad.

Inside the back cover he had taped a picture of his mom. The same picture he remembered his dad holding in his hand and saying, "She was a good woman, Ben. I was a lucky man to have known her, and I guess a very unlucky man to have lost her. She gave you life, she gave me the best years of my life. It's like I told you son, we all must die. It's just a matter of time. And remember, you can't borrow time, nor can you go back in time, only in your memory."

That phrase, "You can't borrow time", was stuck in Ben's mind.

After looking at his mom's picture, for a while, he thought how lucky he was to have met Anna. He loved her, and he would lay down his life for her. Soon, he would ask her to marry him. When and where, he would have to think about that. Then rings crossed his mind. Why wait? Tomorrow would be a good day to look at rings. He would check out the Yorkdale Shopping Mall. He read about it in the paper. It had opened in February 1964. If his mind served him right, at that time, it was the largest indoor shopping mall in the world. He fell asleep thinking about rings for Anna.

At around ten a.m. in the morning, Ben parked his truck at the Yorkdale Shopping Mall. He had never seen such a big parking lot. He entered the mall and was in awe of the enormity of the place. He double checked where he had entered so that he would know where his truck was parked. He had one thousand dollars cash in his pocket. In less than one minute he spotted a jewelry store. He walked in. A dark-haired lady behind the glass counter greeted him. Ben told her he was looking for a set of rings, an engagement and wedding ring. He said to her he was going to ask the most beautiful woman in the world to marry him. The lady smiled and said, "You have come to the right place, young man. What price range are we looking at?" Ben did not know very much about jewelry or rings. He asked the lady to show him different sets and tell him the price of each set. He would then choose a set. The first set she showed him was valued at two hundred and fifty dollars. She said they were very nice. The second set was three hundred and seventy-five. Ben looked at them and said they were beautiful. Then, he spotted another set in the display case. He pointed to them and the lady said these are very expensive, but they are beautiful. The price tag was marked eight hundred and forty-five. Ben said, "I'll take them." The lady said, "Wow, she will be cock-a-hoop with these."

Ben said, "Cock-a-hoop, what does that mean?"

"It means elated, very, very happy," said the lady.

"I guess she will, if she accepts my proposal," said Ben.

"What is her name?" asked the lady.

"Anna," said Ben.

"These rings are size six. Do you know what her size is?" asked the lady.

"No," said Ben, "but I would say, looking at yours, Anna's would be about the same."

"That's fine," said the lady. "You can always bring them back and we will make sure they fit her."

Ben paid the lady who wished him good luck, as he departed the jewelry store a very happy young man. He decided to walk around the mall for a little exercise and see the place.

Half an hour later, he was on his way back to his apartment. While driving back to his apartment an idea popped into his head. It would be a little fun for him at Anna's expense.

He parked at his apartment and reached into the glove compartment and retrieved a match box. It was full of wooden matches. His Dad had told him to always carry matches. In an emergency one could always light a fire and keep warm. He put the match box in his pocket, picked up the little bag containing the rings, and headed for his apartment. He placed the rings and the match box on the table.

He made himself a roast beef sandwich and a mug of tea. Sitting at his table while munching on his sandwich, he thought about the phrase "cock-a-hoop". The lady at the jewelry store was probably right, but he felt he had to check the dictionary and see it for himself. There it was, the lady was correct. He laughed, it amused him.

After finishing his sandwich, he examined the rings. He knew which one was the engagement ring, the lady had pointed it out. He then picked up the match box, opened it completely and let all the matches fall out. Next, he went to the kitchen drawer and picked up scissors. In his den he found a shoe box, and taking the top of the box, he carried it to the table. He proceeded to cut out a rectangle shape to fit inside the match box. He placed the engagement ring flat on the bottom of the match box, and covered it with the little rectangle piece of cardboard. He then put the matches back in the box. The wedding ring he placed on the inside of the top drawer of his dresser in his bedroom. Just in case his truck got stolen, he would not risk putting the match box in the glove compartment until Friday morning. As he often put his keys in one of his boots when visiting someone, he thought of this idea himself. He would never lose his keys. He now placed the match box in one of the boots he would wear on Friday.

Thursday morning Ben went for a good workout at the fitness center. On his way home he stopped at the grocery store to pick-up a few things and see Anna. She invited him for dinner. Cora was picking up chicken. He accepted.

After gorging themselves on chicken, Cora suggested they play strip poker. Ben said, "Sure, I'll have you two naked in no time." Anna said, "No you won't, because we are not playing strip poker." They ended up playing Scrabble. Anna won both games. Ben was home and in bed before midnight. He read until one a.m.

Friday morning Ben ate breakfast, packed his overnight bag, checked the weather forecast, and called Anna at nine-thirty. At nine forty-five he took the match box out of his boot and put it in his pocket. Upon entering his truck, he placed the match box in the glove compartment.

He picked up Anna and they were on their way to Hamilton. After driving only a short while, Ben asked Anna to open the glove compartment and take out the match box. She did as he asked. He then asked her to take a match out and give it to him. She did. He placed it between his teeth and lips as you would a cigarette. She looked at him and said, "Why are you doing that? One end of that is poisonous or at least it's not good for you."

"Don't worry, honey," said Ben, "my dad did this all the time when he was driving. He said it makes you relax." He noticed she had closed the match box, but was still holding it in her right hand. He laughed as he glanced over at her. He did it a few more times, each time with a grin on his face.

"What's so funny?" asked Anna.

"Nothing," said Ben. "I love you so much. You are so concerned about my health. This little match is no danger to a big man like me."

"You are being silly," said Anna, "can I put the match box back in, or might you need another one? A big man like you should maybe have two or three sticking out of his mouth."

Ben really laughed this time.

"No, one is all I need," said Ben. "You can put the match box back in now, thank you very much." He then started to hum a little tune – "You can hold it and never know it." He was definitely having fun at Anna's expense.

Anna shook her head a few times after listening to Ben's humming. Then she said, "What are the lyrics of that little tune you are humming?"

Ben was fast on his feet and fast on his seat. He said, "The lyrics are: I love you more than you'll ever know." It, of course, was not the lyrics he was humming. It was: You can hold it and never know it. Anna never knew that her fingers were only the thickness of the bottom of the match box away from an engagement ring. One bought for her.

They talked about the vacation they were planning in February. Anna said she wanted to buy a new bathing suit before they went. Ben said he would buy it for her and she could choose any one she wanted. Two if she so desired. "Hell," he said, "I'll buy you ten bathing suits."

"I don't need ten," said Anna, "maybe two."

Anna suggested that they should check with a travel agent to find out about the activities on a cruise ship. She knew there were swimming pools on them and lots of good food, but she didn't know where they went. What places would they visit?

Ben assured her they would have loads of fun and he was very much looking forward to going. Anna said she was getting very excited about their vacation.

They arrived at Anna's parents place and were greeted very warmly. They sat and chatted 'til lunch time.

After lunch they decided to take a quick trip to see Niagara Falls. Andrew drove, Audrey sat in the front with him and Anna and Ben sat very close to each other in the back seat. They were holding hands and stealing kisses. Andrew could see them, but Audrey could not. Andrew would smile. He could remember when Audrey and he did the very same thing many years ago, in the back seat of a taxi. His daughter seemed happy which pleased him very much.

It was a beautiful afternoon. It was below freezing, but the sun made it feel a bit warmer. They drove directly to the Falls, took pictures, watched as the water cascaded down over the edge. Ben had never seen the Falls before, and was totally amazed by them. After about forty-five minutes, they headed back to Hamilton. They were back as the sun was going down, a pink and red sky could be seen in the west.

Audrey served roast beef, mashed potatoes, carrots and turnip for dinner. Ben said he had never tasted such tender meat, and he praised Audrey's cooking. That gave him a few brownie points, as he hoped she would become his mother-in-law.

After the dishes were done, the four of them watched T.V. for an hour. Then they played the card game called Hearts, which they had played the first time Anna and Ben came to visit them at Christmas. They played until Andrew said it was past his bedtime. Anna and Ben watched T.V. 'til midnight, at which time Anna went to sleep in the spare bedroom, while Ben would sleep on the big leather sofa in the finished basement. Before falling to sleep Ben thought how lucky he was to be accepted by such a lovely family.

Saturday morning Ben suggested they go out for breakfast, he would treat. Andrew wanted to pay half, but Ben insisted he was treating. Of course, Andrew had no idea that Ben was a millionaire. Ben had contemplated telling Andrew and Audrey about his good fortune, but he decided to wait until he and Anna were engaged. He hoped it would happen soon.

Saturday afternoon they sat and talked, then played Scrabble. They had fun. Audrey made fish and chips for dinner. After dinner they watched T.V. including the hockey game between Toronto and Montreal. They all cheered for Toronto, so there was no disaccord between them.

When the game was over, Andrew said he would retire to the bedroom and read. Audrey watched T.V. with Ben and Anna for a while, then, she too went to bed. Anna and Ben ended up on the basement sofa hugging and kissing with no attempt to keep their hands to themselves. However, they did not violate the house rules. Anna slept in her bed.

Sunday morning Anna served fruit, then hot porridge, toast if you wanted it, tea and juice.

At nine forty-five all four of them headed for church. Ten o'clock service. Ben had not been in church since his dad died. He decided he was not a church-going person. However, when you are in Rome, you do as the Romans do. He went to church that Sunday morning.

Snow was expected Sunday afternoon in the Hamilton area. Ben and Anna decided to hit the road right after lunch. They had been invited to visit anytime. They just wanted a few days' notice so that they wouldn't make plans to go away. Anna said she would give them at least a week's notice. She also told them of their plans for a vacation.

On the outskirts of Hamilton on Friday, Ben had noticed a dirt road on the right side. He was watching for it now as he drove east. Suddenly, there it was, now on the left. He slowed down and turned left onto the dirt road. It had been plowed since the last snowfall.

Anna said, "Where are you going?"

Ben said, "Did you see what they call this road?"

"No," said Anna, "what is it called?"

"It's called Love's Road," said Ben.

"That's a cute name," said Anna, "but it won't take us home."

Just as Anna said that, Ben saw a cleared area on the left side of the road. He turned left into the area and stopped. He was now facing back to the road they had come in. He left the engine running and slid across the seat. He put his right arm around Anna and pulled her close. At the same time, he turned her head with his left hand and kissed her passionately. She kissed him back. It was a prolonged kiss. Anna then pulled away to look around.

"Don't worry," said Ben, "this road probably leads to gravel or sand pit, and this is Sunday. Now, why don't you kiss me again and maybe something will come up."

"Ben Breakwater," said Anna, "if you think you are going to get into my panties in broad daylight on the side of a road, you are dreaming."

"Oh, come on," said Ben, "I bet you never ever had a quickie in the cab of a truck."

"No," said Anna, "and it won't be today, unless you can make it dark."

"Well," said Ben, "I guess it's something to look forward to."

"I guess it is," said Anna, as she reached over and placed her hand on Ben's manhood, and said, "down boy, I will get you up in another place and time."

Ben laughed and kissed her once more. He slid back to the wheel and pulled out onto the main road. They would be in his apartment in less than an hour, where he knew Anna would be more receptive to his advances.

As they turned onto the highway which would take them to Toronto, Anna smiled as she looked over at Ben. She thought about what Ben might have been thinking when he turned and parked on that dirt road called Love's Road. It was presumptuous of him to think she would have sex in his truck, in the afternoon, and on the side of the road. Maybe he was testing her, and had no intention of carrying it through. She suddenly felt mischievous. She reached over and put her left hand on Ben's knee. She moved it slowly up his leg to the upper thigh. She kept her hand there as she slowly massaged his inner thigh.

Ben said, "Don't stop. Don't stop. Don't stop. Don't stop, don't stop," as he talked faster and faster, repeating "Don't stop."

Anna laughed as she moved her hand gently to his manhood.

Ben reached down and removed her hand and told her she could finish the job later but not when he was driving.

"You are right," said Anna, "not when you are driving. Foolish me," and she started to laugh.

Ben said, "You are not driving," as he reached across with his right hand and gently squeezed her left breast. As she removed his hand she said, "Pay attention to your driving, lover boy. Maybe later you might get lucky."

They both got lucky, in Ben's shower a few minutes after arriving at Ben's apartment.

CHAPTER 12

TUESDAY MORNING AT THE FITNESS CENTER BEN TOLD LEON he was ready to try to bench press two hundred and sixty pounds. Leon told him if he did reach that new mark, he had a little reward for him, something he would really enjoy. Leon knew what he was offering Ben was something Ben had never held in his hands before, and he told him so.

Ben was excited, and he was pumped. He positioned himself underneath the bar, lifted it off, lowered it and up it went. Success. The first time he pressed two sixty. Leon smiled and said, "Good work". He then reached into his pocket and handed Ben two tickets. Ben looked at the tickets, then, he looked at Leon. He reached out his hand and said, "Thanks, Leon. I will always remember where I received tickets to see my first professional hockey game. In Ben's hand he held two tickets for Saturday night's game at Maple Leaf Gardens. The Toronto Maple Leafs would take on the Montreal Canadiens.

Ben's dad was a Maple Leaf fan, so naturally, he too cheered for the Maple Leafs. His Dad's favourite player was Tim

Horton. Ben's favourite player was Frank Mahovlich, the Big M, as he became known as.

He sat down and just looked at the tickets. These would take him to a place he had never been before, Maple Leaf Gardens, a place where, since 1931, professional hockey had been played. It was home to the Toronto Maple Leafs, a team that had won nine Stanley Cups before 1964. A place where hockey fans could hear the sound of skates biting into the ice, hockey sticks maneuvering pucks, and pucks hitting the boards. A place where the fans cheered loudly, and music played between referee whistles to stop and start play. It was an atmosphere like no other. It was 'The Canadian Game', graceful, violent at times, and always exciting.

Ben knew that Anna had never been to the Maple Leaf Gardens to see a hockey game. She had watched a few games with him on Saturday nights, and he had explained to her, as his dad had informed him, about how the game is played. He remembered his dad telling him that one had to know the rules of a game, in order to appreciate it and enjoy it.

Tuesday evening Ben called Anna and invited her to have dinner with him on Wednesday. He told her he had something to show her, something that they both would enjoy. Anna wanted to know what it was, however, Ben told her he wanted to show her, not tell her.

Wednesday morning as they were working out, Ben asked Leon where he got the hockey tickets. Leon told him, "Compliments of Tim Horton". Ben said, "You know Tim Horton?" "Course I do," said Leon. "I went to school with him in Cochrane, Ontario. We keep in touch. He has been in here quite a few times." "Wow," said Ben, "he was my dad's favourite player."

"Well," said Leon, "he's been my favourite player ever since he was a boy. Many times, I went to see him play, and I still do. I don't think the Leafs would have won three straight Stanley Cups without him."

"Maybe you are right", said Ben, "but I like Frank Mahovlich. He is the most exciting player with the puck. With those big long strides and his booming slap shot, he sure gets my attention. Plus, he scores a lot of goals."

"Can't argue with you," said Leon. "He certainly is a big part of the team. Enough about hockey, let's get back to work."

Saturday night, an hour before game time, Ben and Anna arrived at Maple Leaf Gardens via a taxi. With a little help from the staff they found their seats. Right at center ice and fifteen rows from the bottom. Ben remarked that they were excellent seats. Anna agreed. They were both elated. They watched with great interest everything that was going on. They had a panoramic view, and watched as the Zamboni prepared the ice for play. The ice looked like a sheet of glass. Soon the players from each team would exit an open gate and onto the ice. They did this with great dexterity. Their skating seemed effortless and graceful. Anna said it was much better than watching it on T.V. She said she felt she was more a part of the action, seeing it live. Ben agreed.

Ben knew many of the players by sight and by their numbers. He was totally in awe. Right there in front of him skated his hockey heroes, as well as his dad's: Tim Horton, Frank Mahovlich, Dave Keon, Red Kelly and Johnny Bower. Then he looked at the other half of the ice and saw Jean Béliveau, Henri Richard, Yvan Cournoyer and Dick Duff, all respected players of the Montreal Canadiens. He had never seen such a spectacle in his life. He would never forget it, and he shed a tear thinking how thrilled his dad would have been to be seated beside him and Anna.

They enjoyed the game immensely. Toronto won the game 3 to 2, and Frank Mahovlich scored two of Toronto's three goals. A taxi was easy to find, as many were parked outside Maple Leaf Gardens. As they sat in the taxi and talked about the night's experience, Ben and Anna knew there were many such nights to come. Ben had the money and they both had the time.

Next on their agenda was a vacation.

Ben had noticed a travel agency in the Yorkdale Mall when he went there shopping for rings for Anna. However, he would not tell Anna that he had been to the mall, for she might be a little ticked that he had not taken her. So, he decided to tell her that Leon had told him about the travel agency in the new Yorkdale Mall.

After a visit to his bank, Ben picked up Anna. It was her day off. The Yorkdale Shopping Mall was their destination. It was a very busy place. Anna told Ben that she had been at the mall several times with Cora. Holding hands, they went directly to the travel agency. There were two couples being looked after, so Ben and Anna decided to walk around and come back later.

Twenty minutes later they were seated at the travel agency and made plans for their vacation.

They would fly to New York City on the second Friday in February. Monday morning, they would board the cruise ship heading to the Caribbean for fifteen days. All transportation required was arranged. They would be on their own for the two days in New York City. Ben paid in cash. They thanked the lady who had been very professional, and left with smiling faces and jubilant anticipation.

They had lunch at a restaurant in the mall.

Ben suggested they go back to his place and celebrate and said he had a very good bottle of wine and a package of condoms.

"That would lead us to do a little giggie-giggie-pushie-push," said Anna, laughing.

"Now where did that come from? Did you just make that up?" asked Ben, as he began laughing.

"No," said Anna, "I think you can guess who I heard say that."

"Let me think…Got it," said Ben, "Cora."

"Right on," said Anna, "one thing Cora is not, and that is a boring person. Yesterday she came home with a book showing many different positions when making love. She called them giggie-giggie-pushie-push positions. We had a good laugh."

"Well," said Ben "if you can remember, we can try some of these positions when we celebrate later."

Anna replied, "If you're 'up' for it."

"Not a problem," said Ben, "let's go celebrate."

The afternoon of the second Friday in February 1965, Ben and Anna checked into the Herald Towers, 34th Street, near Broadway, in New York City. Their room was spacious and very nice, for an older hotel.

They decided to hit the streets and walk around Times Square. They were amazed at the number of people walking in all directions, the size of the well-lit billboards, and the sound of beeping horns. It was dark, nearly six p.m., but you would never know it. So much light from the street lights and giant billboards.

At the corner of Broadway and 42nd Street, is a place Anna will never forget. Amid the lights and crowds of people, Ben suddenly went down on one knee and held Anna's left hand. In his right hand between his thumb and forefinger he held up the engagement ring and said, "Anna Wood, will you marry me?"

It did not take very long for a crowd to gather around them. They were now applauding.

For a moment Anna placed both hands on her face. On removing them, a tear rolled down her left cheek, and with a tearful smile she said, "Yes, yes I will marry you." Ben stood up and as his eyes started to tear up, he placed the ring on Anna's left hand. The applause now grew louder as they kissed, hugged, then, thanked the people for sharing their special moment with them. Soon, the standing crowd was gone and the people who were now walking by, were, of course, oblivious to what had taken place a few minutes ago.

Ben and Anna decided to walk down 42nd Street to look for a restaurant. The sidewalks were not as crowded as they were on Broadway. Within a few minutes they found a very nice restaurant. They waited for half an hour before they were seated at a table.

While they sat and waited, Anna looked at, touched, and moved her ring many times. Her face was aglow with pleasure. Sitting there with Ben, gazing at her ring, she had never felt this happy, never ever before.

Appropriately, they both ordered New York strip steaks. The meal was very pleasing. Usually Ben did not like to share his dessert, however, now he was dining with his future wife for the first time, so they shared dessert.

After dinner they walked back to their hotel. The weather was fine and the temperature was above normal. The waiter at the restaurant said the temperature was forecasted to reach 44 degrees.

The night was young. Tomorrow they planned to do a lot of walking, take a few taxi rides, and ride the subway. Upon entering their room, they flopped down on the bed to relax for a while and reminisced about the day's activities. An hour later, in their large bathtub they took their first bath together, and it was the first time they made love in a bathtub.

Sunday morning, they ate breakfast at the hotel restaurant. After riding the subway, they took a taxi to the Empire State Building in Manhattan, a 1,250-foot sky-scraper that for many years was the world's tallest building. The view from the top was spectacular. Anna was a little scared at first, as she held Ben's hand very tight. And with Ben's assurance, she soon loosened her grip. They both agreed that next to Ben on one knee on the corner of Broadway and 42nd Street, this was the highlight of their trip so far. They stopped in at the gift shop to purchase a few souvenirs. As they walked around the ground floor, Ben noticed a boutique that sold watches. Quickly he made up his mind to buy Anna a watch. After all, he thought, they were in the Big Apple, so he wanted to buy her something substantial. Anna looked at several watches. Soon she walked out wearing a watch that was the same value as the ring she was wearing. She was beaming.

They ate lunch at a quaint little café. Afterwards, they took a taxi to the Museum of Nature. It was huge, beautiful, and they spent the whole afternoon there. They took another taxi back to Times Square, where they had dinner. They asked the waiter where the nearest theatre was, and went to a movie.

They were back at their hotel around eleven p.m. and watched T.V. until midnight.

Monday morning the hotel shuttle bus took them to the cruise ship. It was a very exciting time for both. It would be the first time Anna would see and smell the ocean. This was the first year the Princess Cruise Line operated from New York to Mexico and the Caribbean. Their ship was called The Princess Royal. Ben had chosen an outside cabin with a balcony. It was very nice. They would be cruising in style. The lady at the travel agency had told him if one could afford it, choose an outside cabin. Their cabin was on the second level.

Ben and Anna positioned themselves at a good vantage point and watched as the ropes were cast off, and the big ship's engines came to life, and slowly, the distance increased between the dock and the ship. They were on their way to the beautiful Caribbean.

Anna said, as she embraced Ben, "Let's go to our cabin and start this cruise with a bang."

"Well," said Ben, "am I engaged to modest Anna or not so modest Cora?"

For saying that, he got his nose pinched and little punch to the stomach. Ben laughed, as he reached for her left hand and they headed to their cabin. As Anna lay in the embrace of her lover, for a moment her thoughts went back to the first time she saw him at the grocery store. How handsome he looked, and now she was so in love with him. She was so excited about her future with this rich, young man, and so happy she had taken the job at the grocery store.

As they lay in each other's arms, Ben thought how lucky he was. Anna was so beautiful, inside and out. She had the face and body of a model, the mind of a loving country girl, and the wisdom of a mature woman. He loved her more than words could say.

Food on the ship was available any time of the day. Ben and Anna explored the decks from front to back. They swam in the pool, talked to people, young and old. Sometimes, they would just sit, and people watch.

On the third day they really enjoyed their balcony. The weather was now warm. They even spotted a few dolphins. Dolphins are gregarious and are very strong swimmers. Ben and Anna had never seen them in the wild before. They were told the best place to see them was at the rear of the ship. Dolphins like to ride the wake behind the ship. On this, the third evening on the ship, they ate dinner on their balcony. It was during this time Ben thought of an idea. He smiled and kept winking at Anna. Anna told him he was acting silly again. He just laughed, and told her she was the most beautiful woman on the ship.

An hour after dinner they were in the pool. Then they checked out the entertainment. The comedian on stage was very funny. They really enjoyed the show. After the show they went to a lounge where a man sang and skillfully played the piano. They sipped wine until midnight and went back to their cabin.

Anna asked Ben if he had brought a deck of cards. Ben said he did. She then suggested they play strip poker. Ben was more than happy to oblige. Cora had taught Anna to play poker. Anna pretended she was a novice.

"You will be nude in no time," said Ben.

"Maybe," said Anna, "can we keep it simple?"

"Sure," said Ben, "straight poker or three-card draw, dealer's choice."

"Fine," said Anna, "I think I can manage that."

They began to play.

Anna won the first two hands. Ben lost his socks and his shirt. Ben won the following two hands. Anna lost her blouse and her skirt. Anna won the next hand and Ben lost his pants. Anna now had 2 items left – bra and panties. Ben had only his shorts. The next hand could determine the winner. It was Ben's deal. He called three-card draw. After the deal they both took 3 cards. Anna looked at Ben and smiled. Then she said, "Looks like you are going to lose your shorts."

"Don't think so," said Ben, as he placed a pair of Jacks on the bed.

"Well, well," said Anna, as she also placed a pair of Jacks on the bed. They both laughed.

"I think you are going to lose you bra," said Ben as he placed an ace, a ten, and a seven on the bed.

"Not so fast," said Anna, "drop your shorts," as she placed a pair of fives on the bed.

As Ben dropped his shorts, Anna's bra and panties dropped to the floor. They were horizontal in seconds, on the bed. Ben asked Anna if she felt adventurous. She said, "Maybe, what do you have in mind?"

Ben answered, "Remember at dinner time on the balcony when I kept winking at you."

"Yes," said Anna.

"Well," said Ben, "I was thinking of us making love on the balcony after midnight. It's now after midnight. Are you game?"

"I don't know if I am or not," said Anna.

"I guess then it's maybe," said Ben. "Maybe I can help you." He rolled off the bed, ran to her side, picked her up and proceeded to the door of the balcony. Anna was now laughing as she grabbed the handle and pushed the door open. The warm air felt good on their skin. Ben sat her down on a chair, and told her to stay right there. He went back to get the spare blanket and pillows. They moved the table and chairs, and laid the blanket on the balcony floor. The pillows were placed at one end. As they embraced on the blanket in very dim light, they gently made love.

The next day, early afternoon, Ben and Anna went back to their cabin to relax for a while. Ben fell into a deep sleep. He dreamt he was camping with his dad. They were sitting around the campfire cooking a rabbit for supper. Suddenly, they heard a noise behind them. They both looked up at the same time. There, on her hind legs stood a huge mamma black bear, with a cub beside her. His dad said, "Don't move, put a finger in each of your ears." He reached into his pocket, and quickly stood up, whistle in his right hand. He put that whistle to his lips and blew as hard as he could. His ears were hurting from the sound. The cub ran, and it sounded like it was crying. Mamma bear was now down on all four legs, her head turned watching her cub. Soon they disappeared. Ben said, "I thought we would have to give that bear our rabbit." "No," said his dad, "If we had given her the rabbit, she would be back again. That's how it works with wild animals. They will come back to where they found food. However son, if the whistle didn't work, we would have lost our supper. It would be my last resort, to shoot a bear with a cub."

At that point in the dream, Ben awoke. Anna was sleeping beside him. He closed his eyes and soon he was fast asleep, once again.

A noise, something woke him. He turned, Anna was not there. He sat up in bed and looked around. He could not see

Anna. He sprang to his feet as the balcony door swung open. He checked the washroom, Anna was not there. He ran to the balcony door, then out onto the balcony. He was now in panic mode. He screamed, "Anna," as he looked over into the ocean. A breeze was sufficient to swing the opened door, that's what had awakened him. He looked at the door. Why was it open? They had always kept it closed. His mind was now racing – maybe she forgot to close the door – maybe she went for a walk – the boutiques on the first level – maybe she went there. He ran to the cabin door, ran down the hallway. No shoes or socks. Down the stairs to each of the boutiques. No Anna. He was losing his mind, he just couldn't think anymore. The one he loved more than his own life was missing. Without thinking he was now headed back to the cabin. He was running once again. He was now mad with grief. He entered the cabin shouting "Anna, Anna, I will save you". Quickly he moved to the balcony door, then he was on the balcony. He threw off his shirt, then his pants and leapt over the railing. He was falling, falling. Then a voice called his name, an arm held him and squeezed him, and he heard his name again. He screamed as he sat up in the bed. He turned his head and there was Anna. Tears rolled down his cheeks, he embraced her, kissing her as he called her name. Anna knew he must have been dreaming because of his movements on the bed.

"You were dreaming," said Anna.

"An awful, awful dream," said Ben. "The absolute worst dream I've ever had." The dream was vivid in his mind as he relayed it to Anna. When he got to the part where he leapt over the balcony railing, Anna couldn't stop her tears from falling. She knew now, how much Ben loved her, even though it was a crazy dream.

The first stop was Freeport in the Bahamas. Taxi cabs were parked near the dock. Upon leaving the ship, you were on your own. Ben and Anna hopped into a cab and they were in town in a few minutes. The weather was lovely. They walked around, and stopped at a few stores. They each bought a hat. They would need them from now on. They heard music. They were in what was called the Market Place. They arrived at a large stone patio with umbrellas shading each table. Many people sat around listening to the Bahamian music, and enjoying a drink. Ben and Anna decided to try their first Piña Colada, but it wouldn't be their last as they both enjoyed it very much. After finishing their drinks, they took a taxi to the nearest beach. The water was spectacular. They walked in the sand near the water's edge, and wished they had time to swim. The taxi waited for them and took them back to the cruise ship.

The next stop was Nassau, where they spent two hours on the beach and in the water. They had a great time. They had two Piña Coladas each, before heading back to their ship.

The next port would be Kingston, Jamaica, in the Caribbean Sea. Sunshine and hot every day. Ben and Anna were in the pool morning and afternoon.

The day after leaving Nassau, while having breakfast, they met another young couple. A small world, this couple was also from Toronto. Kevin and Sue. Kevin was twenty-four and Sue was twenty-thee. Kevin worked as an auto body repairman, while Sue was a hairdresser. Ben asked Kevin where in Toronto did he work? Kevin said he used to work at Tony's Auto Body in Mississauga, but now he worked at Jim Bob's Auto Shop on Elm Street in Toronto. Ben said, "I know where that is, it's not far from the Ford dealership where I bought my truck." Ben was not about to tell him the Jim Bob story.

Anna and Sue had their own conversation going. Sue worked in the hair salon at the Yorkdale Mall. Anna remembered walking by the salon when she and Ben went to the travel agency.

They exchanged phone numbers and saw each other a few more times at breakfast and in the evening in the lounge.

Ben did not have any more dreams during the trip. He told Anna if she ever witnessed him acting like he did when he dreamed she was missing, to wake him immediately.

They arrived in Kingston, Jamaica, where the ship would dock for forty-eight hours.

Ben read the leaflet about Jamaica that was available on the ship.

Kingston was founded in 1692, when an earthquake destroyed the nearby city of Port Royal. It became the capital of Jamaica in 1872. It is located on the southeast coast of Jamaica and has a deep-water harbour. The population now was around 355,000. Northeast of the city are the Blue Mountains, a renowned coffee growing region, with trails and waterfalls. Kingston Harbour is the 7th largest natural harbour in the world.

Jamaica was a British Colony from 1655 to 1962. It gained its independence in 1962. Slavery existed in Jamaica until 1833.

Ben and Anna were the first to disembark the cruise ship after it docked in Kingston, Jamaica. Ben carried his Dad's old backpack which now contained a canteen of water and towels. They took a taxi to Buccaneer Beach. The white sand was a sight to see and stretched for miles. They rented a large umbrella, and spent the whole afternoon on the beach.

At five forty-five they took a taxi to a restaurant with a stone patio on the waterfront, on Port Royal Street. They tasted the local cuisine, enjoyed the live music while sipping on Piña Coladas. They were back on board their ship by ten p.m. They had enjoyed the afternoon very much.

The next morning a taxi took them to the Blue Mountains. The driver old them there were lots of good trails, and if they wanted to see a very nice waterfall, he could take them to a trail where the falls were not very far from where he would park and wait for them. Both Ben and Anna were wearing new hiking shoes they had purchased for their vacation so they were more than ready for a short hike.

A ten-minute walk and they were at the waterfall. It was only twenty feet from the trail. A well-worn path led to the bottom of the falls. The spray would drench your clothing if you stayed there for too long. Ben estimated the falls to be thirty feet high. As they were leaving, several other people arrived at the falls admiring their beauty.

Ben and Anna decided to hike a while longer. Fifteen minutes after leaving the falls, the trail narrowed and turned rather sharply to the right. Just as they made it to the turn, a man stepped out from behind a large palm tree. He was holding a machete and a bandanna covered the bottom half of his face. He stepped closer and was only three or four feet from Anna who was on Ben's right. Pointing the machete at Anna, he said, "Be quick about it, drop your watches, your ring young lady, all your money and then remove these nice shoes. Do as I say and the young lady won't bleed all over that nice blouse." Ben thought for a few seconds and decided he would not jeopardize Anna's safety, so he told her to do as the man asked.

After they had complied with the man's wishes, he told them to turn around and walk back the way they had come.

Ben and Anna had only taken about ten steps when Anna started to cry. Ben looked back only to see the man pick up what must have been the last item that was on the ground, and then he vanished. Ben had noticed a narrow path just past the corner that went to the right. He thought the man had taken that path. He held Anna as she wept. He felt very frustrated, but there was no other option. He really could not have done anything different.

Between her sobs, Anna said, "That bastard took my ring".

"It's okay Anna," said Ben, "the ring can be replaced. What is more important, we were not harmed. Let's go back to the waiting taxi."

The trail was fairly smooth. Ben asked Anna if he could carry her on his back. She said, "No, I will walk. I am so mad, I don't feel my feet."

Ben looked away and smiled, saying to himself – what a woman, she has more spunk that I thought.

As they approached the taxi, the driver rolled down the car window and said, "What the hell, what happened to your shoes?"

"We got robbed," said Ben.

The driver was now out of his car and opened the back door for Anna. When they were all seated, the driver turned his head and said, "Damnedest thing I ever heard, two people had their shoes robbed while they were standing in them."

"We had more than our shoes robbed," said Ben. "We were walking along the trail, and suddenly a man with his face half covered, stepped out from behind a tree and pointed a machete at us. He threatened to use it if we didn't do what he commanded. On the ground in front of us we placed our watches, my fiancée's ring, the money I had in my wallet and our shoes. He then told us to start backtracking. I looked back as he vanished. So here we are."

The driver said, "Sorry man, I didn't mean to make a joke on seeing you barefoot."

"That's okay," said Ben, "please take us to a place where we can buy shoes."

"Yes, yes," said the taxi driver, "I am so sorry for your misfortune. I feel sad now because I chose that trail for you."

"I do not hold that against you, man," said Ben. "The falls were lovely."

As they drove back into the city Ben knew as a small consolation he had, to a point, outsmarted that thief. He had read a book some time ago, about a man on vacation who got robbed at knife point. He kept all his money in his wallet. He lost it all. Ben realized there was a lesson to be learned here. He had heard his dad say, never put all your eggs in one basket. Therefore, before leaving the ship he put most of his money in two pockets, and did not have very much in his wallet, mainly small bills.

After purchasing new shoes, Anna wanted to go back to the safe confines of the ship. Ben agreed they would, but first they would take a taxi ride to the police station to report what had happened to them on the Blue Mountain trail.

The policeman listened very intently to their story. He was also sympathetic. He told Ben and Anna that fighting crime was ongoing, and they were short-staffed. Furthermore, he told them he hoped to send an undercover cop to that trail to try and catch that thief. He thanked them for reporting it.

Ben and Anna went back to the ship. It was now lunch time. During lunch, Ben asked Anna if she wanted to go back to the beach, where they had spent yesterday afternoon. Anna said maybe. She would often look at her left hand and a tear would roll down her cheek. Ben knew it would take a long time for Anna to forget having to take off her ring and just lay it on the ground and walk away. Ben told her he would buy her another one just like it, as soon as they got back to Toronto.

After lunch they went back to their cabin to relax. Later they went to the beach for a couple of hours. They ate dinner on board the ship and ended up meeting Keven and Sue in the same lounge as before. The entertainment was good and so were the Piña Coladas. Sue noticed that Anna was not wearing her ring. Anna explained what had happened. Sue said, "Oh my God, we hiked that same trail this afternoon." Ben said, "That bandit won't be back on that trail for a few days anyway. After he pawns what he got from us, it will keep him going for a while."

The next morning, Ben and Anna took a taxi to a Jewelry store. Ben bought a watch for himself and one for Anna. Their ship was due to leave at noon. They were back on board by eleven a.m.

Sharp at 12 noon, their ship left the Kingston dock. The weather was lovely. There was a gentle warm breeze on their faces as Anna and Ben sat on their balcony. Their vacation was more than half over.

Ben read the leaflet left at the door of their cabin. The ship would stop for eight hours in Nassau. Then the next stop would be the New York City dock, where they had started the cruise.

The next two days went by much too fast. Kevin and Sue came to their balcony both days and they played cards for a couple of hours. Sue was very jovial and quite the extrovert.

Anna mentioned to Ben that Sue was very much like Cora. Ben agreed, and said Sue and Cora would be the life of any party.

About four in the afternoon on the second day after leaving Jamaica, Ben and Anna went for a walk around the ship. They were passing by a small lounge with a bar that served drinks in the afternoon. They decided to stop and enjoy a Piña Colada before dinner. As they were walking to a table with their drinks, Ben said, "It can't be. Yes, it is, it's him."

Anna said, "Who, where, what are you talking about?"

"That man sitting over there by the far window. I know him."

Anna looked and saw the man Ben was referring to.

"Who is he?" asked Anna.

"That is Joseph Blackmore, Private Detective, from Toronto. My, my, it's a small world," said Ben.

Anna thought for a few seconds and then she said, "Is he the one that you hired to find out where Uncle George lived in Halifax?"

"The very man," said Ben. "Let's go talk to him."

"I don't know if I want to," said Anna.

"He doesn't know you exist, Anna," said Ben. "I did not reveal the reason I wanted to know where George lived."

"Oh," said Anna, "that was foresight on your part. You are very smart, for a teenager. Okay, let's go see the man."

"Smart for a teenager eh," said Ben. "I guess that makes you a cradle robber," and he chuckled.

Anna, as she often did, gave him a punch in the shoulder, and he almost lost his drink.

"Let's go see the man in the Hawaiian shirt," said Ben.

As they approached his table, the man looked up, then he sat tall, he looked at Ben and said, "Well I'll be a monkey's uncle, if it isn't young Ben Breakwater." He stood up and held out his hand. Ben took it and gave it a firm squeeze.

"And who is this beautiful young lady on your arm?" asked Joseph.

"This is my fiancée Anna," said Ben. "Anna, this is Mr. Joseph Blackmore, a detective from Toronto."

"Pleased to meet you, Mr. Blackmore," said Anna.

"Have a seat," said Joseph. "Well, well, guess one never knows who might be travelling in the same direction you are."

"I guess we just proved that," said Ben.

"How was your trip to Halifax?" asked Joseph.

"Everything worked out just fine," said Ben. "Are you travelling alone?"

"No," said Joseph, "my wife is in our cabin, resting, she didn't sleep well last night. I was planning to go wake her after I finish this drink. I left her about two hours ago. I told her I was coming here to read and enjoy a couple of drinks. Oh, I guess I won't have to go wake her, here she comes."

It did not take Anna long to realize Joseph's wife was much younger than he was, twenty years at least. She was gorgeous. Long blond hair and dressed to kill. Anna reached over and took hold of Ben's left hand that was resting on the arm of the chair. She wanted to signal to this beautiful creature that Ben was her man, just in case she had any ideas. Joseph was not a good-looking man; however, Ben was.

As she approached them, Joseph stood up and held out his hand. She held his hand. Ben and Anna were now standing as well.

"Angelina," said Joseph, "meet my new friends, Ben and Anna." Greetings ensued. Joseph went to the bar and brought back a drink for Angelina.

Joseph pulled another chair over to the little table, and Ben and Anna shuffled over to make room for Angelina's chair. She sat down. Joseph explained to her that he had done a little investigating for Ben a few months ago. He said he was reading his book, he looked up and there they were. "Small world, that's for sure," he said. Joseph did most of the talking.

Anna could see in her peripheral vision that Angelina's eyes were often glancing at Ben. She had no reason to be jealous of this married woman, but a sense of insecurity came over her. She knew Ben loved her very much. However, this woman exuded confidence, and Anna said to her self – "Maybe my imagination is taking me to a place I don't need to be, but, I'll bet this woman gets whatever she wants, but she is not getting Ben. Relax, relax, Anna, enjoy, you are on vacation. Maybe we will never see this woman ever again."

Just as Anna finished her thought that they might never see this woman again, Angelina said, "You two should come and visit us in Toronto sometime. We could hang out in our pool."

These were the last words Anna wanted to hear. She reached for her drink and finished it, as she heard Ben say, "Yes, thank you for the invite." Then he looked at Joseph and said, "I still have your business card. I will give you a call."

"You do that," said Joseph. "Oh, by the way, other than Piña Coladas, what do you two like to drink?"

"A glass of wine would be fine," said Ben. "We both like wine."

"That's poetic," said Angelina. "Are you a poet?"

"No," said Ben, "however, I could say yes and prove it by saying – I'm a poet and I know it, I can rhyme any ole time, my feet are Longfellow's and they smell like the Dickens." They all had a good laugh.

Anna thought she should do a little talking instead of thinking. She asked Angelina if they had any children.

"Joseph and I have no children; however, Joseph has two from a previous marriage," said Angelina.

"Yes," said Joseph. "My son, Stanley, is one year older than Angelina, and my daughter, Barbara, is one year younger."

Angelina spoke up and said, "Yea, he robbed the cradle."

"That's right," said Joseph, "you are my baby, cause you are my lady, the love of my life," and he blew her a kiss.

"Well," said Ben, "I think we will move along and leave you two lovebirds alone."

"Maybe we will see you again before we reach New York," said Angelina. "Nice to have met you."

"It was nice meeting you," said Anna. "Bye for now."

They each waved to the other.

Anna felt a little foolish in retrospect. Her first impressions of Angelina may have been wrong. She now hoped they were. She wasn't sure she wanted to go and swim in their pool. If her initial feelings persisted she would have to talk to Ben about it.

The ship docked in Nassau at nine a.m. The weather was beach weather, and that is where Ben and Anna spent most of the eight-hour stop. They did take a taxi to the town center and enjoyed more Bahama island music. It was there they learned (by talking to a local man) that the Bahamas consisted of 700 islands, and only 20 islands were inhabited.

Five p.m., Ben and Anna watched for the last time the lines being cast off, and once again the big ship was moving.

They then headed for the back of the ship looking for dolphins. They saw several, following the ship.

Back in their cabin, they followed their usual routine. A shower, dinner and a visit to the lounge to enjoy the live music and a few Piña Coladas.

It seemed that after three Piña Coladas Anna wanted to play strip Poker. On this occasion she had four, lost the game but won the night. Ben had to use a second condom.

After lunch, the day they left Nassau, Ben and Anna decided to walk around the ship for exercise. As they were climbing the stairs to the third level, they heard someone whistling. They both looked back and saw a young crew member who quickly passed them because he was taking two steps at a time. As they began walking down the hallway, the young crew member walked up beside a lady and put his arm around her. The lady dropped her left hand and placed it on the young man's buttocks. After a few steps they stopped in front of a cabin door. The young man placed a key in the door and they stepped inside and the door closed.

Anna was watching every move they had made.

"Did you see that?" she asked Ben.

"See what?" said Ben.

"Ben Breakwater, do you know who that lady was that just entered a cabin with that young crew member who just passed us on the steps?" asked Anna.

"No," said Ben, "I didn't pay much attention. I was looking at the fancy door trimmings and the shiny numbers on those cabin doors."

"It was Angelina, Joseph's wife," said Anna.

"You're kidding me," said Ben.

"No, I am not," said Anna. "As soon as I saw her hair I knew it was Angelina. I also saw her profile as she turned and entered the cabin."

"Well I guess it's none of our business," said Ben.

"You are right Ben, it's not our business," said Anna.

"Maybe Joseph knows she cheats on him, and for some reason he doesn't care. Maybe he can't get it up, who knows," said Ben.

"I think I'll just forget about it," said Anna.

"I already have," said Ben.

For Anna, it was easier to say than do. She thought back to her original feelings about Angelina. Maybe she was right. But then, Ben had a point with his line of reasoning. Would she ever know? She would think about it from time to time. To her, it was like a problem she couldn't solve. She thought about Joseph. He seemed like a nice man. She hoped time would soften the memory.

As they reached cooler water in their northward journey, they spent less time on their balcony. At their last dinner on the ship, they talked about what they liked most about the cruise. Anna said what she liked best was the beach in Kingston. Ben said what he liked best was the romp on the balcony, but he also liked the beach.

They saw Kevin and Sue one final time at breakfast before the ship docked in New York.

They caught the shuttle bus back to the Herald Towers Hotel. Another bus took them to the airport. They arrived back in Toronto at five thirty that day which was Monday.

The first thing Anna did after arriving at her apartment was to call her mom. She told her mom what had happened in Times Square, and how happy she was to be engaged to Ben. She also told her some of the highlights of their cruise to the Caribbean, minus the thief on the Blue Mountain trail. Her mother was very happy for her, and wished her all the best. She reminded Anna that her dad was now on the phone and she repeated what she had told her mom. Her dad congratulated her.

Anna knew her parents liked Ben very much. On the 27th of March, her dad's birthday, she would inform them that Ben was a very rich young man, whom she would marry, even if he were poor.

After she finished talking to her dad, she called Ben and told him she had just talked to her mom and dad. She told him how happy they were for her. She also informed him of her dad's birthday, and that she said they would be there. Ben agreed, and said he enjoyed visiting her parents.

Ben's first order of business the day after arriving home from their vacation was to replace Anna's engagement ring. Ten a.m., he was at the jewelry store in the Yorkdale Mall, where he had purchased the rings for Anna. In his pocket he had the wedding ring and the bill of sale. The same lady that had showed him the rings the first time he went there was behind the counter. She recognized him and asked him if the rings he bought were the correct size. Ben said they were, but he needed to buy another engagement ring. From his pocket he took out the wedding ring and the bill of sale.

The lady asked Ben what happened to the engagement ring that he had bought. Ben explained what had happened in Kingston, Jamaica. The lady said she was so sorry to hear of their misfortune, and that Anna must have been devastated.

Ben said, "Yes she was, but I told her I would buy her another one, so here I am."

"Well," said the lady, "it may take a while to get just the engagement ring."

"How long?" asked Ben.

"Maybe a couple of months or longer", she said, "and the cost will be almost what you paid for the set.

"Do you have another set here like the one I bought?" asked Ben, "or very similar."

"Yes, I am sure we do. Let me see that ring." The lady found another set of rings that were almost identical. She showed Ben pictures of both sets in her catalogue. Ben could not see any difference. He bought the new set.

On the way home Ben thought about the extra ring he now had. Maybe Anna would wear it on her right hand, at least until they were married. However, on second thought, that was not a good idea. Then he thought of the simple solution. After they were married he would give it to Anna, and she could do whatever she wanted with the ring. If she didn't want to wear it, he might suggest she give it to Cora as a present.

Ben parked his truck at his apartment building. He reached into his jacket pocket for the little bag containing the new rings. It was time to do a little thinking. When and how was he going to present Anna with her new engagement ring? Looking at the dashboard of his truck, his eyes moved slowly back and forth. Then they became fixated on the glove compartment door. The match box. He had totally forgotten to tell Anna about the match box with the ring inside. He now recalled how much he enjoyed that little joke he played on Anna. He could do it again. However, this time the ending would be different. Thinking about it for a while, he formulated a plan.

He opened the glove compartment door and took out the match box. As he did before, he emptied the box, placed the engagement ring underneath the little rectangle, and replaced the matches. He placed the match box back in the compartment.

With a smile on his face he exited his truck and entered his apartment.

He needed groceries, he had been gone two weeks. After making a list, he went back out to his truck and headed for the grocery store where he knew Anna would be working.

Upon entering the store Ben noticed there were only three line-ups. Anna was working on number five cash, where he had seen her for the very first time. He picked up his groceries and proceeded to number five.

Anna didn't notice him until he started to place his groceries on the belt. When the lady who was ahead of him moved away Ben said, "Hello gorgeous". Anna smiled and said, "Hello handsome". Ben said, "I am cooking dinner, what time can I pick you up?"

"How about six?" said Anna.

"Six it is," said Ben. Then he leaned over and whispered in her ear, "I'll be wearing my panty remover cologne."

Anna laughed.

Ben picked up his groceries and left.

The lady next in line was a regular customer. She said, "Hi Anna, how are you?"

"Just fine," said Anna. "I just got back from a two-week vacation."

"You were conspicuous by your absence," said the lady. "Hope you had a good time."

"I had a lovely time," said Anna.

"It sounded like you know that handsome young man that was ahead of me," said the lady.

"Yes, I do indeed," said Anna. "I am going to marry him one of these days."

"Is that a hope or have you had a proposal?" said the lady.

"A proposal," said Anna. "It happened two weeks ago in Times Square, New York City."

"Lucky Lady," said the woman, and she moved slowly into the short line-up leaving the store.

Ben picked up Anna at the agreed time, six p.m. Just before they reached Ben's apartment building, Ben asked Anna to get him a match from the box in the glove compartment.

As she opened the box to get a match, she asked Ben why he wanted one now, because they were almost to his place. Ben just smiled as he placed the match between his lips. He then parked his truck in his usual parking space.

Still holding the box of matches, Anna looked at Ben as he took the match from his mouth and placed it in his right hand. He then told Anna to take out all of the matches and put them with the lone match.

"Ben Breakwater," said Anna. She always said his full name when she was annoyed with him. "What silly game are you playing?"

He laughed as she placed the matches in his right hand.

"Now what?" said Anna.

"I love you so much," said Ben.

Anna was now shaking her head, as she looked at him.

Then he said, "Anna, I want you to separate the little box from the cover." She did, and there was her engagement ring. As the ring appeared, Ben said, "You still want to marry me? That is your new engagement ring."

Anna just looked at the ring, then, tears rolled down her cheeks as she looked up at Ben, who reached over and picked up the ring. She turned over her left hand, and he slipped the ring on her finger. They came together on the seat, kissed and hugged. Ben said, "Please don't lose this one." They both laughed.

Before leaving the cab of the truck, as Ben was putting the matches back in the box, he told Anna about the other ring that was in the box when they drove to visit her parents.

Anna said, "So that's why you were having so much fun at my expense. I was holding my ring and didn't know it."

"Right on," said Ben.

"What on earth will you do next," said Anna.

"That's easy," said Ben. "I will serve you dinner and then I will serve you some lovin'."

The Saturday after Anna got back from vacation, both she and Cora had the day off. They made plans to go shopping at the Yorkdale Mall. Anna had invited Ben for dinner. She was making a chicken casserole. Cora's boyfriend, Sammy, was picking her up at six-thirty. They were going out for dinner and Cora was staying overnight at his place. Ben would be Anna's company overnight.

Anna called Ben when she returned home from the mall. Ben was there half an hour later. Anna had the casserole in the oven. Ben sat on the chesterfield turning the pages of a magazine. Anna and Cora had disappeared into the bedroom, to change the bed sheets.

Ben was reading an article in the magazine. Anna and Cora came out of the bedroom and stood where Ben could see them, but he did not look their way. Anna said, "Is that an interesting article, Ben?"

"Yes," said Ben.

"More interesting than us?" said Anna.

Ben looked up and saw Anna and Cora standing there in their mini-skirts.

"Well," said Cora, "do you approve?"

"Nice legs," said Ben. "Did you wash these skirts in hot water or what?"

"No," said Anna, "we just bought them today, they are called mini-skirts, the new female fashion."

"Well," said Ben, "they sure reveal a lot of leg. I think come warm weather they will cause a lot of car accidents."

Cora and Anna thought that was funny and they laughed, as they headed back into the bedroom, leaving Ben shaking his head.

After Cora and Anna changed back into their regular clothes, the three of them played cards until Sammy came to pick up Cora.

Ben and Anna ate dinner, washed the dishes, and watched T.V., Hockey Night in Canada. The Detroit Red Wings were playing the Toronto Maple Leafs.

At the end of the first period, Anna asked Ben if he liked her mini-skirt.

"You sure look good in it," said Ben. "However, it's a bit short to wear out on the street."

"It's the new fashion," said Anna, "lots of young women will be wearing them."

"Well," said Ben, "I just don't relish the thought of a young buck walking behind you with a hard-on, because he can almost see your panties."

"You are being ridiculous," said Anna.

"Maybe," said Ben, "Do you think your mother would approve of you wearing that skirt out on the streets of Toronto?"

"No, I guess she wouldn't," said Anna, "and my dad would agree with her big time. However, they don't have to know I wear one anyway, you know, what the eyes don't see…"

"Well," said Ben, "I am not the boss of you, I wouldn't tell you not to wear it, but you know how I feel. If I didn't love you, I wouldn't care what you wore. The second period is starting."

Watching the game, Anna thought about the mini-skirt issue. It would be more than two months before she could wear it outside. Anyway, she had an idea.

When the second period ended, Anna asked Ben if he would like her to wear her mini-skirt when he came to her place. Ben said he would, but he would have a hard time keeping his hands off her and therefore, the skirt would not stay on very long.

"Maybe I'll have to teach you a little control," said Anna. "After the game is over we will practice control."

"Sounds good to me," said Ben.

When the game was over, Anna asked Ben to open a bottle of wine that was in the fridge. Anna slipped into the bedroom and came out wearing her mini-skirt. Ben whistled when he saw her. He placed the two glasses of wine on the coffee table and sat down. Anna paraded back and forth out of his reach. Then she said, "You see, honey, you men have to learn to control yourselves when you see legs, because this is the way it's gonna be." She picked up her glass of wine, took a sip, sat it back down, and continued her sexy stride back and forth. (Ben was showing more restraint than she thought he would.)

"Okay, okay," said Ben, "I get it, now come and sit here beside me and drink your wine."

She sat down and smiled.

Ben looked down at her legs and skirt, and remarked, "That thing sure don't cover much when you sit down, Anna Wood."

"Covers more than my bathing suit," Anna said, "and I wear it at a public beach."

"I guess you got a point there," said Ben.

They sat and sipped wine, talked about their vacation and where they would like to go on their next vacation. Occasionally, Ben would put his hand on Anna's knee and slowly move it up to the mini-skirt.

Anna said, "Let's turn on the radio and find music we can dance to. I feel like dancing."

"Good idea," said Ben. "It will be the first time I danced with a lady in a mini-skirt."

Anna found appropriate music and they danced. They finished the bottle of wine. Anna was now losing her inhibitions, and it was time for a little payback. Ben was sitting on the chesterfield. Anna walked up and stood in front of him. She said, "Lucky man, you win the prize." She lifted her skirt and revealed the fact that she was not wearing panties.

Ben grabbed her and pulled her down on top of him as he fell prone on the chesterfield. He laughed, and said, "You sat beside me, we talked, then we danced, and all this time you were not wearing any panties." She laughed. Ben said, "I guess the score is one, one. Me and my match box, you and your bare box." Anna could not stop laughing. Finally, she said, "Ben Breakwater, you sure have a way with words."

They made love on the chesterfield, Anna still wearing her mini-skirt.

Ben left Anna's apartment Sunday afternoon, just before Cora came home. Cora told Anna that her boyfriend Sammy had asked her to move in with him. She said she had told him she could not just leave her best friend to pay for the apartment alone.

Anna said she thought about moving in with Ben, but could not for same reason, however, now that has changed, if you want to move in with Sammy.

"Well, I guess that is good timing," said Cora. "Our lease is up at the end of next month. We have paid for this month and next month is already paid, so we both can leave this place anytime."

"I guess we could," said Anna. "I will miss you. It's been fun sharing this apartment."

"I will miss you too," said Cora. "Sammy and Ben will be very happy, that's for sure. We will still see each other, just not as much as we used to."

They hugged. Cora called Sammy to tell him the good news. Anna wanted to tell Ben the next time she saw him, and not on the phone. She did call him and told him something had come up and she would drop by after work Monday evening to talk about it. She told him not to worry, he would be happy about it.

At six fifteen Monday evening, Anna walked into Ben's apartment.

"So, what is the good news?" said Ben.

"Well," said Anna, "I am moving out of that dingy little apartment and I am moving someplace else."

"Oh," said Ben, "did you and Cora have a fight?"

"No, nothing like that. She is moving in with Sammy, and I am moving in with you, if you will have me."

"Have you!" said Ben. "Why that news makes me the happiest man in the world." He then kissed her, swept her off her feet and did a couple of three sixties, holding her in his arms.

"I can move in anytime," said Anna, "so I guess it will be on my next day off, which is Friday. I am working Saturday. This will give me lots of time to pack what little I have. I have decided to give Cora most of the furniture. I don't want to crowd your apartment."

"Whatever you decide, Anna, is fine with me," said Ben. "Let's go out for dinner, maybe that little café where we went on our first date."

"Let's go," said Anna, "I'll drive, you can treat."

During dinner they talked about several things. When they would get married, buying a house, and when would Anna start the dental assistant course. They also talked about the ramifications of telling Anna's parents that Ben was a rich young man. Ben said he thought it would be wise for them to get married before Anna started the dental course. In doing so, her parents wouldn't have to help pay for her course. Ben said if he were in her parents' shoes, and his daughter was married to a rich man, he would not feel obligated to pay for further education. Anna agreed that it was quite logical thinking.

Anna said she didn't see why they had to rush anything. However, she thought that buying a house would be a wise move, because paying rent was a waste of money, whereas a house was an investment.

Ben nodded his head and said, "You are not just a pretty face, Anna Wood, you are a very astute young lady. Why am I renting when I have the money to buy a house? That is our next project. We will buy a house as soon as we find one we both like."

Anna said they would be smart to buy a bungalow, four bedrooms, two bathrooms and a powder room. She said if they have two kids, a boy and a girl, they would need three bedrooms, the other one would be a bedroom for guests.

"And a two-car garage," said Ben.

"This is getting exciting," said Anna. "In just a few months, I go from a small apartment to a spacious apartment, to a four-bedroom house. How lucky can a girl be?"

Ben leaned over and gave her a kiss and said, "Just lucky enough to have met me, that's all. However, I think I am the lucky one. Lucky to have found John Dillon, and lucky to have met you."

After Anna dropped him at his apartment, Ben sat in his leather chair and did some thinking. His lease was up in September, but if he paid rent to August, he could leave anytime. He picked up the phone book off of the coffee table and found the real estate section. At the top of the listings was Adam's Real Estate. He noted the number and wrote it on the inside cover of the phone book. He thought it was going to be fun, him and Anna looking at houses.

The next morning, after his workout, he called the number to Adam's Real Estate. He talked to a man named Malcolm, and told him what he was looking for. Malcolm checked his listings and said he had four houses that he could show him. One was vacant, the others could be seen any afternoon or on Saturday. He told Ben when he was ready to look at the houses, to call him and he would pick him up.

Ben told him he would call him the following day.

Ben called Anna after dinner and informed her of the four houses they could go and see. Anna suggested they should go and see them Friday afternoon. They could move all her things in the morning, from her apartment to his. Ben said he would call Malcolm the very next morning.

Ben helped Cora and Anna pack her stuff and they had it all moved to Ben's place before noon on Friday. Malcolm picked up Ben and Anna at one p.m. They saw all four houses before five p.m. The one they really liked was at 46 Robin Hood Road. Ben said he would buy the house. They would move in on August 1st, that's when it would become available.

Anna called her mom and dad on Friday night and told them she had moved in with Ben. She also told them about the house they would move into in August. Her mom asked her about their wedding plans. Anna told her she would be the first to know when they set a date. Anna told her she was looking forward to August when they would be in their own house, and they could come and visit her and Ben for a change.

Saturday morning Anna served breakfast in bed. Fruit and French toast with maple syrup. Ben said it was the first time he ate breakfast in bed, he liked it very much. Anna said she was happy that she was the first one to serve him breakfast in bed, however, she wouldn't be doing it on demand, only if she wanted to. Ben said he would never demand, that was not his style, he was not a male chauvinist. However, he said he might try and smooth talk her into doing something, but he would do something in return.

After breakfast, while still lying in bed, Ben asked Anna if she still wanted to take the dental assistant course. Anna said she did. He then told her she should give her notice at the grocery store and sign up for the course. He said, "Now that we are living together, best friends and lovers, plus being engaged, he would pay for the course.

"Thank you," said Anna, "I will find out when the next course starts at the University of Toronto.

Anna shed her housecoat, she wore nothing underneath. She slipped into bed beside a nude Ben and snuggled close. She reached out and rubbed his chest, circling his nipples. She nibbled on both his ears, told him she needed him and kissed him passionately. She moved her right hand down over his stomach to reach his pubic hair. Slowly she stroked his now erect manhood. She was now kneeling perpendicular to him. He reached for her breasts and gently massaged them. Anna then moved and sat on his stomach. She leaned forward, and Ben's mouth and tongue worked over her breasts. Then came passionate kisses. Ben reached under the pillow for a condom and slipped it on. Anna moved her body further down and inserted Ben's manhood into her. This was the first time she had adopted the dominating position in their lovemaking.

CHAPTER 14

BEN AND ANNA HELPED CORA PACK FOR HER MOVE WHICH would take place the following Saturday morning, a week after Anna moved. Sammy had a friend in the moving business who would send two men and a truck to move Cora to his place.

Anna checked with the University of Toronto and found out the next dental assistant course would start on the 2nd of April. She would give the grocery store two weeks' notice on the 15th of March.

Ben made a trip to Metro Toronto Police Headquarters and informed them that he would like to become a police officer. They would interview him on the 15th of March.

One morning, after breakfast, Ben suggested to Anna that he should call Joseph and Angelina and ask them if the invitation to swim in their pool was still on. Anna had forgotten about Angelina. Now the memories on the cruise ship came back to her. However, her pride would not allow her to indicate to Ben that she saw Angelina as a threat, because she was a beautiful woman.

"Well," said Ben, "should I call them or not, or do you want to call them?"

"No," said Anna, "you call them, and if they give us an option as to when we can visit, let's make it a Sunday afternoon."

"I will call them this evening," said Ben. "I can't wait to see their house. I'll bet it's huge."

After Anna left for work, Ben washed the breakfast dishes and headed to the club for his workout.

Ben was in the locker room getting dressed after his workout when a friendly man who was also getting dressed started talking to him. He said his name was Larry Whitmore, and he had just joined the club. He said he worked for the TTC (Toronto Transportation Commission). He operated a streetcar. His hometown was Gander, Newfoundland, and he had been in Toronto about ten years. He had an uncle who worked for the TTC.

Ben told him how long he had been in Toronto and that he hoped to join the Metro Police Force.

Larry told him it was a noble thing to do, wished him good luck and said, "Gotta go to work. See ya later."

Ben said, "Have a good day." And he was gone.

After dinner, Ben found Joseph Blackmore's business card and called his home number. Joseph answered. Ben was impressed that he knew who was calling. It had been nearly four months since Ben talked to Joseph on the phone. They chatted for a while. Joseph asked him when they were coming for a visit. Ben suggested Sunday afternoon. Joseph checked his calendar and told Ben this coming Sunday would be fine, and he was looking forward to seeing them again. He also said that it was only a couple of days ago that Angelina had mentioned him and Anna, and wondered if you would call as you said you would.

"Well," said Ben, "now that I have followed through on my promise, what is your address?"

"Fifty-two Nottingham Drive," said Joseph.

"Oh," said Ben, "a while ago, Anna and I looked at a house for sale on Nottingham Drive. However, we didn't buy it. We are buying one on Robin Hood Road, which is only one street over from where you are."

"What are the chances," said Joseph. "You pick my name in the Yellow Pages, we meet on the same cruise ship, and now we will be almost neighbours, hot damn."

"Pretty amazing, I guess," said Ben. "We will see you guys on Sunday." He hung up the phone.

Anna was sitting beside Ben while he talked to Joseph. After he hung up, she asked him what was amazing. Ben told her what Joseph had said. Anna agreed.

Ben was thinking – if they became good friends with Joseph and Angelina, maybe they would have pool parties every now and then. That would be fun.

Anna was thinking - living so close to Angelina could be detrimental to her marriage – there I go again – feeling insecure – why do I do this to myself? Maybe I need to see Lynn again. She helped me before. Should I tell Ben? Lynn will know what I should do.

Ben asked Anna how things were at the grocery store. Anna said they were fine. Then she told him about the man who came through her cash today. She said she caught him looking at her a couple of times. Before he left, he leaned over and said in a whisper, "If you were not wearing that ring, I would buy a new broom and try to sweep you off your feet, gorgeous one."

"Course you are gorgeous," said Ben. "I didn't use a broom, but I swept you off your feet. I don't think I told you, but I was so happy the second time I saw you and saw that you were not wearing a ring. Too bad, so sad, for that guy. He will have to look elsewhere."

"So will any other guy except the one that put the ring on my finger," said Anna.

"And a lucky guy he is," said Ben.

Anna just smiled and blew him a kiss.

Sunday afternoon Ben and Anna were on their way to Nottingham Drive to see Joseph and Angelina. Anna had made up her mind that she was not going to jump to conclusions as to what Angelina's intentions were, or what she might do. She planned to relax and let the chips fall where they may.

As they pulled into the driveway at number 52, Ben said, "Wow, just as I suspected, big brick driveway, two-car garage and a big house."

They rang the doorbell and Joseph answered. He welcomed them to his house, took their coats and hung them in the closet. He then provided them with knitted slippers, and led them to the big leather chesterfield in the living room. The room was beautifully decorated and the carpet was plush.

Just as they were seated, Angelina walked into the room carrying a tray that contained crackers, cheese and pâté. She greeted them and said she was happy to see them again. She was wearing a low-cut blouse and a mini-skirt. She sat in the chair on Anna's right.

Joseph asked if they would like a glass of white wine. Ben and Anna both answered yes. He returned with a tray on which there were four glasses of wine. They sipped wine and ate crackers, cheese and the pâté.

They chatted for half an hour. Ben and Anna learned that Angelina worked at a dance school. She taught dancing. Most of her clients were single men, but she also taught couples.

After they had finished their wine, Joseph suggested that they should get into pool attire and hit the pool. He said he would get towels for them.

Ben went out to his truck to get the overnight bag which contained Anna's two-piece swim suit and his swim trunks. Angelina, who was already in her skimpy two-piece swim suit, showed them where the change rooms were. In a few minutes, they were all in the pool.

Angelina was a very good swimmer. She was doing laps of the pool like an Olympic swimmer, using a different stroke for each lap of the pool. Joseph remarked to Anna and Ben that the pool was where Angelina did her workout. Twice a day on weekends and holidays, otherwise, once a day.

Ben, like his Dad, was a strong swimmer. He swam in the lake near Breakwater with his Dad many times. Every time he swam he thought of the many times as a boy, his Dad would be in their boat moving along beside him. When he got tired, they would switch, and his Dad would swim.

Anna and Joseph were not very much like fish in the water. They could swim, but only for short distances. Just being in the water made them happy.

Ben decided to tread water in the deep end of the pool. Angelina was swimming underwater. She would swim the length of the pool underwater and come to the surface at each end. Suddenly, Ben felt his swim trunks were being pulled down to his knees. He immediately went underwater only to see Angelina swimming away. He pulled his trunks up and kept on treading water. He watched as Angelina came up in the shallow end of the pool. She had a big smile on her face, as she stood and walked over to where Anna was standing, up to her waist in the water. Ben could see that they were talking, but he could not hear them. He doubted that Angelina was telling Anna what she had just done, nor would he. Did she do it to be mischievous or was there an ulterior motive. Anna was now walking toward the shallow end while Angelina was looking at Ben. Ben shook his head and gave her a thumbs-down. Again, a big smile on her face. Ben decided to swim to the shallow end. Before he arrived, Anna was back in the pool carrying what looked like a medicine ball and Joseph had started swimming back from the deep end.

Angelina announced that they were going to play a game called O.U.T. They were to spread out in the pool and throw the ball to whomever you choose. Bad throws were not counted. The first time you drop the ball would be O, second time U and the third time T, and you were out of the game.

They had a lot of fun, and a good exercise for the arms. Joseph was the first out, Anna the second out. It seemed Angelina was very athletic. Ben was tempted to let her win because she was the hostess, but it was against his nature to let anyone win in any competition.

Anna cheered for Ben, Joseph cheered for Angelina. They both had an O. Ben decided to throw the ball with a little spin that went undetected for a couple of times. He then increased the spin and Angelina dropped the ball. She now had a U. She saw the ball spinning as it came toward her, however, she did not say a word. She tried to spin the ball on her next throw, and Ben almost lost the ball as he moved to his right to catch it. He gave her a thumbs- up. She laughed. Ben now decided to change his tactic. This time when he threw the ball he spun it in the opposite direction. It worked, as the ball spun out of Angelina's hands, for an O.U.T.

Anna cheered and applauded.

Angelina said, "Well done, young man, that is the first time I lost a game of OUT since high school."

Ben just turned his palms up and said, "Sorry to break your winning streak. You are very athletic."

Joseph said he was thirsty and suggested they sit by the pool and have another glass of wine.

They chatted about their experiences on the cruise ship, where they met. Angelina said she had a great time and she wanted to do it again. Anna was thinking again – I bet you want to do it again – you and your love boy crew member in that cabin – stop it, it's none of your business – enjoy the nice hospitality – and she's not flirting with Ben. Little did she know.

Joseph asked if anyone had a good joke.

Ben said, "Did you hear about the gay midget?"

Joseph said, "No."

Ben said, "Yea, he came out of the cupboard."

They all laughed. Joseph said it was a good one, and then he said, "I've got one. The old farmer said to his grandson, son if your girlfriend never farts when she's around you, you might wonder what else she might be holding back." More laughter.

Joseph said, "More wine anyone?"

Ben and Anna declined. Angelina reached for the bottle and poured wine in Joseph's glass and her own.

Ben said he would do a few laps of the pool and they would be on their way.

After about ten laps, Ben and Anna changed, thanked Joseph and Angelina for a lovely time. As they were leaving,

Angelina told them not to wait too long before calling them again, and thanked them for coming.

On the way home Ben and Anna talked about how much they enjoyed the afternoon. Ben commented that Joseph and Angelina were very nice people and knew how to treat their guests. Anna said Angelina acted like a lady, and she was now comfortable around her. She was looking forward to visiting them again. (Ben was now convinced that he could not tell Anna what happened in the pool. If he did tell her, he knew she would never set foot in their house ever again.)

Monday morning Ben walked to the fitness club. As he walked into the locker room he noticed Larry sitting at the far end. This time Ben started the conversation. It appeared Larry did not see him come in. They chatted as they changed into their workout attire.

Evidently, Larry loved music, mainly Folk and Country. He said he sang and played guitar all through his teens, to entertain his parents and friends. He also wrote songs. He told Ben that learning to play guitar was one of the most important things he had done in his whole life. He said that playing guitar kept him grounded, and entertaining others made him feel good.

Ben really felt that Larry meant every word he said. His passion for music was real. Suddenly, Ben felt the need to be like Larry. He had never really found his passion in life. Yes, he had found love, and he had money, yet he lacked what Larry had. Being able to do something you love, and make others happy at the same time, must be something special. The concept intrigued him.

He then told Larry he remembered his dad listening to the radio on Saturday nights, oblivious to anything else that went on. He said it was the Grand Ole Opry from Nashville, Tennessee.

"I watch it on T.V. now," said Larry. "Only the best of the best get to sing and play on the Grand Ole Opry stage. I could sit here for hours and talk about the many stars that sang on that stage. Maybe you should come to my place some evening and we can talk music. Hell, I will sing a few songs while you are enjoying a beer."

"I would like that very much," said Ben. "I'll get your phone number before I leave."

As they were leaving the locker room, Larry informed Ben that the Grand Ole Opry was founded in 1925 by a guy named George D. Hay. Ben always enjoyed learning something new.

After their workout, Larry told Ben he was working mornings for the next two weeks, and he could call him after three in the afternoon. He gave Ben his phone number and his address.

Ben told Anna about Larry, and that he was going to his place and hang out with him some evening. Anna told him Cora and her were going out for dinner on Wednesday, that would be a good time to go.

Ben called Larry Tuesday afternoon, and Larry told him Wednesday evening would be just great, any time after six p.m.

Six-fifteen Ben rang the doorbell at 192 Elm Street. Larry opened the door and said, "Come on in Ben, and make yourself at home. I have beer, wine and whiskey."

"Wine would be nice," said Ben.

Larry poured Ben a glass of wine and he opened a beer for himself.

Ben asked Larry where his wife Cathy was. He said she went out with a friend, shopping. Ben told him his fiancée Anna was out with a friend as well.

Larry said, "Maybe the next time we get together there will be four of us."

"Sounds good to me," said Ben.

"Well," said Larry, "I guess you are here to talk music. Do you listen to music Ben?"

"Not really," said Ben. "I do turn on my truck radio, but I never find anything that I want to listen to. I danced to music in high school, but I never really listened to it."

"Never too late to start," said Larry. "You are only a few years older than I was when I got interested in music. Did you ever play an instrument?"

"No," said Ben, "but I think I would like to try."

"Maybe I should get my guitar and give you a little concert, just to see if you enjoy what I call my passion. Come with me."

Ben followed Larry to his basement. In a small room in his basement he kept his two Martin guitars. He told Ben that the Martin Company that made these guitars kept their factory at around fifty percent humidity and seventy-two degrees Fahrenheit. Larry picked up one of his guitars and they went back up to the living room.

Larry sat on the chesterfield and sang a few old country classics. Ben enjoyed every second. He then told Ben the next song he would sing was one that he wrote. He said the song came to fruition because of a true story his Uncle Len Whitmore told him, the same uncle who worked for the TTC. He then relayed the story to Ben.

Len had married at the young age of twenty. His young bride Jane was the same age. Len was assertive, and Jane was not, she went along with most of his decisions. Whatever Len wanted to do he did. The marriage, for various reasons, broke down. They divorced. Two years later Len married Mary, who was as assertive as he was. One Saturday night, shortly after they were married, Len was doing what he had done for several years - he was watching hockey on T.V. Mary came into the room and said, "I hope you are not going to watch hockey all night. It would be nice if I got as much attention as that T.V." Well, Len up and told her that he always watches the hockey game on Saturday nights, and he was going to continue to do so. These words led to their first verbal match.

Larry told Ben after he heard the story he thought maybe there was a song to be written about a man who wanted to watch hockey, and a woman who wanted attention at the same time. He said he didn't know how he came up with the title, it just flashed through his mind. The title was: "Why Do Women Want Sex on a Saturday night."

Ben just shook his head and laughed.

Larry then sang the song.

The lyrics of the song:

It always amazes me and the cause of many a fight
Why do women want sex on a Saturday night?
Oh why do they do it I guess I'll never know
How can a man get in the game
How can he watch the show
When along comes that woman and lays that old guilt trick
I'm playing second fiddle to men with a twenty dollar stick

Hockey night on T.V. is a very popular show
And why most women disagree

I guess I'll never know
Unlike the players in the game who cause a great uproar
I just like to sit it out, I don't want to score

It always amazes me and the cause of many a fight
Why do women want sex on a hockey night?

After Larry had finished the song, Ben remarked, "If that doesn't tickle your funny bone, then you don't have one."

Larry replied that "yes, every time he sang that song it got a lot of smiles and laughter."

Ben asked him how many songs had he written. Larry said, "Around sixty. I haven't counted lately."

Ben told him that his dad wrote poems, and that he has his dad's book of poems at his place, and periodically he reads them.

Larry said, "A poem consists of words, just like a song. You just have to come up with a melody and sing it like a song."

"Are you saying you could take one of my dad's poems and sing it like a song? asked Ben.

"Yes, I think so," said Larry. "I may have to change or add a few words, but it can be done."

"Next time we get together I'll bring the book with me, and you can work on any poem you like," said Ben. "I can't wait for you to sing one of my dad's poems. That would be awesome."

"You do that," said Larry, "I will do my best."

Larry told Ben that he never took guitar lessons. He taught himself. He bought a chord book, learned a dozen chords and practiced. However, he told Ben, if one had the money, they should take lessons from a professional.

Ben said he would, if he decided he wanted to play guitar.

Larry sang a few more songs and they chatted about things they liked to do. When Larry said he liked camping, it was music to Ben's ears. Nobody would or could replace his dad as a camping partner, but he thought that Larry would be a very fine camping friend. He left Larry's house a very happy young man.

At ten a.m. on the 15th of March 1965, Ben was seated at Metro Toronto Police Headquarters waiting for his scheduled interview. He was given a clipboard on which there was a form that he was asked to complete. Full name, date of birth, address, etc., etc. When he read total monetary assets on the form, he started thinking. As of now, only two people knew he was a millionaire, Robert Pebble and Anna Wood. He now realized that he would have to reveal to the Police Department his much-guarded secret. He filled in the blank space, $1,000,000.00. He completed the form. From a large envelope he had brought with him, he took out his high school diploma and another sheet of paper which he placed under the completed form. It was a bank statement that listed his monetary assets as $1,030,000.00.

It was not very long before a Police Sergeant came down the hallway and approached him. He said, "Ben Breakwater, I assume." Ben stood up smartly and said, "Yes sir, that's me." They shook hands. Ben made sure he made a firm grip. The man said, "I am Sergeant Ken Browning. I'll take that clipboard Ben, please follow me."

He led the way to the office at the end of the hallway, told Ben to have a seat, and he closed the door. He walked around the desk and sat in a big leather chair. "First things first, young man," he said. "I need you to show me a piece of identification." Ben gave him his driver's licence, and watched as the Police Sergeant's eyes moved down the form he had completed. Suddenly, he looked up and said, "Young man, did you honestly complete this form, or is this some kind of a joke? This is not the 1st of April."

"Sir," said Ben, "I can assure you that every entry I made on that form is exact, except the monetary assets figure."

"I thought so," said the Sergeant. "Am I correct in saying there are too many zeros?"

"Yes sir," said Ben, "One of the zeros should be a three. I thought the number looked better using all zeros after the one. You will find the exact figure in my bank statement underneath the form."

He flipped the page and looked at the bank statement. Then Sergeant Ken Browning dropped the clipboard on the desk and sat back in the chair. He shook his head and a big smile came across his face. "Simply amazing. A first for me" he said. "A young man, not yet nineteen years old, who is a millionaire, and he wants to become a police officer."

"Yes sir," said Ben, "that's why I am here."

The Sergeant leaned forward over his desk toward Ben and said, "Would you mind telling me, Ben, how you attained such a large sum of money?" He then sat back in his chair.

Ben once again relayed the story of how he found John Dillon, the man who made him rich. He noticed the Sergeant took a few notes. When he finished the story, the Sergeant shook his head once again. Then he said, "I am intrigued by your story Ben. As a matter of fact, I know all about the John Dillon case. I was in the force about two years, when he went to jail."

Ben reached into his pocket and pulled out his wallet. He said, "I have something here I want you to see, sir." He took out a folded sheet of paper, unfolded it and handed it to the Sergeant. It was a copy of a police report clearing Ben Breakwater of any wrong doing in the death of one Mr. John Dillon.

The Sergeant nodded his head after reading the report and then he told Ben they would keep all his documents until his next interview. He also told him he would receive a phone call within the next two weeks as to the time and place of his next interview.

Once more the Police Sergeant looked at the form on the clipboard. "I have been remiss in congratulating you on your academic achievement in your final year of school. You indicated you were an honour student."

"Yes sir, my diploma is underneath, on the clipboard." The Sergeant lifted the other papers and saw the diploma. He looked up at Ben and just said, "Wow, a 97% average. That is the highest I have ever seen. One has to be very intelligent to achieve such high marks."

"Whatever I am sir," said Ben, "I give credit to my mom and dad."

"Well spoken, young man," said the Police Sergeant. "I must say this has been the most interesting interview I've conducted in my many years in the force."

He wished Benn all the best and hoped he would see him in a police uniform in the near future.

Ben replied, "You will sir, and maybe in the future I will have your job."

"Shoot higher, Ben, much higher," said Sergeant Browning.

They shook hands, and Ben walked smartly down the hallway and out to his truck.

CHAPTER 15

ANDREW, ANNA'S DAD, WAS CELEBRATING HIS FORTY-FIFTH birthday on the 17th of March 1965. Anna called her mom on the 16th of March to find out what she was planning for the birthday celebration. Audrey, her mom, told her she was baking a cake, had wrapped a few presents, and was taking Andrew out for dinner. Anna asked if anyone else was invited. Audrey said no, just the four of them. (She knew Anna and Ben were coming.) Anna did not want any more surprises like the last time when her Uncle George was there visiting.

On the way to Hamilton, on March 17th, Ben and Anna discussed whether they would tell Andrew and Audrey that Ben was a wealthy man. Anna had already informed them that she was starting the dental course on the 2nd of April. They would be expecting to pay three quarters of the cost of the dental course. They had agreed to pay, some time ago. Ben now decided he would inform them of his good fortune, on Andrew's birthday.

They arrived in the early afternoon, and as usual, Andrew and Audrey were very happy to see them. They congratulated Anna and Ben on their engagement.

After chatting for a while, they played the card game "Hearts". This time they cut the cards. The two with the highest cards would be partners. It would be men against the ladies. The ladies won two games, the men one.

When the card game was over, they celebrated Andrew's birthday. The candles on the cake were extinguished, they sang Happy Birthday, the gifts were unwrapped, and wine was served.

Ben then announced that he was joining the Metro Toronto Police Force, and that he had his first interview on the 15th of March, two days ago. He also informed them that he was waiting for a call for his next interview, in about two weeks. He thought now was a good time to break the news of his good fortune.

He started out by saying he had a good news story to tell. He explained that he had waited until he and Anna had fallen in love before he had told her the same story that he was now going to tell them.

Once again, Ben relayed how he found Mr. John Dillon, the man who gave him his fortune. Andrew and Audrey were wide-eyed, and shaking their heads slowly, looking at Ben and occasionally at Anna. After Ben said the words "in the safety deposit box was one million in Canada Savings Bonds," Audrey said, "Oh my goodness." For Ben and Anna, tears of joy now ran down her cheeks. She then stood up and said, "This is very deserving of a group hug." She motioned with her hands to stand, and the four of them hugged. After the group hug, Audrey hugged Anna and Ben. Andrew shook

THE YOUNG MILLIONAIRE FROM BREAKWATER

Ben's hand and congratulated him. He then said the thought that Anna would marry a millionaire never ever crossed his mind, but he was very happy for both of them.

Ben then told Andrew and Audrey that he would be taking care of Anna's dental course and any future financial needs. Also, he would be treating them to dinner each and every time they were out together. He reached into his shirt pocket, unfolded an envelope and handed it to Andrew, saying, "Your next vacation is on me, enjoy, and once again, Happy Birthday."

Andrew opened the envelope – a cheque for $1,000.00. He told Ben he didn't have to do this, then, thanked him for being so generous.

Anna said she was getting hungry and they should head out to the restaurant. She reminded her dad that it was his birthday and that he was to choose the restaurant. Andrew said he would be happy to choose one, and that he was driving. Fifteen minutes later they were on their way.

On the way home from the restaurant everyone was in a good mood. Audrey was telling Ben about some of the things that Anna did or said when she was little. She told the story about what Anna said when she was about three years old. She said that sometimes Anna would sleep with her and Andrew. One night the three of them were in bed. After a story had been read and it was time to go to sleep, Audrey had asked Anna to go and turn out the overhead light. She did, and the room was now in total darkness. After a few seconds a little voice said, "Where I am". Audrey said at the time they could not stop laughing, as little Anna tried to find her way back to the bed. After everyone stopped laughing, Anna said she had a funny story to tell about a little boy whose name was Billy.

He was four years old and she was seven. She said they were playing baseball near Billy's house. The yard was small, so they had just one base. Anna was up next. She hit the ball and as she was running toward the base, she yelled at Billy and said, "Billy run home." Billy did. He ran and did not stop until he reached his front door. Anna said she stood on the base and could not stop laughing. She said that Billy grew up to be the best baseball player on his high school team.

Just as Anna finished her story about Billy, Andrew turned onto his street. After they came around the turn just before reaching his house, Andrew saw the police car. Its lights were flashing. Then he saw firetrucks. It looked like they were near his house. Next, he saw flames as they were shooting up higher than the firetrucks. He could not tell for sure what house was on fire. As he drove closer to the police car, the policemen stepped out and approached his car. Andrew cranked the window down and asked him what was the number of the house that was on fire. The policeman said "421, and you cannot go any further."

"That it is my house," said Andrew. Audrey started crying.

"Sorry, sir," said the policeman, "they are doing their best to put out the fire. He turned and walked back to the police car. Andrew was trying to console Audrey. He told her they had insurance and they could build a new house. Through her tears Audrey said, "There was so much that could not be replaced and that made her sad."

They decided to wait a while before leaving the scene. Ten minutes later the policeman and a fireman walked over to their car. The fireman was the head fireman on the scene. He told Andrew that part of the house would be saved, however, no one would be allowed to enter the house until it was inspected and deemed safe to do so. He told Andrew to call his insurance company as soon as possible. He gave Andrew his business card and asked him to call him in the afternoon of the next day.

Andrew started the car and they headed for a hotel. Anna suggested they stop at a drug store and buy toothbrushes and toothpaste.

By nine p.m. they were in hotel rooms. Ben thought it would be a good idea for them to go visit Andrew and Audrey in their room. He said after what just happened they may appreciate some company. Anna hugged Ben and told him he was very thoughtful and they proceeded down the hallway of the hotel and knocked on their door. Andrew opened the door and said, "Thanks for coming. We could sure use the company." Audrey was drying her eyes as Anna walked over and gave her a hug. Anna told her that everything would be okay, and the most important thing was that they were safe. Audrey agreed, and thanked them for checking on them.

Andrew excused himself and said he had to go to his car for something. He came back with a deck of cards in his hand. To try and get their minds off the burning house, they sat on the carpet and played cards until their backs were sore. Then Ben and Anna went back to their room. They had agreed to meet at eight a.m. for breakfast.

During breakfast, Audrey discussed the fact that they were really good friends with their next-door neighbours. They had house-sat for each other a few times. She hoped that the fire had not damaged their house. She said that their son had joined the Canadian Army a few months ago, and she knew that if she were to ask them, they would be happy to accommodate them till their own house was ready to move into. Andrew agreed, and said he would ask them. Their names were Marvin and Lola.

They drove back to the hotel and checked out. Andrew called and talked to Marvin. Evidently, there was no damage to their house. After he hung up the phone, he said that Marvin had invited them to his house.

As they approached their house, they could see that one third had been burnt. They parked in Marvin's driveway. Marvin answered the doorbell. Ben and Anna observed that Marvin and Lola acted more like family than neighbours. They were very nice people. After discussing the fire, Marvin offered to accommodate them for as long as it took to rebuild their house. Andrew thanked them for their kindness.

Lola then stated that they were planning to fly to Halifax, Nova Scotia, to visit her parents at the end of the month. They were going for two weeks, but she said since Andrew and Audrey would now be living in their house, they might stay in Halifax for a month.

They then decided to go out and take a good look at the fire damaged house. Marvin said it would be better to build a new one than to try to repair it. Andrew agreed.

Andrew called the fire department. He was told that two fire inspectors would need access to his house at one thirty p.m. today. Andrew told him that he was staying at his neighbours' house next door, number 419.

The house was inspected, and a copy of the findings was given to Andrew. It was determined that the fire started in the electric box in the basement. Andrew, Audrey, Ben and Anna were escorted into the house to recover some of their belongings. They were happy to find many things that were not damaged – photo albums, briefcase containing important documents, and clothes in a couple of closets.

One of the inspectors told Andrew to call the same number as he had called to set up a time to re-enter his house to remove undamaged items out of the house.

Anna and Ben recovered their overnight bag. Ben's truck was safe, as it was parked on the street. They said good-bye and asked to be kept informed as to how long it would take before their new house was built. Ben reminded them that he and Anna would be moving into their house on the 1st of August, and they would be expecting a visit from them.

Anna was still working at the grocery store. Ben was attending the fitness club daily and cooking dinner on the days that Anna worked. Their first disagreement was about to take place.

Anna was getting a little irritated with Ben as he sometimes entered the kitchen and supervised her activities. She had made up her mind that it had to stop. She would tell him next time where to go.

It was a Saturday. Anna was in the kitchen washing dishes. She was placing the dishes in the drying rack. Suddenly, Ben showed up. He started to re-arrange the dishes. He told Anna that some of the dishes would not dry because of the way she had placed them in the rack. Anna told him to get lost and said, "You are pressing my last nerve. I will place the dishes anyway I want. Leave me alone."

Ben stormed out of the kitchen and headed for the chesterfield.

To show her annoyance she decided to dry the dishes. She would bang the cupboard doors after placing each dish. A loud voice came from the living room – "If you break these cupboard doors, I will not fix them."

The banging then became louder. Ben was now thinking that Anna was losing it. However, he decided not to add fuel to the fire.

After about five minutes, the banging stopped. Ben decided to go for a walk. He did not see Anna as he went to the door, slipped into his boots and jacket. He shouted, "I am going for a walk." There was no reply. He left the apartment.

His first thoughts as he started walking were of Anna. He had never seen her get so upset, so quickly. He thought he was trying to help, as he had done many times before. Then he realized what he had been doing. He said to himself – The apple doesn't fall far from the tree (unless there is a tornado). He was a chip off the old block, his dad. He remembered the many times his dad would supervise his activities. He now realized he was doing that very same thing to Anna. That is why she became so annoyed. In future, he would ask her if she needed help.

He had been walking for about ten minutes.

It was time to go back and apologize to Anna.

Upon entering the apartment, he called her name. She answered by saying, "I am in the bedroom." (She was laying on the bed reading a book.)

Ben walked to the left side of the bed. He usually slept on that side. He lay down and immediately apologized for his interference. He told her that he didn't realize that he was so controlling. He then relayed to her that his dad had been very controlling, and he should have known better than to do that very same thing.

Anna said she accepted his apology. She turned on her side to face him. She placed her right hand on the side of his face and said, "Thank you for realizing what you were doing, and I promise I won't bang any more cupboard doors."

Ben laughed and said, "I meant it when I said I would not fix them." It was Anna's turn to laugh. They hugged and kissed. All was well.

Ben received a call from the Metro Toronto Police Force on the 27th of March. He was to report to the Toronto Police College for his 2nd interview on the 30th of March at ten a.m.

He arrived at nine-thirty. At ten a.m. he was greeted by another Sergeant whose name was Bruce Logan. He was an instructor at the College. The interview was short. Ben was told they were very impressed with his academic achievement, and that he had been highly recommended by Sergeant Ken Browning, who had conducted his first interview. He was now told if he passed a physical he would be accepted, and the next training course would start on the 15th of May. The initial training would be six weeks. Then he would be paired with an experienced officer for further on-the-job training.

He was given the name and address of Doctor R. Bowden, who did physicals for anyone joining the police force. He would be called as to the date and time.

Sergeant Logan wished him good luck, and said he hoped to see him on the 15th of May.

Ben walked out of the College a very happy young man. Only six weeks, and he would be in training to be a police officer.

As he drove back to his apartment, he asked himself a question: What training, other than the work-outs he was already doing, could he do to better prepare himself for police work. He felt confident he could handle the mental aspect. Could he handle the physical? Maybe he should take karate lessons. Every police officer should know how to defend himself.

He decided he would run longer distances at the club to build his cardio. He would ask Leon if he could recommend a location where he could take karate lessons.

Ben had not seen Larry, his new friend, at the fitness club in the past week. He knew Larry must be working mornings. He decided to call him and invite him and his wife Cathy over for dinner. He would ask him to bring his guitar.

After what Ben had said about him, Anna said she looked forward to meeting him and Cathy as well.

Ben made the call. The date was set. It would be Friday afternoon, four p.m., as suggested by Ben.

Larry and Cathy arrived right on time. Ben had just placed the roast beef in the oven. The vegetables were sitting in a large bowl. They would be tossed in with the roast later. His dad taught him to cook a roast beef dinner this way. He remembered his dad saying, "One meal, one pan, no muss, no fuss."

After introductions were made, Ben offered wine. They sat in the living room and chatted.

Anna was intrigued by Larry's 'Newfie' accent. She thought he was a very genuine man and witty. He repeated phrases that she had never heard before, and some of them were very funny. She didn't ask him if they were his own or not. She knew he was a songwriter. She also thought that he was somewhat of a philosopher and deep thinker.

He said that he liked to read quotes by famous people. He said he had written a few himself, and asked if they would like to hear some of them.

Ben and Anna said yes, they would.

He began:

A question I often ponder: Who will write the story when the world ends?

In the political realm, we have three identities, the left, the right, and those who say they are both wrong.

When you follow your dream, sometimes it becomes a nightmare.

Time is not renewable, don't waste it.

Common sense and intelligence need not dwell in the same place.

Larry then recited the limerick that his Uncle Don had told him:

I see said the blind man
As a man with no arms waved,
I saw that, said a man who could not speak,
Then a man with no legs,
In disgust, walked away.

"Very funny," said Ben, "I think that is the best one I've heard yet." He then stood up and said, "Excuse me, I have to slip into the kitchen and put the veggies in with the roast."

When Ben returned, Anna asked Larry to get his guitar and sing a few songs. She said nobody in her family sang or played an instrument.

"Well," said Larry, as he took his guitar out of the case, "music is just part of living in Newfoundland. That's just the way it is. Some sing and play, others just sing. Maybe that is why Newfoundland is called Canada's Happy Province."

"Okay, here's one I wrote called 'Life's Other Side'"

The lyrics:

> *I once knew a man he lived just down the road*
> *And many would say a brick shy of a load*
> *On a cold day in his wood stove he burnt his backdoor*
> *His elevator never did go to the top floor*
>
> *Chorus:*
> *He lived in a cabin he lived all alone*
> *Even with the lights on there was nobody home*
> *Some lose their marbles others lose their locks*
> *Some not the brightest crayon in the box*
>
> *One could say he never played with a full deck*
> *On a cold day in April he would swim in the lake*
> *No doubt he would never become a father*
> *For he never did have both oars in the water*
>
> *On purpose he bent his old shotgun barrow*
> *He never did shoot with any straight arrow*
> *He was one of a kind we don't need any more*
> *He was not the sharpest knife in the drawer*
>
> *Chorus:*

After he finished the song, he said one of his sisters asked him if he had written the song about their uncle Lenny, who lived in a cabin, and alone. However, he told her he didn't. No doubt uncle Lenny was not her favourite uncle.

Larry sang until Anna served dinner. He sung ballads, love songs, comedy, and gospel, and they were loved by all.

Cathy commented that it was a very enjoyable dinner. Larry said, "Compliments to the chef."

Ice cream was served for dessert. Both Ben and Anna said that baking was not their forte.

When dinner was finished, they played Scrabble.

Larry had to get up early in the morning, so they headed home after the game. Before leaving Cathy said they would be the host the next time they got together.

Ben was now taking karate lessons at the fitness club every other day. The lessons were at eight a.m., so these days he had to get up much earlier than for his usual work-out.

Anna had started her 2nd week at the dental school. Monday evening Ben suggested that they go out for dinner on Tuesday.

Anna had worn her mini-skirt to class on Tuesday. When she came home she found Ben asleep on the chesterfield. He had been reading a book and it was now on the floor. She bent over and kissed his cheek. He was lying on his back. She then noticed the bulge in his jeans. She reached down and placed her hand on his erection, and gently rubbed. His eyes came open, and he smiled.

She said, "I hope you were dreaming about me."

"As a matter of fact, I was," he said. Then he saw her mini-skirt.

"Did you wear that skirt to your dental school?"

"Of course, I did. Lots of girls are wearing them."

Sitting up, he said, "I don't like it, it shows too much leg."

"It doesn't show any more than the other girls who wear them," said Anna.

"I don't care about the others, I care about you."

"If you cared, maybe you would respect my choice to wear whatever I want to. Why are you trying to control me?"

"In my mind I am not trying to control you. I am concerned about how much skin you are showing. You know men will think you are loose and available. If you were not my girl, I wouldn't care how much you revealed."

"You are making far too much of this. I am not putting myself on display. I walk to my car, drive to class, walk into the building. There is only one man I see in the building and he teaches us all about equipment, and he is old."

"Never too old to look, I'd say."

"So what, it's the new fashion, look but don't touch."

"I give up. I guess I am an old-fashioned teenager."

"Yes, you are, but I love you, and thank you for caring. From now on I will only wear my mini on days that end in ay."

Ben started to laugh. Then he said, "Now that is funny. One good thing about mini-skirts, they are built for quick and easy access." He reached under Anna's mini-skirt and was planning to hook a finger under her panties. His fingers found pubic hair, no panties.

She laughed.

He did not.

"Don't tell me you went out in the mini-skirt and no panties. Anna Wood, you are going to drive me crazy, I declare," said Ben.

Anna just looked at him and smiled.

"I guess now you are going to tell me you forgot to put on your panties," said Ben.

"No Ben. But I remembered to take them off before I woke you up.

"Okay, you got me," said Ben. They both started laughing.

"I am sticking with my story. Mini-skirts were built for quick and easy access," said Ben.

Dinner would be delayed.

CHAPTER 16

ANNA WAS DOING VERY WELL AT THE DENTAL SCHOOL. SHE was near the top of the class.

Ben was reading anything he could find regarding police work.

Ben and Anna decided to make a trip to the Yorkdale Mall. It was Saturday afternoon. The radio in Ben's truck was on. It was tuned to a Toronto station. Just before they were about to park at the mall, the local news came on. The man said there had been a serious accident on Highway 401. The only details were that two trucks and a car were involved in the crash. Two people, a man and a woman were taken to the Toronto Hospital.

Ben parked his truck and then they went into the mall.

They were at the mall for a couple of hours. As they were driving home, the three-p.m. news came on. There was no further news as to the identity of the man and the woman who had been taken to the hospital. They were trying to locate the next of kin.

Two days later, on Monday, Ben picked up the Toronto Star newspaper, as he was accustomed to doing. On page 2 there was a photo of the accident that had happened on Saturday on Highway 401. He began to read the story – and the victims of the crash were Sammy Pender, 24 years old, and Cora Roberts, 23 years old. They are in serious condition in the Toronto Hospital.

Ben could hardly believe his eyes. Immediately he thought of Anna. She would be very despondent when she heard this unfortunate news. He would have to inform her of the sad circumstances. How would he tell her, when would he tell her? Did she already know? Maybe not. His mind kept racing. If she did not know, should he wait until after dinner to tell her? She probably would not eat dinner if he told her. He made up his mind. He would wait until after dinner. There was no doubt in his mind she would want to rush to the hospital to see Cora.

He located the phone book, found the phone number of the hospital. He called to see if Cora could have visitors. He was told only family was allowed to see her. She was in ICU (Intensive Care Unit).

Ben planned for an early dinner.

Anna came home at five p.m. Ben informed her he was planning an early dinner. He was hungry. Anna said she was hungry also.

Ben tried to keep a conversation going until they finished dinner. He had rehearsed how he would tell Anna the bad news.

He said, "Anna I have news that will upset you. However, death is not part of the story. That car accident on the 401 Saturday, it was Sammy and Cora who were taken to the

Toronto Hospital. They are in intensive care and they are in good hands. I read it in today's paper."

Anna started to cry. Ben held her and told her he was sorry that this had happened.

Anna, through her tears, said, "I want to go and see her now."

Ben said, "I know you do, however, I called the hospital and only family can see her right now." He then asked her if she knew Cora's parents. She said she did. Ben suggested they could go to the hospital café, hang out there, and hope Cora's parents showed up to get something to eat. He said he couldn't think of anything else. Anna thought it was a very good idea.

At six forty-five p.m., they were in the hospital café. Ben bought a soda pop for himself and Anna. They chose a table that was a good vantage point to the entrance of the cafe. Ben did not know Cora's parents, so he read a book. Anna watched each and every person that entered or left the café.

An hour later, they were still sitting there. Suddenly, Anna said, "There they are." She stood and rushed to meet Mr. and Mrs. Roberts as they entered. They both recognized Anna, and gave her a hug. (Ben stayed at the table, he was a stranger to them and he decided to lay low.)

They were very close to his table, so he heard every word that was said. Both Cora and Sammy were still in ICU. However, Cora was now stable, and the outlook for her was good. Sammy was not doing well. His injuries were more severe.

They were only talking for about a minute, then, Anna introduced Ben.

Mr. Roberts said they would be back after picking up something to eat.

After they left, Ben said, "That was good news and bad news." Anna just shook her head and said, "They are taking this very well."

"And so they should," said Ben. "The outcome could have been a lot worse. It's amazing they survived the crash."

"I know," said Anna, "but it's still a grave situation."

"Yes, it is," said Ben.

The Roberts returned to the table with their food. Anna did most of the talking while they ate.

When she had finished eating, Mrs. Roberts told them that Cora had been sedated and she was very weak. She talked in only a whisper. The doctor told them she had suffered head blows, and in one area a small skull fracture.

Before parting, they exchanged phone numbers. They would let Anna know when she could see Cora.

Ben and Anna left the hospital and went home.

Two days later Mrs. Roberts called to say Cora's condition had improved a little. They expected she would be out of ICU in a couple of days. Sammy, however, was not doing very well. He had internal injuries, as well as head injuries. She would let Anna know when Cora was out of the ICU.

This was the most difficult time Anna had ever faced. Ben really did not know what to do or say to help her through this unfortunate circumstance. He remembered when his dad had died. He felt he was alone in the world. Anna at least had him for company when she wasn't at dental school.

Two days later Anna received the call she had been waiting for. Cora was out of ICU, and she could visit her. However, the good news was followed by bad news. Sammy had passed away. Mrs. Roberts told Anna that Cora was not informed of Sammy's passing. She had asked about him and was told that he was still in ICU, where she had been. Mrs. Roberts asked Anna not to mention Sammy, and if Cora asked about him, just say he was still in ICU. She said she would consult with the doctor before telling Cora about Sammy.

Ben and Anna picked up a bouquet of flowers and a card on their way to the hospital to see Cora.

As they approached Cora's room, a nurse was just leaving, and she told them Cora was sleeping. She said Cora was doing well. She had talked to her about twenty minutes ago.

Anna's tears rolled down her cheeks when she saw Cora. Her best friend in the whole world, excluding Ben. Anna loved Cora like a sister.

Ben told her she should try and be strong for Cora. He said when she opens her eyes and sees you, it would be better if she saw you smiling. Anna nodded her head and started to dry her tears.

Ben said, "She will be so happy to see you."

Then, a loud noise. Someone had dropped something in the hallway near Cora's room.

Cora opened her eyes. She smiled upon seeing Anna. Anna smiled back, trying very hard not to cry. Ben then moved over so that Cora could see him. He winked, and her smile grew wider. Anna reached for her hand and held it. Cora gently squeezed her hand. In a soft weak voice, she said, "Thank you for coming."

"We love you," said Anna. "You are going to be just fine."

"I want to see Sammy," said Cora.

Ben told her they could not see Sammy. "He is in ICU, where you were, and only family can visit him. We could not visit you when you were in there," said Ben.

"That's what my mom told me," said Cora.

Anna then said, "I think we better go and let you rest. We were told not to stay long, you need your rest."

"Okay," said Cora. "See you later alligator." She often used that phrase when they parted.

Anna and Ben waved and blew her a kiss as they left her room.

"She is doing very well," said Ben. "She's got lots of spunk. I told you she'll be just fine."

"I am concerned with her finding out that Sammy has passed," said Anna.

"Well," said Ben, "she has to know, there is no other choice. We cannot keep it from her much longer. I think it would be best if her mom, alone, would tell her. The least number of people at her bedside when she is told would be a better situation."

"I will leave that to her mom," said Anna.

As they drove home, Anna said she would ask Mrs. Roberts to let her know when Cora had been informed about Sammy. She said she needed to know, to avoid an awkward situation with Cora. If she knew she could act accordingly. Anna then told Ben that Cora had told her, that she hoped Sammy would ask her to marry him.

Ben and Anna visited Cora every evening. She was up and walking the hallway several times a day, as long as she had someone with her. She could not yet walk alone, because a fall would be detrimental to her recovery.

One evening as Ben and Anna were walking down the hallway, they met Mr. and Mrs. Roberts, who were on their way to the café. Mrs. Roberts told them she would be telling Cora about Sammy as soon as she got back from the café. She also informed them that the doctor recommended both she and Mr. Roberts should be present, just in case Cora needed to be restrained. The doctor explained that any sudden movement might set back Cora's recovery.

Ben and Anna decided they would wait in the café for fifteen minutes after Mr. and Mrs. Roberts went back to break the tragic news to Cora.

Cora was sitting in her chair when her parents entered her room. She said, "Mom, I have a feeling that you are trying to protect me from the truth. Sammy should be out of ICU by now. I need to know what is going on."

Her mom took both her hands in hers. She said, "You are right Cora, Sammy is not in the ICU anymore. I am so sorry, Sammy did not make it. His injuries were very severe."

Tears streamed down Cora's face. She said, "No, no, no, I love him. He can't leave me. I don't want to live without him."

Both her mom and dad tried to comfort her. They held her hands and wiped away her tears and cried with her.

Cora kept repeating that she loved him and wanted to be with him.

Her dad told her that Sammy would want her to go on with her life. He said if it was you who did not make it, wouldn't you want Sammy to go on with his life?

Cora nodded her head.

Ben and Anna were slowly walking down the hallway to Cora's room. Ben had been thinking. He told Anna that maybe she should go alone. He said, "She just found out that she has lost her boyfriend, so I think it's not right if you walked in with me. If she asks where I am, just tell her I am pumping up a tire on my truck that was a little low." He said he would wait a while and read his book.

Anna walked into Cora's room. After greeting her she said, "I am so sorry Cora, I know how much you loved Sammy. We will help you get through this." Anna tried very hard to control her emotions, however, tears slowly rolled down her cheeks. They held hands and Anna told her she loved her and considered her a sister.

Cora thanked her and told her they had been sisters for a long time. She then thanked her for the flowers and the card.

Mrs. Roberts said they were stepping out for a while, but they would return.

Ben, sitting in a chair at the end of the hallway, did not see them coming. As they approached him, Mr. Roberts said, "Good book Ben?"

Ben looked up and said, "Yes, it is."

Mrs. Roberts saw Ben before her husband. She was now asking herself why didn't Ben accompany Anna in to see Cora. She knew Ben and Anna had been visiting Cora every evening since she came out of ICU. Then she thought she had the answer. She didn't know whose idea it was, but she knew it was very mature of them. They had been thinking of Cora, who just found out she had lost her boyfriend. So they decided it would be psychologically easier on Cora if she did not see them together, at least not right now.

Just to confirm her thoughts, she asked Ben why he had not gone with Anna to see Cora. Adding I think I know the answer. (Ben's answer confirmed her thoughts.)

Mrs. Roberts thanked him for his thoughtfulness.

After her parents left the room, Cora asked Anna where Ben was.

Anna told her one of the tires on his truck was a bit low, and he was using a hand pump to inflate it to the correct pressure. She said he would be here soon.

As Ben turned the page in his book, he realized it was time for him to make an appearance. He placed the bookmark on the page and headed down the hallway to Cora's room.

He entered slowly, waved his hand as Cora and Anna acknowledged his presence. He smiled and asked Cora how she was feeling, and told her she was looking good. He then told her he could not express in words how he felt when he heard of Sammy's passing and if there was anything he could do, he would be there for her.

Through her tears, she thanked him for his kindness.

Anna asked her if she would like to go for a walk. She nodded and stood up from her chair. Anna held her hand, and they left the room. Ben decided to stay in the room.

They met Cora's parents before they reached the end of the hallway. Her Dad mentioned how impressed he was with her progress. He told her that she would be coming home soon. Cora said she was looking forward to leaving the hospital and hoped it would be soon.

They walked up and down the hallway a few times before going back to Cora's room.

Anna and Ben wished her well and they left.

Cora and her parents discussed what would happen when she was released from the hospital. Cora said she did not want to go back to the apartment that she shared with Sammy. She couldn't afford the apartment on her own, anyway. She didn't have any choice really, but to live with her parents, which she agreed to do.

Cora had told both her parents, as well as Anna and Ben, that Sammy had no family in Toronto. His mom was in Europe, and he had no contact with her. He had been raised by his grandmother who had died two years ago. He did not know who his dad was.

After her parents left, Cora cried. She tried to be brave and control her emotions when people were around, as best she could. When she was alone, she mourned for her lost love, Sammy.

Mrs. Roberts called Ben and Anna after they arrived home. They discussed their visits to see Cora. They decided that they each would visit her every other evening. She also told them they were hiring movers to move everything out of Cora's and Sammy's apartment and into storage. She told Anna that Cora's mail would now be delivered to their house.

Ten days later, Cora was released from the hospital, and went back home to live with her parents in North Toronto.

Ben kept himself busy. Working out, running, karate lessons, cooking, and part-time house-husband, as he called it, although he was not yet a husband. He thought maybe at some time he would write a poem called "House Husband". He would ask Larry to come up with a melody and sing it.

He was now bench pressing two hundred and ninety pounds. He was very pleased with his progress. He was learning a lot about self-defence in his karate lessons.

He had talked to Leon about getting hockey tickets for next season. Leon told him to call the Toronto Maple Leafs ticket office to find out what was available. He did, and there were two tickets for a ten-game package that was not picked up or paid for, and the date for payment had expired. Ben told the lady to hold them for him, and that he would be there to get them in the next hour. He was a very happy young man as he drove back to his apartment with the tickets.

When Anna came home that evening, Ben showed her the tickets. He was as happy as a kid who was told he was going to Disney World. He also had the calendar marked, and the time of each game.

Anna received a phone call from her mom on the 28th of April. She said their old house was demolished, and the new one was taking shape. They expected to be in it early July.

That same evening Ben told Anna they should discuss wedding plans, like when, where, people they would invite, who would marry them, bridesmaid and best man, and the reception.

Anna said she would like to be a June bride.

Ben said, "Why don't we get married on my birthday. You would be the best birthday present I would ever get."

"Okay," said Anna, "the 24th of June it is. What year?"

"The month after next," said Ben, "and it's on a Saturday."

Ben said he would hire someone to help plan the wedding. Then he asked Anna where would she like to get married.

Anna did not hesitate, she said, "Near the falls in Niagara Falls."

"Very good choice," said Ben. "I like it."

They talked about who they would invite, and where they might hold the reception. Anna said she would ask Cora to be her bridesmaid. Ben said he would ask Leon to be his best man.

Ben asked Anna if she would like to visit Joseph and Angelina again. She said she would, and asked Ben to call them. That afternoon, Ben called. This time Angelina answered the phone. After telling her who he was, Ben asked her if there was still water in the pool. She said there was, and she hoped he could keep his swim trunks on if he wanted to swim in her pool.

"Very funny," said Ben. "That won't happen again even if you were to try. I will be wearing my trunks that tie at the waist and not the ones with the elastic band at the waist."

She replied, "Oh, I guess I will have to think of something different to have some fun at your expense."

"I will be watching you," said Ben.

"I hope you do," said Angelina, "I might just throw in a few extra wiggles, in that case."

"Nothing wrong with a wiggle or a jiggle," said Ben.

"Why don't you and Anna join us around two p.m. this Saturday," said Angelina. "Wilbur and Julie, our neighbours, will be here as well."

"See you Saturday afternoon," said Ben, and he hung up the phone.

Saturday afternoon Ben and Anna were greeted at the door by Joseph. They were introduced to Wilbur and Julie. They sat in the living room and talked while sipping wine. After they finished their wine, they went to the pool.

Just before four p.m. they had changed and were back in the living room with a fresh glass of wine.

Angelina and Anna were in the change room together after they swam. She asked Anna if she would like to play a little trick on Ben. She explained what would take place, and Anna thought it would be fun. She would do it.

At four-fifteen, Angelina served cheese and crackers. After a few minutes she announced that they were going to play a game. It was called "Under the blanket". She said that Anna, being a good sport, volunteered to be the first one to be under the blanket.

Angelina asked everyone to take a good look at Anna. Anna then sat on the floor in the middle of the living room. Angelina covered her with the Queen size blanket. She said nobody is allowed to touch the blanket. Then she explained that each of them would ask Anna to take off something she was wearing and toss it outside the blanket onto the floor. She asked Ben if he would like to start.

Ben was thinking – I don't know if I like this game. However, she did say nobody could touch the blanket. Anna is a very modest woman, she knows what she is doing. He would play along,

"Take off one of your slippers," said Ben.

A slipper was thrown outside the blanket.

Joseph was next and said, "Take off the other slipper."

The second slipper landed near the first one.

Julie said, "Take off an earring."

An earring was tossed out.

Wilbur called for the other earring.

It too was now outside the blanket.

Angelina said, "The ribbon in your hair."

The ribbon was tossed onto the floor.

It was now Ben's turn again. Again, he was thinking – blouse or shorts. Then he thought about her ring, and he said, "Take off your ring".

The ring was gently placed on the floor just outside the blanket.

Joseph called for the blouse.

The blouse was tossed out after a slight delay.

Ben started to show concern. Angelina watched him in his uncomfortable state, with a smile on her face.

Julie said, "Let's have the shorts."

The shorts came flying out and landed on Julie.

Everyone except Ben laughed.

Wilbur shouted, "Toss out the bra."

Anna waited. Then she said, "Do I have to?"

Angelina said, "The game is not over, and you agreed to play to the end."

Out came the bra. It landed in Joseph's lap. Once again there was laughter. Ben tried to smile, but did not. The look on his face was one of deep concern.

Angelina said, "Last but not least, throw out your panties."

Another delay, longer than before. Slowly the panties were placed on the floor just outside the blanket. However, she was still holding them.

Angelina said, "What a sport Anna is, let's give her a big round of applause." Everyone did, except Ben.

Suddenly, Anna threw off the blanket as she stood up. She was wearing a bathing suit.

Everyone started the applause again.

Anna threw her panties in Ben's lap as she wore a big smile on her face. She pointed a finger at Ben and said, "Got yea."

Ben pulled the panties over his head, and everyone cheered and there was more applause. Anna walked over and sat on his knee, pulled the panties off his head and gave him a kiss. Ben looked over at Angelina and she winked at him. Then a thought passed through his mind – she got me again.

Joseph said, "Join the crowd Ben. Both Wilbur and I went through the very same experience you just did. However, you can now have a little fun watching another unsuspecting friend, when his wife or girlfriend is under the blanket."

Ben said, "I've already got someone in mind."

Anna went into the change room to change into her clothes. She would never tell Ben that the panties she wore when she was under the blanket were a new pair that Angelina had given her. But she would tell him that the bathing suit she wore was Angelina's. She said she had never worn it.

Ben and Anna left around five-thirty. They were invited to dinner at Cora's parents' place.

Cora was very happy to see them. She was doing very well. She said she wanted to go back to work part-time soon. She hoped to get a transfer to the Dominion grocery store that was only a block away. She said she had an appointment at the Toronto Hospital in two weeks, and she was hoping to be cleared to go back to work.

It was a lovely visit, and it seemed Cora was getting back to her old self, that everyone loved so much. However, Anna knew that she would be grieving for Sammy for maybe years to come.

CHAPTER 17

ONE AFTERNOON BEN DECIDED TO CHECK THE YELLOW PAGES of the Toronto phone book looking for wedding planners or event planners. There were several numbers listed for event planners. After thinking about it, he decided to first check with Joseph or Larry or Leon. He knew Leon married a younger woman about two years ago, and he most likely had help.

The next morning at the fitness club he asked Leon if he could recommend anyone that could help plan his wedding. Leon said he could indeed. He reached into his pocket for his wallet, and from his wallet he pulled out a business card. He handed it to Ben. The lady's name was Debra Stone, Event Planner.

After lunch he called the number on Debra's business card. Ben identified himself and told her he was getting married in June. She told him that weddings were her speciality and that she demanded good money for good work. Ben told her that would not be a problem.

Two days later all the information was given to Debra, and the wedding plans were set in motion.

The 5th of May 1965, Ben became a member of the Metro Toronto Police Force. The 15th of May, Ben reported to the Police College along with nine other candidates. They were all welcomed by Sergeant Bruce Logan, the officer who had interviewed Ben.

Ben knew some of the training would be intense, but he was willing to do whatever was necessary to become a police officer. He was confident he had what it took to be a competent one. He knew that the officers at the College were experienced, and he planned to absorb every word that was said, in and out of the classroom.

Anna's twenty-first birthday was the 30th of May. Ben planned two surprises for her.

He made reservations at a restaurant (a private room in the back) where he would take her to dinner. They had been there twice before, and he knew Anna really liked that restaurant. What he did not tell her was that there would be others dining with them. He had called her parents, Andrew and Audrey, Cora and her parents, Joseph and Angelina, Larry and Cathy (their Newfie friends), as well as Leon and his wife Colleen. Anna did not know Leon or Colleen. However, Ben decided it was time she met them. Leon would be his best man. Ben had informed everyone that he would be picking up the tab for dinner. He had said that an uncle had died and left him some cash. He knew the odds were good that everyone would be there. His dad had told him some time ago that if people were invited to any function and the food was free, they would be there. He had not yet proved this theory, but he knew his dad was usually right.

Anna's birthday was on a Saturday. Her parents called her in the morning to wish her a happy birthday. So did Cora.

After they had lunch, Ben asked Anna if she would like to accompany him to the Yorkdale Mall. He wanted to buy a new pair of shoes to wear on their wedding day. Anna agreed to go, and she said she would look at shoes as well.

They went out to the parking lot. Anna was looking at Ben as he was talking to her. Suddenly, Ben said, "Anna, my truck is gone. It's not in my parking space. There is a car parked there, looks like it's decorated for a wedding procession."

Anna said, "Oh Ben, we better call the police."

Ben said, "Yea, but let's take a closer look at that car."

As they got real close, Ben said, "Happy Birthday, Anna. There (pointing) is your new car."

Tears of joy rolled down Anna's cheeks. Then she saw the tag on the pink ribbon bow on the front of the car. It read – To Anna, with love, Ben. She threw her arms around him, kissed him, hugged him and said, "Thank you. My first new car." It was a 1965 Ford Mustang.

Ben went around to the driver's side rear wheel. He bent down and retrieved the car key that was hidden in behind the tire. He handed her the key and said, "Check it out."

Anna said, "How did you know the key was there?"

Ben told her that he told the salesman to place it there. He said the car was parked there only twenty minutes ago.

They sat in the car. Anna said she just loved the smell of a new car.

Ben said, "As much as you love me?"

"Almost," said Anna, and she laughed.

Ben said, "I didn't know a new car would be my competition."

"Well now you know," said Anna.

"Take her for a spin," said Ben, "just don't scare me."

"I doubt that very much," said Anna.

She started the engine, put the shifter in drive, and stepped on the gas pedal, the tires squealed, and the car lurched forward. Anna quickly applied the brake. "My old car doesn't do that," said Anna. "I don't know if I can handle so much power."

"Sure you can," said Ben, "you will do just fine after you drive it a little while. Just press the gas pedal slowly that's all. Let's go."

Anna drove out of the parking lot and unto the street. There were no vehicles ahead of her. She pressed the gas pedal, the car lurched forward. She liked the surge of power. She yelled, "I love it."

As she was driving back to their apartment she asked Ben what were they going to do with her old car. Ben told her the Ford dealer where he bought the car would buy it.

That evening Anna drove her new car to the restaurant where Ben had made the reservations.

They were greeted as they walked into the restaurant. Ben informed the lady at the front that they had made a reservation. The lady knew when Ben gave her his name that a surprise party had been booked in the back room for them. She asked them to wait a minute because she wanted to check and make sure their table was ready. She went to the back room and informed everyone that the birthday lady had arrived.

As Ben and Anna entered the room everyone was standing behind a chair at the large table, and they shouted, "Happy Birthday". Anna was very surprised. In the room were all the people that Ben had invited, including Anna's parents,

Andrew and Audrey, who drove from Hamilton to be at their daughter's birthday party. Anna was thrilled.

After everyone finished dinner, a large cake was delivered with 21 candles aflame. Anna blew out the candles and everyone enjoyed a generous portion of cake.

Anna thanked everyone for coming and for the gifts and cards. She then announced that Ben had bought her a new car, a Mustang. Everyone applauded.

Before they left the parking lot, everyone gathered around Anna's new Mustang. She was all smiles as everyone told her how lucky she was. Angelina moved close to Ben who was standing in the background, and in a low voice said, "I bet you will get lucky tonight."

In a low voice Ben replied, "I get lucky every night."

He then winked at Angelina and walked to the passenger side of Anna's car.

As they had planned, Andrew and Audrey followed them back to their apartment. They would visit them for a while before going to their hotel.

Audrey wanted to see the house Ben and Anna were moving into in August. Anna and Ben drove to their hotel on Sunday morning and the four of them went to Robin Hood Road to view house number 46.

Audrey said it looked lovely, and she could hardly wait to see the inside.

Ben said, "It's just a house, however, Anna and I plan to make it a home. It will be a home to eight or ten kids."

"No, it will not, Ben Breakwater," said Anna. "I've not agreed to that many kids, nor will I ever."

"Just kidding," said Ben. He and Andrew laughed.

"She is an assertive woman, Ben, just like her mother," said Andrew.

"I know," said Ben, "I wouldn't want it any other way. I love her just the way she is."

"I am very happy to hear that," said Andrey. "True love is unconditional. You may not like what a loved one does or says, but you still love them."

"That's the kind of love my dad said he had for my mom," said Ben. "He once told me that love does not really make the world go around, but it sure makes the world a better place to live in."

"Well said," Andrew replied.

They dropped Anna's parents at their hotel, said their good-byes, and went back to their apartment.

On the way back, Ben was feeling frisky. He reached over and rubbed Anna's knee. Then he moved his hand up her thigh on the outside. Back down to her knee, this time his hand moved slowly up the inside of her leg. Anna did not say a word. She took her right hand off the steering wheel, reached down and held Ben's left hand so that he could not move it any further. Then she said, "Sorry to spoil your fun, but I am driving. You will have to wait. You can give me another birthday present later when I am in my birthday suit." Ten minutes later, they left a trail of clothes from their apartment door to the bedroom. One birthday, two in their birthday suits.

Cora was now working part-time in the Dominion grocery store near her parents' home.

She had gone to visit Sammy's gravesite many times.

One afternoon when she arrived home from work, her mother told her there was an envelope for her on the kitchen table. The letter was from the Royal Bank of Canada in Toronto. It stated that she was the beneficiary to an account of a Mr. Sammy Pender, now deceased. She was asked to call and schedule an appointment. Cora called the bank. Two days later she parked her car and entered the bank.

She was greeted by a middle-aged man and they proceeded to his office. Cora produced ID and was given a bank statement. She was the beneficiary of an account worth ten thousand dollars.

After leaving the bank, she sat in her car and cried. She had been saving money to attend teachers' college. She had been informed that a new teachers' college was opening in London, Ontario, and she wanted to attend. Thanks to Sammy, she could now quit working at the grocery store and go to the college in London. Her life-long dream was to become a teacher. Her priority would now be to find out when the next program would start at the teachers' college. She would then look for a room to rent near the college.

As she drove home she could not stop thinking of Sammy. She wondered what would he have done with the money he had saved. Maybe he was saving for a down payment on a house. She quickly made up her mind. After she started teaching, she would buy a house. In death, Sammy was providing for her. Tears started falling once again.

Cora obtained the address of the Teachers' College in London. She drove there accompanied by her mom. She completed the application and was accepted. The program would start on the 2nd of August. They checked the London newspaper and found a room for rent only a five-minute walk from the college.

Ben was really enjoying the police training. He especially liked the unarmed combat sessions. He was very pleased that he had taken karate lessons. The instructor was very impressed with Ben's ability in the combat sessions. Ben was now six-foot one and weighed two hundred and ten pounds. He could bench press three hundred pounds.

He also enjoyed the target shooting. He had never fired a pistol before. The only firearm he ever used before was a 22-calibre rifle that his dad had. He gave it to Mr. Pebbles who liked to hunt wild turkeys.

At the police college Ben was given the name BB.

One afternoon, Ben received a phone call from Debra, who was planning his wedding. She knew that the wedding would be in Niagara Falls, Ontario. She asked Ben if he and Anna would like to be married on the Maid of the Mist, the boat that takes people close to the falls. Ben knew about the boat because Anna had told him she had been on it. The Maid of the Mist II began operation in 1956. There were several before her. The Maid of the Mist II was involved in the rescue of Roger Woodward, a seven-year-old boy who became the first person to survive a plunge over the Horseshoe Falls on July 9th, 1960. He was wearing just a life jacket.

Ben said he would check with Anna and call her back. Debra told Ben she hoped to book their wedding for the 24th of June, on the Maid of the Mist if that was what they wanted. She also said that they may already be booked for other weddings.

That evening Ben told Anna that Debra had called.

"What did she want?" said Anna.

198

"She wanted to know if we would like to be married on the Maid of the Mist in Niagara Falls," said Ben.

"You are kidding me," said Anna.

"No, that's what she wanted to know," said Ben. "I told her I would check with you and call her back."

"That would be fun," said Anna, "let's go for it"

Ben called Debra and told her to book the boat for the whole wedding party.

Debra called back two days later to say it was a go for the wedding on the Maid of the Mist II on the 24th of June.

Ben and Anna were elated.

They were married on the Maid of the Mist II at four p.m. on the 24th of June 1965. Anna's brother who lived in British Columbia also attended the wedding.

A reception was held at a hotel banquet hall overlooking the Horseshoe Falls. For Anna and Ben, it was the happiest day of their lives. They would plan a honeymoon after Ben finished police training and Anna completed the dental course.

On their wedding night in Niagara Falls, Ben told Anna from now on he would not be using a condom. Anna replied that she would let him know when he should start using them again.

On the July 1st long weekend Ben and Anna went camping. It would be their first camping trip together. Ben didn't know how much Anna knew about camping. He had purchased more camping gear and they would have many more amenities than he and his dad had when they camped.

Ben had done a little research and found out that a new provincial park called Bon Echo had opened only a few weeks ago. With the camping gear loaded in his truck they headed for Bon Echo on Friday morning.

They arrived at noon and there were only a few camping sites left. They were very happy with the site they were given. Ben liked a secluded site and that is what they got.

They unloaded almost everything and went to get firewood. Anna watched as Ben, who was very skilled with an axe, cut a few pieces of slash into kindling. He had brought newspaper which he crushed into softball size paper balls. He placed them in the fire pit, stacked the kindling around the paper balls to form a teepee. He then lit the paper and soon the kindling wall was all ablaze.

Anna asked what he would do if he had no paper. He told her he would use his sharp knife and cut into the kindling and create shavings which could be set afire with a match, no need for paper. He also told her that a little birch bark from a birch tree could also be used instead of paper. He said that this is what his dad always used.

They added wood to the fire, and then proceeded to set up the tent. When there were only embers left in the fire pit, Ben placed a grille on top of the stones which formed the fire pit. The grille was about three inches above the embers. Wieners were placed on the grille and heated in a few minutes. They ate hot dogs and potato chips for lunch.

After lunch they inflated the double mattress, put up a clothesline and set up the hammock. Ben said a hammock was the best place to relax, and he would never leave home without it. The hammock was a one-person hammock, but if you really got close, two could fit in it. Ben and Anna liked to get close, and they did. Ben said it would be a tricky place to make love.

It was a beautiful Sunday and warm. They relaxed on a blanket on the sandy beach. Next, they walked barefoot along the water's edge. Anna said walking along the beach near the water was very soothing and sure felt good. Ben agreed.

They cooked steaks for dinner on the grille over the fire pit as they had heated the wieners they had for lunch. Ben commented that food tasted much better outside surrounded by trees, then in a restaurant.

After dinner they went for a walk on a three-mile hiking trail.

Anna remembered the last time they went hiking. It was in Kingston, Jamaica, and they got robbed. She would never forget how she felt losing her engagement ring. She mentioned this to Ben as they walked along. Ben replied that the chance of that happening again was very slim, and it was the last thing on his mind.

They saw two deer, wild turkeys and many birds. They met several hikers on the trail who had stopped to feed the chickadees. They would hold out their hand which contained bird seed, and the chickadees would fly and perch on their fingers to eat the seed. One lady gave Anna a handful of bird seed. Anna thanked her, placed the seed on her right hand and held it out. Within seconds a chickadee landed on her pinky finger and with its little beak, pecked at the seed. She was thrilled. She later told Ben that was the most fun she'd ever had with her clothes on. She said it was something special to feel the little bird's claws wrapped around her finger, a very unique feeling, akin to being part of nature.

After the trail walk they drove to the shower building for a shower. Back at the campsite Anna started the fire. It would be dark soon, so they prepared their campsite for the night. Ben tied the plastic bag that contained garbage and placed it in the truck so that the animals could not get it. They checked their flashlights and secured the tent so that the mosquitoes would not get in. Ben said, "A little thought and preparation makes for less aggravation. I got that line from my dad."

Anna laughed and said, "Your dad must have been a special man."

"Yes, he was," said Ben. "He was my mentor and he will always be with me."

Anna held his head as tears rolled down his cheeks. They sat by the fire and reminisced about some of the events of their lives from their first date to their wedding. They took turns replenishing the hungry fire.

All was quiet except for the crackling sound of the fire and their own quiet voices. Ben asked Anna if she was hungry.

Anna said, "What did you have in mind?"

"A cup of tea and toast," said Ben. "My dad and I always had tea and toast around midnight. Toast made from the heat of wood embers taste better than from a toaster."

They had tea and toast and brushed their teeth.

Anna said, "Remember when we made love on the balcony of the cruise ship?"

"Course I do," said Ben.

"Why don't we do something to remember our first camping trip?" said Anna.

"And what might that be?" asked Ben.

"Sex in the sand," said Anna. "Bet you have never made love in the sand."

"No," said Ben, "but I bet those who have, know the meaning of true grit."

Anna laughed. She said, "We could use a blanket that might eliminate some grit."

"Yes, it would," said Ben, "but that would be like cheating."

"Okay then," said Anna, "no blanket. Let's go. If you are game, so am I."

On the warm night, under the stars, on the sandy beach at Bon Echo camping ground, Ben and Anna made love in the sand. Without much grit.

On their second day Ben and Anna rented a canoe and paddled around the lake.

Anna saw the green canoe before Ben. It was moving from the shore toward them. The man in the canoe was not wearing a life jacket. The canoe was lurching from side to side. The man was not a smooth paddler. Anna and Ben watched as the man stood up in the canoe, lost his balance and fell overboard. The canoe flipped and was now bottom up. He was now splashing around in the water and calling "Help".

Ben and Anna quickly paddled toward him. Ben said, "I am going in the water, and don't you come too close to him."

As Ben swam toward the man, he knew from his training at the police college that if you get too close to a person in the water who is frantic and not swimming, they would drag you under the water. Ben was a strong swimmer. Just before he reached the man, he flipped onto his back, removed his life jacket, and pushed it toward the man. The man saw the life jacket and grabbed it. Ben told him to put it under his chest and kick with his legs. He repeated the instructions. The man's head was now above water and he seemed to be doing fine. Once again Ben told him and directed him toward shore. Anna followed in their canoe.

As they approached the shore, Ben saw two men who were watching them. They were lifeguards, and they were now walking out into the water. They stopped when they got waist deep and waited.

Ben heard one of the lifeguards say: "That must be him, he has a beard and that overturned canoe is green."

Ben was now standing in the water near the two lifeguards, as was the bearded man Ben had saved from drowning.

One of the men asked Ben what his name was. Ben told him. He then asked the bearded man what his name was. The man in slurred speech said his name was Allen Robson.

The other lifeguard said, "Allen, I think you better come along with us. We are making a citizen's arrest, and you stole that canoe and we don't like thieves in our campground."

Again, in slurred speech the bearded man said, "I just borrowed it, I was meaning to bring it back."

The lifeguards just shook their heads. They thanked Ben for saving the man's life. They moved forward and held the man's arms and headed for the shore.

Ben looked out and saw the overturned canoe. He asked the lifeguards if they would like him to bring the canoe in to the shore. One of them said, "Thanks that would be much appreciated."

Anna paddled the canoe to the shore. Ben got back in the canoe after putting on his life jacket, and they proceeded to recover the overturned canoe, and left it high and dry on the shore.

They paddled for another half hour and went back to their campsite.

They were relaxing in the hammock later in the afternoon, when a Provincial Park patrol vehicle stopped near their site. A man stepped out and walked toward them. Ben recognized him as one of the lifeguards that arrested the canoe thief.

He said, "Hi folks. I've come to thank you again for saving that man's life. I would like to inform you that not only did you save his life, you apprehended a fugitive. That canoe thief was not Allen Robson, he was Jack R. Jennings, better known as Jack Rabbit Jennings, who committed armed robbery. He robbed a bank in Ottawa, Ontario, our nation's capital, about three months ago. He is now in custody. To show our appreciation you have been granted free access to our park for the remaining of the summer. You can pick up your free pass at the office."

He shook Ben's hand as well as Anna's. He waved a good-bye and headed for the vehicle.

Ben and Anna looked at each other. Anna said, "You are my hero, Ben Breakwater. You'll make a real fine cop one day."

Ben just shook his head and said, "I'm no hero, too much to live up to."

They went back to the hammock and they both fell asleep.

CHAPTER 18

ANNA'S PREGNANCY WAS CONFIRMED ON THE 21ST OF JULY. She was three weeks pregnant, three weeks after their first camping trip.

Ben told her maybe she had conceived the night they made love on the beach. Later they were discussing baby names. Ben suggested a couple of names. He told Anna that since she may have conceived in the sand, if it was a boy, call him Sanford, and if it was a girl, call her Sandra.

Anna said, "Ben Breakwater, only you would use that reasoning to name our baby. However, I do like the names." She then told Ben that she would like to include her mother's name if it was a girl, and her father's name if it was a boy. Ben agreed that would be the right thing to do.

Ben and Anna moved into their house on Robin Hood Road, #46, on the first of August 1965. They had a house-warming party on the 10th of August. Except for Anna's brother and Cora, everyone that had attended her 21st birthday party was there, including her parents, whose new house would not be ready for occupancy until the end of August.

Ben was now doing OJT (On the job training) with an experienced police officer named Blake Bradley. He was a big man, six-foot three and weighed two hundred and forty pounds.

One day they were cruising around the streets of Toronto, Blake was driving. He told Ben that drugs were becoming a problem, suppliers and buyers, and we would only catch a small percentage of the suppliers. He said the drug problem was a difficult one to solve, and he didn't think it would ever be solved, but we would not stop trying. He then told Ben he had written a poem about kids on drugs on the streets. He recited the poem to Ben. He called his poem *Streets of Broken Hearts*.

Streets of Broken Hearts
Kids on the street each other meet
They live from day to day
Drugs and booze they over use
What a price they will have to pay

Sometimes too young to realize
That it's not wise to start
And it's so sad to see them
On the streets of broken hearts

Some were loved and had the chance
To make a better start
But the rebel in their blood
Overcame the heart

And now with minds all clouded
Together or apart
Hand in hand they take a stand
On the streets of broken hearts

Ben liked the poem. He told Blake that his dad wrote many poems, and that he had a book of poems written by his dad.

Blake relayed a story that happened about ten years ago, when he was training. He said one of the guys commented that writing poetry was for sissies.

"I hope you set him straight," said Ben.

"Yes, I did," said Blake. "Boxing was part of the training back then. The next time I boxed against him, I said, "I write poetry as you know." Then I proceeded to bloody his nose. Later he apologized, and said that he had been wrong to make such a statement.

"Good for you," said Ben. It was now noon, so they parked the police car and went into a restaurant for lunch.

During lunch Ben told Blake the story about the boxing match he had with Mr. Big Mouth, it had reminded him of a story his father-in-law Andrew had told him.

Andrew's friend, Gary Lawson, had been a boxer in the Canadian Army back in 1950's. He was transferred from Gagetown, New Brunswick to Winnipeg, Manitoba. There was a dance at the Junior Ranks Club on Saturday night, shortly after he arrived in Winnipeg. Gary was dancing with a pretty young lady. As the song finished playing, a young man stepped up close to Gary and said, "My turn to dance with the lady." She knew him and wanted no part of him. She said, "No, I don't want to dance with you." The young man said, "Why not? I am just as good looking as he is." She said, "I said no, now go away."

Gary then said, "The lady said no. What part of no don't you understand? Now, move on."

The young man said, "Maybe you and I could move outside and have a little dance, if you know what I mean." Two young men were now standing beside him.

Gary said, "I didn't come here to fight, I came here to dance. Maybe you've had too much to drink. I would appreciate it if you and your friends would just move along."

A couple of days later Gary was in the boxing ring in the gym, sparring with another boxer. They were doing some serious sparring. They stopped for a drink of water. Gary then saw the three young men. They had been standing there watching the sparring match.

Gary then noticed that they were the three men he had met on the dance floor, and one of them had challenged him. He said, "You there in the blue shirt. Do you remember me? I'm the guy you wanted to fight. You challenged me in front of the lady I was dancing with, and you called me a chicken. Now it's my turn. Why don't you put on a pair of gloves and step into this ring, or are you chicken? Cluck, cluck."

The young man said, "I'm not a boxer." He started to back away. He then turned and walked away. His two friends followed him.

Gary, in a loud voice, said, "Be careful who you challenge."

Blake said, "That sure did top my story. That one deserves the line, who taught who the cold hard facts of life."

"I guess it does," said Ben.

They finished their lunch and went back to the police car.

It was Ben's turn to drive. He drove east on Queen Street. The light turned red at Victoria Street. Just before it turned green, a black pick-up truck made a right turn and proceeded east on Queen. Ben saw it and suddenly had a flashback. He stepped on the gas. The pick-up was now just ahead of him, it had a white tail-gate. He noted the license plate number and asked Blake to write it down. Blake did so and said, "That is the plate number of that truck just ahead of us."

"That is correct," said Ben, "you are very observant." Blake looked at Ben and remarked, "Smart ass rookie." Ben laughed.

He then told Blake that the truck ahead of them could be the same truck that Jimmy Falls rode into the hotel parking lot in, and tried to commit armed robbery. He looked at Blake and said, "Remember, a black pick-up with a white tail-gate."

"I'll be damned," said Blake. "May be your lucky day."

Ben said he would like to see the driver's face. He was sure he would recognize him if he was the same man who drove away and left Jimmy that day.

The light up ahead turned red. Ben said, "You are correct, Blake, this is my lucky day. The brake light on the pick-up is not working, we can pull him over for that. We don't need to make up an excuse."

"Right you are Ben," said Blake, as he switched on the cruiser's lights.

Ben drove up behind the pick-up and followed it. The driver did not pull over.

Ben said, "Some people just don't look in their rear views and therefore they don't know what is going on behind them."

Blake was about to switch on the siren, when the pick-up turned right at the next side street and stopped.

Blake said, "I don't see a passenger. You stay here, I'll be right back."

Ben said, "Okay. Good thinking. He might recognize me and drive away in a panic."

He rolled down the window and watched as Blake approached the driver. He could hear what was being said. He heard Blake say "Good afternoon sir, we pulled you over because your brake light is not working. May I see your driver license and vehicle registration?" Ben watched as Blake accepted the two documents and he heard Blake say, "You stay right where you are, I will return these in a short while."

Blake was now back in the cruiser. He showed Ben the man's driver's license. Ben read the name – Jimmy J. Falls. "That's him, that's the bastard," said Ben.

"Well," said Blake, "he has done his time and he is now probably on probation. The only thing we can do to him is to give him a ticket. However, he said he didn't know his brake light was out. We can't prove otherwise, so I will give him a warning. That is all we can do."

Blake went back and gave Jimmy back his documents and the warning.

Jimmy said, "Thank you officer. I will get my brake light fixed." He drove away.

While Blake was writing out the warning, Ben noted Jimmy's address. He repeated it over and over so that he would remember it. He wasn't sure why.

Before the end of the day, Ben had written three tickets, two for stop sign violations and one for speeding.

Upon arriving in his driveway, Ben wrote down Jimmy's address and placed it in his wallet. 79 Wellesley Street, East

Toronto. He had a gut feeling Jimmy was not on the straight and narrow.

Ben was now serving with the Central Field Command Headquarters at Eglinton Avenue. That is where he reported in for duty every day.

Ben could not erase Jimmy J. Falls from his mind. He decided to pay a little visit and check out the neighbourhood.

His next day off was Saturday. On his way home Friday evening he stopped at a rent-a-car and asked the man behind the counter if he could leave his truck in the lot if he were to rent a car. The man told him that would not be a problem. Ben said he wanted a car and he would pick it up in the morning at seven a.m.

After picking up the car Ben drove to Jimmy's address. There were several cars parked on the street. Ben parked the car and had a good vantage point. He would be able to see any activity in Jimmy's driveway. He wore his old ragged ball cap. He had grown a mustache and he thought even if Jimmy saw him, he would not recognize him.

He placed the car seat as far back as possible and kept a close eye on the driveway. It was now eight a.m. He felt a little guilty. He now had a man under surveillance without due cause, however, his gut feeling told him otherwise.

Eight-thirty – nothing happening. Nine – all quiet. He looked in the driver's side mirror and saw a man walking on the street. The man stopped, unlocked car door two cars behind him. He backed the car up then drove past him and on up the street. He watched the car until it turned right on the next street. His eyes came to Jimmy's driveway, just in time to see a pick-up truck turn into the driveway. A man stepped out of the cab, closed the door and walked to the front door and knocked four times. He wore a brown jacket. In a few seconds the door opened, and the man stepped inside and closed the door. After about five minutes, the man emerged, got back in the truck, backed out of the driveway, turned and drove away.

In the next two hours a total of seven vehicles visited Jimmy's place. Each doing the same routine, and they all wore jackets.

Ben wrote down the make and the license plate numbers of all seven vehicles.

He waited another hour and left.

He picked up his truck and went home.

After parking his truck, he sat there and wondered what he had just witnessed. Seven men visited Jimmy in two hours. Why? He did not see them carry anything in or out. However, they all wore jackets. Jackets had pockets that were big enough to carry a good supply of drugs. If it were drugs, then Jimmy was a drug dealer. He decided he would do a repeat performance on his next day off, which was Saturday.

Many times the following week, as he and Blake drove around the Toronto streets, he was tempted to tell Blake what he had done. He decided not to.

The following Saturday morning, Ben parked his rented car in the same area as he had before, not far from Jimmy Falls' driveway. It was a very quiet street. Most houses were surrounded by hedges. Jimmy had picked a good location to do his business.

Ben checked his watch – eight-forty a.m. When he looked up, a car pulled into Jimmy's driveway. He recorded the make and license plate number. He checked, he had not listed this vehicle before, and he marked it with an asterisk.

As he did last Saturday, he watched as eight vehicles, five that he had noted last week, and three new ones, drove into Jimmy's driveway, and left within five minutes. He recognized four men he had seen last week.

Once again, he waited for one hour after the last visitor before he left. Driving back to pick up his truck he wondered if other days were like Saturdays at Jimmy's place. But, he had seen enough. The question now was, what was he going to do about it? Who could he tell – what if he got in trouble over his spying on Jimmy. He did not want trouble. His mind started to race. Maybe he should tell Blake. If what he had done was not kosher, he hoped Blake would overlook it, because he was a rookie. An idea popped into his head. A dream. Yes, he would tell Blake he had a dream and that in the dream he went to spy on Jimmy. He would get his reaction and go from there. He thought about the phrase his dad had used a few times when he had a good idea, or he solved a problem – "My mamma never raised no fool." He laughed at himself as he pulled into the lot where his truck was parked.

Monday, Ben and Blake were once again patrolling the downtown streets of Toronto. A couple of times they parked the police car and did a little foot patrolling.

As usual, they ate lunch at a restaurant. Ben usually treated. He told Blake a rich aunt had left him a few grand. Blake said, "I'll eat to that." Ben thought that was very funny. He was starting to have a good rapport with Blake. He had a good sense of humour.

After they placed their order, Ben looked at Blake and said, "Had a dream last night."

"Yea," said Blake. "What about? Hope I didn't get shot."

"No nothing like that," said Ben. He then relayed to Blake as a dream, what in reality, he had done – spying on Jimmy.

"Wow," said Blake. "If I were to analyze your dream I would say your Mr. Jimmy is selling drugs."

"Yea," said Ben, "that's what I thought, after I woke up. Do you think my dream might be an omen?"

"Don't know," said Blake. "Some people give dreams a meaning. I don't give them much thought."

Ben gave Blake one of his serious looks. He asked Blake if police officers followed the rules at all times.

Blake said, "I would like to think they do." But he said that sometimes the rules are stretched when things get difficult. He said, "short cuts sometimes yield info quicker. I guess in all walks of life little white lies are told. Don't you think, Ben?"

Ben agreed.

Blake then told Ben that his mom had always told him to tell the truth, and he always kept that in mind. "However," he said, "there are times when a lie could save someone's life. Case in point – you are in an alley and a young girl comes running pass you and makes a right turn at the next street. Then you see a man with a knife in his hand. When he sees you he hides the knife in his jacket pocket. He asks you which way the girl went. Do you lie or tell him the truth?"

"I would lie," said Ben.

"So would I," said Blake.

Lunch came and was consumed. They both liked to eat, especially Blake.

Ben asked him which would he choose, sex or the best steak money could buy.

"The steak," said Blake. "Just kidding. However, I would say I would like a ratio of one in five."

"What do you mean?" asked Ben.

"Steak once and sex five times," said Blake.

Ben laughed.

They left the restaurant.

After they were seated in the police car, Ben said, "I have a confession to make. The dream I told you about before lunch was not a dream at all. I actually did what I told you was a dream."

Blake gave Ben a very serious look. "You should not have done it Ben. There is no judge in the land that will give us a warrant to search Jimmy's house because you had no cause to do what you did," said Blake.

"I kind a figured that," said Ben. "I guess I let my gut over rule my brain."

"Maybe we can figure something out here," said Blake. "I hate to see a drug dealer go unpunished. You say you have ten license plate numbers. Let's start there. We could run the numbers and get names. We may get lucky. One or more might be on probation for drug dealing. We will go back early today and see what we come up with." They found one man whose name was Rodney Gibbons, who did jail time for trying to sell drugs to an undercover police officer one year ago. He was now on probation.

Blake told Ben he would try and think of a plan of action, and if he couldn't they would drop the whole thing.

The next morning Blake revealed his plan to Ben. He told Ben that it might not work, but it was worth a try.

The plan: Blake was on duty this coming Saturday, and he would have an unmarked police car. He would pick up Ben and they would park in the same area as Ben had parked to observe Jimmy's driveway. If Rodney showed up, they would follow him and hope he would do something whereby they could pull him over. Blake said they would fake a reason if they had to. Like tell him his brake light was not working. Blake said he hoped Rodney would throw the drugs into the ditch if they stopped him. He said they could not search him.

Saturday morning Blake parked the unmarked police car and they watched Jimmy's driveway. Several vehicles pulled into Jimmy's driveway for a few minutes and then left. Blake and Ben were looking for Rodney's car – a white Chevy.

Ben said, "Maybe he won't come today."

As he said the word today, a white Chevy turned into Jimmy's driveway. Blake checked the plate number. It was Rodney's car.

A few minutes later the white Chevy left the driveway and headed up the street. Blake and Ben followed.

There was a stop sign up ahead. The white Chevy did not stop at the stop sign. It had slowed down only.

"Got him," said Blake, and he turned on the lights. After a minute or so the car stopped.

Blake stopped behind him. He told Ben to watch the passenger side of the car. He got out and cautiously moved to the driver's window which was now down. As Blake looked at the driver he knew it was not Rodney Gibbons. He was a very young man and he looked scared. He said, "I know I did not stop at that stop sign, I am sorry officer. Please don't give me a ticket."

Ben was now standing beside Blake. Blake asked him for his driver's license and the vehicle registration. The young man's hands were shaking as he fumbled in the glove compartment for the registration. He found it and gave it to Blake.

"Your driver's license," said Blake.

"I don't have my license with me," he said. "I lost my wallet."

"You don't have your license?" Blake repeated.

"No sir," said the young man.

"Do you have an ID?" asked Blake.

"No sir," he said. "My name is Steve Johns."

"Steve Johns. That's your name," said Blake.

"Yes sir," he said.

"I see this vehicle belongs to a Mr. Rodney Gibbons. Did you steal it?" asked Blake.

"No sir," he said, "I am his cousin. He asked me to pick up something for him, because he lost his driver's license last week."

Blake looked at Ben and said, "Sounds like a bullshit story to me, how about you?"

"Sounds to me like you are in a heap of trouble. I believe you stole this vehicle," said Ben.

The young man looked at Blake with tears in his eyes.

Blake said, "Maybe we will give you a break."

The young man looked at him.

"I'll tell you what I will do," said Blake. "If you show me the package you picked up for Rodney and you give me the address where you picked up the package, I will let you go – no ticket. You will be free to be on your way in thirty seconds."

"Really," he said, "I'll be free to go."

"Yes, that's what I said," repeated Blake.

"Okay," he said, as he reached into his jacket pocket and handed the brown bag to Blake. (Blake looked in and saw the plastic bag that contained drugs, and he thought it was LSD.) Then Steve gave Blake Jimmy's address, which Blake already knew.

Blake said, "Steve, you have been very cooperative, however, I am arresting you for possession of drugs. You are coming with us."

Blake had been on the Drug Squad a few years ago. He always carried with him his small backpack which contained a wig, a fake mustache, an old pair of shorts, a ball cap and a tee-shirt. He changed in the cruiser. They went back to Jimmy's place. Blake walked up to the door and knocked four times as Ben had told him. The door opened, and Blake stepped inside.

Blake told Ben that as soon as he mentioned Rodney's name, Jimmy didn't blink an eye. He reached into an old backpack, Blake handed him the cash and Jimmy handed him the brown paper bag. Blake said he looked into the bag and nodded his head. He then walked back outside and waved to Ben. They both then entered and showed their badges and arrested Jimmy.

Jimmy was found guilty of drug trafficking. Because of the circumstances, Steve was given a suspended sentence, with conditions he would have to adhere to or he would be arrested.

CHAPTER 19

SEPTEMBER LONG WEEKEND BEN DECIDED TO TAKE ANNA TO see his hometown of Breakwater. They arrived early Saturday afternoon.

After visiting the falls, Ben showed Anna the house he had lived in, which now had a new owner. Then he drove to the school that he attended. It was now four p.m. They found the door unlocked. They entered. Ben knew where Mr. Pebbles' office was, and as they approached he was just leaving.

He was very surprised to see Ben.

Ben introduced Anna, and stated that he was very proud to announce that Anna was almost three months pregnant.

Robert congratulated them both.

He asked how long they were planning to be in town. Ben told him they would be heading back to Toronto on Monday.

Robert said he hoped they had not checked into the hotel in Breakwater.

Ben said, "No not yet. That's where we were headed next."

"Don't bother," said Robert. "I have lots of room at my place. You are welcome to stay anytime. I could use the company."

"Okay," said Ben, "as long as you let me treat you to dinner."

"Let's go," he said, "to my place, and you can tell me all about your endeavors since we last chatted."

They sat in Robert's living room and talked for an hour or so. Ben told him everything that had happened to him since leaving Breakwater except the incident with Tommy in the parking lot in Toronto. Ben didn't see any point in telling Robert that one of his students was a druggie on the streets of Toronto. He did, however, tell him that he heard Billy Brooks died from a stab wound about a year ago, on some street in Toronto. Both Ben and Anna noticed a change in Robert's demeanor when he had been told of Billy's death. He had closed his eyes and lowered his head, but did not say a word. They thought it was very strange behaviour, for Billy had been his student for many years.

A while later they went out for dinner. Robert insisted that he drive his car.

Sunday afternoon Ben and Anna visited the falls once again. They sat on a bench facing the falls. A short time later a young man walked past them and sat on another bench that was facing the falls.

Anna saw him and she immediately thought of the King of the Cowboys, Roy Rogers. He wore a white Stetson, a fancy shirt, jeans and cowboy boots. She whispered in Ben's ear, "Do you know him?"

Ben shrugged his shoulders and in a low voice said, "I don't know, I didn't see his face."

Just as he said the word face, the young man turned and looked in their direction.

Ben saw his face and shouted, "Tommy, Tommy Seal."

Tommy stood and said, "Ben Breakwater, fancy seeing you here. Thought you were in the Big City, Toronto."

"Thought you were too," said Ben.

They were now very close, and they shook hands. Anna joined them and Ben introduced her. Anna knew all about Tommy Seal. Ben had told her.

"Since when did Tommy Seal become a cowboy?" asked Ben. "Last time I saw you…"

"Let's not go there" said Tommy, "I am clean now and I have a job, right here in Breakwater.

"Good for you," said Ben. "Is there a horse ranch around here now?"

"No, I am working at my Uncle Gordon's used car dealership. I sell more cars than he does," said Tommy. "I'll bet I am the only cowboy car salesman in the whole area, including the city of Ottawa."

"Yes, I bet you are," said Ben. "Was it your idea or your Uncle Gordon's?"

"No, it wasn't planned," said Tommy, "it just happened. Let's sit and I will tell you."

"After I cleaned up my act, I came back home to Breakwater. My Uncle Gordon gave me the job selling cars. After receiving my first paycheque I went to the bank to open an account. The young lady behind the counter was very friendly. She told me I looked like Roy Rogers, King of the Cowboys. She said she loved Roy Rogers, he was so good looking, and he could sing and yodel. I told her I could sing and yodel. She said but you ain't no cowboy like Roy. I said no I ain't. I then asked her if she was new in town because I had not seen her before. She said she was. I said see you later gorgeous, and I left the bank."

"I sat in my old car, one that Uncle Gordon gave me, and a few things ran through my mind. If the young lady thought I looked like Roy Rogers, and she said Roy was good looking, then maybe I had a chance to get a date. Furthermore, I thought, hell, if I were to dress like Roy, I would have a better chance of getting a date. However, I didn't have the cash to buy the attire I needed. I played drums on the steering wheel. Then it hit me. I had equity – this old car. I sold it the next day, and in the evening, I borrowed my dad's car, drove into Ottawa and bought what you're looking at now, plus a change, except for the boots."

"The next day I showed up for work in my new cowboy attire. Uncle Gordon looked at me and smiled. He said, "Now why didn't I think of that. A cowboy car salesman. A first in Breakwater. Way to go Tommy. I knew I hired the right man."

Then I told him I sold the car he had given me in order to purchase my new look. He just laughed and said I would have to earn my next one, no more freebies.

I said, "Just watch me. I'm gonna sing and yodel while I work, and I will outsell you until the new wears off my cowboy hat." Uncle Gordon said he would be a winner either way.

The next time I went to the bank to deposit my paycheque, the same lady was behind the counter. As I walked up to the counter she was shaking her head. I nodded my head up and down as if to say yes, yes, it's me again, here comes your Roy Rogers look-a-like. How do you like me now?

I said, "Hi, Roy couldn't come, so he sent me."

She had a big smile on her face and it stayed.

After the deposit was made I asked her if she was free Sunday afternoon. I could meet her at the waterfall. I told her there would be other people around, and anyway, I wouldn't hurt a mosquito unless it was biting me. She laughed. Then she said, "Okay, two p.m. at the Falls."

"That was three weeks ago, and we are in love. Her name is Suzie Walsh. She was born in Almonte, Ontario and she is twenty-one years old. Oh, I already told you she is gorgeous. My rose from Almonte."

"That is quite a story," said Ben. "A young man sells his car to dress like a cowboy and get the girl of his dreams."

"Yep, that's how it happened," said Tommy.

"Congratulations Tommy," said Anna. "I am so happy for you."

"Thank you, Anna," said Tommy. "I think Ben is as lucky as I am." (Ben didn't see him wink at Anna.)

Ben asked him if he had another car yet.

Tommy said, "Not one I own; however, Uncle Gordon lets me drive the oldest car on his lot until I have the money to buy one."

He then asked Ben how long did he plan to be in town. Ben told him they were leaving for Toronto in the morning.

"Guess you got a good paying job Ben," said Tommy.

"Well," said Ben, "not as good as some, but better than others. I joined the Toronto Police Force."

"Wow," said Tommy, "you always were a brave one. I am sure you will be an excellent addition to the Force. You sure have all the attributes. With your brain power, Ben, you could do anything your little ole heart desires."

"Thanks Tommy," said Ben, "and I have you to thank that I didn't drown a few years ago."

"What are friends for Ben," said Tommy. "You would have done the same."

Anna asked where Suzie was. Tommy said she had gone to Almonte, visiting friends. He said they get together every few months.

Ben asked him if he had plans for dinner.

Tommy said he had no plans.

Ben asked him to join them.

Tommy said he would love to.

"I guess you are staying at the one and only hotel in town," Tommy said.

"No," said Ben, "we are staying at Robert Pebbles place."

"Oh," said Tommy, as he shook his head.

Ben asked, "Why was he shaking his head?"

Tommy said, "Maybe it's better if I keep my mouth shut."

"About what?" said Ben. "You know something about Robert I don't know?"

"Yes, Ben I do," said Tommy.

"Tell me. It must be something serious," said Ben.

"It's a story only Billy and Robert knew until Billy told me," said Tommy.

"You're talking about Billy Brooks," said Ben.

Tommy nodded his head.

"I told you that Billy died from a stab wound he received on a street in Toronto. Well, a few days before that happened he told me the reason he wanted to leave Breakwater. It was his idea that him and I head for Toronto. He said he didn't want to stay in Breakwater any longer, and at the time he did not tell me the real reason why. He just said he was bored, and wanted more excitement in his life."

"As you know, Ben, Billy was not the brightest kid in our school. He had a learning disability I guess. You also know that Billy would stay after the class was dismissed in the afternoon and Robert would spend extra time helping him. This went on for years, until Billy quit school when he was sixteen."

"Billy didn't go into much detail, however, he said that Robert stole his innocence. He said it came about slowly. He said he was about seven when it started. He said Robert would expose himself and ask Billy to play with him. He said that Robert told him if he wanted to move to the next grade with his friends, this was the only way he would get extra help to move on. Robert told him not to tell anyone, and if he did, Robert would tell everyone that Billy was a liar. He also said, without his help Billy would be called a dummy by all his school friends, because he would have to repeat the same grade. Billy said he made up his mind that he would do anything not to be called a dummy."

"Billy said when he was about thirteen, Robert would give him money. He said he quit school at sixteen because he knew he could never pass an arithmetic exam, no matter how much help he got. He said he didn't see any point in Robert giving him a pass, because if he got a job, and he had to work with numbers, he would still look like a dummy, so he might as well quit school."

Tommy said he asked Billy how did he explain to his parents where he got the money to buy things. He said he told them that he did chores for the teacher Mr. Pebbles on Saturdays.

Ben looked at Tommy and said, "And nobody knew."

"Nobody but Robert and Billy," said Tommy. "However, now there are four of us who know."

"I never would have guessed in a million years," said Ben, "that Robert was capable of such child abuse. I always thought he was a pillar in our community."

"A wolf in sheep's clothing," said Anna.

She then told Ben she did not want to see Robert Pebbles ever again. "We have to get a room at the hotel tonight Ben," she said.

"Okay," said Ben, "let's go and get a room. Then we will have dinner."

After they placed their order at the restaurant, Ben asked Anna what would he tell Robert as to why they were not staying at his place. He said it was going to be an awkward situation for him.

Anna was quick to respond. She said, "Tell him I caught a cold or something and I am sneezing and coughing, and I didn't want to pass it on. Or, you could tell him that I saw a spider in the bedroom, and I am terrified of spiders. Your choice."

Tommy said, "You are not only beautiful, you are very clever, to think of that so quickly."

"Thanks for the compliment Tommy," said Anna.

While Anna and Tommy were talking, Ben was thinking he had already thanked Tommy several times for saving his life. The time had come for him to show how grateful he was and give him something. After all, he was a rich man.

He reached for his wallet. He always carried a couple of blank cheques. He took one out of his wallet, and with a pen he took from his shirt pocket, he wrote Tommy a cheque – three thousand dollars. He handed it to Tommy and said, "Here Tommy, buy yourself a good set of wheels. This is my gift to the only cowboy car salesman I know."

Tommy slowly reached for the cheque. He looked at it, then he looked at Ben and said, "I can't accept this Ben.

How can you afford to write a cheque like this on a first-year policeman's pay?"

"You are right Tommy," said Ben. "With my paycheque only, I could not write you that cheque. However, I was lucky to inherit quite a sum of money. In the past year or so, I bought a new truck, wedding rings, a house, and Anna and I took a vacation to Jamaica. So, you see Tommy, I have more money than my paycheque."

Tommy looked at the cheque one more time. Again, he looked back at Ben. Tears rolled down his cheeks. He looked at Anna. She gave him a big smile and said, "Thank you for your efforts in saving my husband's life. I will forever be grateful. Now go buy yourself a set of wheels like Ben said, Cowboy, or you could buy yourself a couple of horses." All three of them laughed.

"Maybe," said Ben, "if you have enough left after you buy your wheels or horses, you might want to buy your cowgirl attire to match yours."

Tommy wiped his eyes, a smile returned to his face, as he picked up the cheque and slipped it into his fancy shirt pocket. He said, "Thank you both, thank you very much. A cowboy could not ask or wish for more thoughtful friends than you two. Seems to me you are very deserving of each other."

Ben said, "Why don't you and Suzie come and visit us in Toronto. We have lots of room. Take a spin and check out your new wheels."

Anna said, "Please do, I would love to meet Suzie." Anna dug into her purse and found paper and pen. She wrote down their address and phone number, and gave it to Tommy.

Before they left the restaurant, Ben told Tommy he should call the O.P.P. (Ontario Provincial Police) and inform them of the child abuse of Billy Brooks by Robert Pebbles. Ben said it's very important you do that.

Tommy said he would.

Ben and Anna said good-bye to Tommy outside the restaurant. They then drove to Robert's place. Anna waited in the truck.

Ben retrieved their overnight bags at Robert's house. He told him that Anna had contracted a cold and was sneezing and coughing and they decided to take a room at the hotel. As he walked to the door, he told Robert that he would drop by and say good-bye before leaving for Toronto. He had no intention of doing so. He would never shake Robert Pebble's hand, ever again.

A little more than three weeks later, on a Wednesday evening, the phone rang. Anna answered. It was Tommy. He wanted to know if this coming weekend would be a good time for him and Suzie to come visit them. Anna told him they had no plans for the weekend, and would be looking forward to seeing them.

After she hung up the phone, Ben returned from outside. She told him they would have visitors this coming weekend.

"Who?" asked Ben.

"Tommy and Suzie," said Anna. "They will be here Saturday afternoon."

"You mean Roy and Dale," said Ben.

"Who's Dale?" asked Anna.

"Thought you knew," said Ben. "Dale Evans, she is Roy Roger's wife."

"Let's just stick with Tommy and Suzie, okay?" said Anna.

"As you wish, gorgeous one," said Ben.

He then told Anna he was very anxious to hear what happened in Breakwater after Tommy talked to the police.

Anna said, "I guess you will know this Saturday when Tommy and Suzie arrive."

"I just hope Tommy did call the O.P.P. Robert may be abusing some other kid, and nobody would know, just like he did with Billy."

"My guess is Tommy did," said Anna.

"We will find out soon," said Ben.

Anna said, "I am very proud of you for writing that cheque for Tommy. He has two good reasons to stay clean, you and Suzie. Remember he shed tears when you gave him the cheque. Then there is Suzie. He said they were in love. He will have to stay clean if he wants to keep her."

"Guess you are right," said Ben.

They were sitting on the chesterfield, close to each other as usual. The lower part of their legs was intertwined.

Ben broke the few moments of silence. He said, "These past fifteen months sure has been interesting. My life has changed so much since that day I found John Dillon in the forest near Breakwater. If I had not gone for a stroll that day, where would I be today?"

"How could you ever know," said Anna.

"I guess I might have sold my dad's house, packed my back-pack and headed out to see the world. Maybe to Europe, I don't know. But here I am, lots of money in the bank, that led me to meeting and marrying a beautiful, intelligent, young, vibrant woman, who will in about six months, give life to a child that will never have to worry about a mortgage payment or any payment for that matter. We have a nice home and lots to be thankful for. Oh, yes, and I have a father-in-law who thinks

I am special, and a mother-in-law that I think the world of. What more could a man ask for."

"I guess you are a very lucky man, Ben Breakwater," said Anna. "And if you had gone to Europe, I would still be working at the Dominion grocery store, minus morning sickness."

"Maybe not," said Ben. "Some other guy would have swept you off your feet, and you still would have morning sickness."

Anna leaned over and gave him a passionate kiss. "I am happy it was you," she said. She kissed him again, as she reached between his legs and felt his manhood grow. She said, "Maybe we should go and do a little practicing, I want more than one kid." (Once again, they left a trail of clothes from the chesterfield to the bedroom.)

It rained Saturday morning. However, it was sunny when Tommy and Suzie arrived at 46 Robin Hood Road. After greetings and introductions, Ben and Tommy went out to the driveway. Ben wanted to check out Tommy's new wheels. (He didn't buy horses.) Tommy had bought a 1964 Chevy pick-up, blue in colour. Tommy said he got a real good deal. The bank had repossessed it. He said his Uncle Gordon knew the bank manager. When they had a vehicle, they would call him and Gordon always bought it, and at a good price.

Tommy once again shook Ben's hand and thanked him for his generous gift, that of three grand.

They sat in the living room and chatted. Tommy and Suzie were not wearing cowboy and cowgirl attire. They said they did not want to be conspicuous on the streets of Toronto or at the Yorkdale Mall which they planned to visit.

Ben asked Tommy if he had called the O.P.P. as he said he would.

Tommy said he called the O.P.P. Monday morning. Two officers came to see him at his uncle's used car dealership. He said he told the officers the same story he had told them. Tommy said he didn't hear a thing until his Uncle Gordon, who is a friend of the Mayor of Breakwater, told him that Robert Pebble was dead. The Mayor told him Robert had died of a heart attack. Tommy said he didn't believe that. Robert was a fit man. Only forty years old, or not much over that. Tommy said he thinks Robert committed suicide, and if that was the reason given, there would have been questions asked. To say he had a heart attack – no questions, all soon forgotten.

Ben said his logic was quite believable, but he would sure like to know the truth. "More than one person knew what had happened," said Ben, "and someday, I may find out."

Ben had cooked his famous spaghetti meat sauce dinner. Suzie said it was the best she had ever tasted.

Anna and Suzie had a lot in common. They both were strong women with a good sense of humour. They both loved their miniskirts, although Suzie could not wear one while working in the bank. The bank had a dress code. Suzie loved western movies. Her favourite actor was Roy Rogers, although her favourite movie was Shane. Anna said she saw Shane and thought it was excellent.

Ben was happy to hear them laughing as they cleaned up after dinner. The two young women seemed very comfortable in each other's company. He was hoping they would develop a lasting friendship. He remembered his Dad telling him that good friends make one's life more complete, and that friends who call you only when they need something, are not really friends.

Tommy sure acted like a man in love. It seemed he couldn't get close enough to Suzie as they sat on the chesterfield. And they would always hold hands.

Ben knew that these two lovebirds had only been together for a month and a half however, he had a feeling that there would be a wedding in Breakwater in the not too distant future. They reminded him of himself and Anna.

It was a fun weekend for the four of them. They went downtown, walked around, ate lunch at a quaint little café then went to see the movie The Sound of Music, which had just debuted.

After the movie, Ben treated them to a steak dinner.

Monday morning Ben made everyone breakfast. He was now working evenings. Anna said good-bye and left for class, but not before saying how much she had enjoyed the weekend. She told Tommy and Suzie to please come again soon.

Tommy and Suzie left shortly after Anna, for their drive back to Breakwater.

Ben sat in the leather chair in the living room. He put his feet up. The house was full of silence. The laughing and joking that he had enjoyed these last two days no longer could be heard. He thought of Tommy and he smiled. Tommy Seal, the cowboy, car salesman and a young man in love. It warmed his heart. Then his thoughts turned to Billy. A sadness came over him. To think that he was violated by a man whom he held in such high esteem. When he lost his father, Robert had been there for him. Robert was the first person to know that he was a millionaire. Now he was dead. He did not feel sad, he felt betrayed. He knew it would take time to process it all. He went and poured himself a glass of water. His mind was working again. Were there any positives he could take from the situation concerning Billy and Robert? Maybe he had now gained insight into human behaviour. There must be other adults who were taking advantage of children. He thought of Anna and her Uncle George – now Billy. He realized that the only person you really, really know is yourself. Unless one could read minds, how would you truly know? However, he knew there had to be many, many more honest individuals than deceitful ones. That was the best positive he could rationalize.

CHAPTER 20

ANNA DID NOT KNOW IF IT WAS AN ACCIDENTAL OR NOT. IT was the first time that Peter, the dental lab technician, had ever touched her. His full name was Peter Kyle Kenley. He had expert knowledge of all dental equipment. He was the only male instructor at the dental school. The director of the program was also a male, Mr. Chad Winter.

Peter was a very small man. He could have been a jockey. All the students were female, and they were all taller than Peter. Anna was much taller than Peter, and she felt a little self-conscious whenever he was close to her. She had to look down at him while he looked up at her.

It happened in the lab. Anna, like the rest of the students, was sitting on a stool at a counter that was rather high. Peter was handing out reading material associated with the lab work they would be doing that morning. Anna had both her elbows on the counter and her hands were resting on both sides of her face. She was looking a little to her right. Suddenly, something brushed against her left breast. She looked down and realized it was Peter's arm. He had passed the handout between her chest and her elbow and onto the counter in front of her. Then he moved behind her to the next girl. It happened so quickly, and she watched as he passed the handout over the next girl's arm, which was also on top of the counter. Anna now asked herself why did he pass the handout to her in such a way that he touched her. She then looked again at the girl on her right. Then it hit her. The girl on her right had small breasts. Anna knew she had rather large breasts, and no doubt Peter had noticed. The question she now asked herself – Did he do it on purpose? Or was it accidental? How could one prove it was on purpose? He must have known that his arm touched her. He did not apologize. Anna did not want to cause a scene, and decided to think about what she might do or say about what had just happened.

During lunch Anna thought about her dilemma – should she tell Peter that he had inappropriately touched her in the lab. If she did, and he replied that if he did it was not done on purpose, and that he was sorry if he touched her, she might now become the black sheep of the class. She now thought she was caught between a rock and a hard place.

She had not observed Peter commit any improprieties in the class or otherwise. However, that did not mean he had not done so. Maybe one or more of the girls had experienced inappropriate behaviour by Peter, and they were thinking the same way she was, afraid to rock the boat because of possible retaliation by Peter. Then she thought – Why not ask them? How could I narrow it down? I would need to get each one alone. If I could find just one other girl who was in my position, we could go to the Director and tell him.

Mid-afternoon Anna was in the washroom. One of the girls walked in soon after she did. Her name was Serina. Anna took extra time at the sink. When Serina came to the sinks, Anna said, "I have a question for you Serina."

Serina said, "What is it?"

Anna then asked her if Peter had ever touched her or acted improper in any way.

She said, "No, however, I think he is a bit creepy, but if he did touch me, I would have slapped his face. Did he touch you?"

"Yes," said Anna. "But I do not know for sure if it was intentional." She explained to Serina what had happened in the lab. She then told Serina that she was trying to find another girl who may have experienced anything similar to her. If so, she would tell the director.

Serina told her she was doing the right thing.

Anna told her to please keep their conversation confidential.

Serina said she would, and left the washroom.

Anna checked the time. Another ten minutes before class re-convened.

A few seconds later a girl named Rhonda came in. Anna stood at the sink and combed her hair. She went through the same routine with Rhonda, and received the same answer. Anna left the washroom with Rhonda and they went back to the classroom.

After class finished that afternoon, Anna stood in the hallway near the washroom door. She pretended she was looking for something in her purse. Tammy, whom she had talked to many times and was very friendly, was coming toward her. Anna hoped she was headed for the washroom.

As she approached, Anna said, "Tammy, I would like to ask you a question. Let's step into the washroom."

Tammy said, "Sure, that's where I was headed."

Anna once again went through the same scenario as she had done with Serina and Rhonda. As soon as she mentioned the circumstances whereby Peter had touched her left breast Tammy said, "Oh my God, he did the same thing to me. He pushed the handout under my arm and touched me. I thought I may have moved and caused the contact, I wasn't sure. A few times he has moved really close and almost touched me."

"Well," said Anna, "I think our little Peter likes big boobs. I talked to Rhonda and Serina who do not have large breasts, and he had never touched them. Although Serina did say he is a bit creepy."

"He is that," said Tammy.

"I think we should go and tell the director about Peter's behaviour," said Anna. "I think he has to go."

"I agree with you Anna," said Tammy. "But first I will ask Eva if she experienced anything like us. She has even bigger boobs than we do."

"Okay," said Anna, "three would be better than two."

The next day Tammy arrived early. She waited in her car until Eva arrived. Before Eva got out of her car Tammy approached the driver's side door. When Eva opened the door, Tammy said, "Hi Eva, may I sit in, I have a question for you."

"Sure, sit in," said Eva, and she closed the door.

Tammy asked her if short ass Peter (that's what Eva called him) ever touched her or did anything inappropriate. She then explained why she asked the question.

Eva just said, "The son-of-a-b."

She then told Tammy she had noticed a few times that he was staring at her. She also observed him staring at Anna and Tammy. Once she said Peter had stood real close to her and puckered his lips, like he was thinking, then he turned, and Eva said if she had not moved back, his shoulder would have touched her breast.

Tammy then asked her if she would accompany her and Anna to the director's office to see Mr. Chad Winter. Eva said she would.

At lunch break, Anna, Tammy and Eva walked into the director's office. He was just about to leave for the café, when they arrived. Anna had agreed to be the spokeswoman. Anna told him they had a concern and would like to express such.

He invited them in and he sat behind his desk.

Anna relayed her story. Tammy and Eva did the same.

Anna, at first, thought he was taking them lightly. After Eva finished speaking, Anna told him there would be serious trouble if Peter ever touched her again.

He said he would speak to Peter and he was quite confident there would be no further trouble with Peter.

They left the director's office and went back to the lunch room.

Tammy said she wasn't sure Chad believed them. Eva said he had better believe, or the next time she visited his office, she would be using words that were not very lady-like.

Anna, Tammy and Eva agreed they would keep a close eye on Peter. And they did.

It was Thursday afternoon. They were all in the lab, sitting at the counter. Peter was once again handing out reading material. Eva was sitting at the end on the left, and she was the first to receive the handout. She was looking to her right, Tammy was talking to her. Suddenly, she felt something touch her left breast. She immediately looked down and saw Peter's arm. Instinctively, she lifted her left arm and quickly forced her elbow into Peter's face. The elbow is the strongest point on a human. Peter drew back in pain. Eva shouted, "You S.O.B., you touched my breast."

Everyone was now looking at Peter.

He quickly placed the handouts on the counter, turned and walked away.

Eva asked if anyone had seen what had just happened. Two of the girls said they did. Eva asked them to accompany her to the director's office. They did.

Eva told the Director, Mr. Chad Winter, what had just happened in the lab. The two witnesses confirmed what Eva had said.

The director immediately apologized to Eva.

He asked them if they knew where Peter was. Eva said that he had left the lab, that's all she knew.

He told them to go back to the lab and he would be with them in a few minutes. After they left he went to look for Peter. He could not find him.

He then went to the lab and apologized to everyone. He said, "I can assure you ladies that behaviour that took place here in the lab this afternoon, will never happen again. Peter has been fired." Eva was the first to applaud and the rest joined her.

He then told them they would have a long weekend. He would see them Monday morning.

Peter called Chad just as he arrived in his office Monday morning. Peter said that he was quitting. Chad told him he was late with that news, and that he had been fired Thursday afternoon. Chad told him he would mail him his last cheque. He also told him not to use his name as a reference if he ever applied for a job. He hung up the phone.

Chad Winter never did see the shiner that Peter was sporting during the phone call on Monday. Neither did Eva, she would have been so proud.

CHAPTER 21

CORA HAD FINISHED HER COURSE AT THE TEACHERS' COLLEGE in London. She was temporarily living with her mom and dad. She was planning on buying her own house as soon as she found full or part-time work as a teacher.

She would like to teach at a West Toronto school, as well as find a house in the general area. She would love to find a house near Anna. She had missed Anna very much, especially since Sammy died. She enjoyed her time with her mom and dad, but it was not the same. The conversations were much different. Her and Anna were the same age, experiencing the same things, talking about men, and what their future might hold.

She had called Anna the day she arrived back to Toronto. Anna invited her to come and stay the following weekend. She had accepted, and was looking forward to spending time with Anna. Friday evening was only three days away. Anna had told her that Ben was working the graveyard shift, so they would have lots of time for conversation. Just the two of them, like it had been eighteen months ago.

Cora had asked Anna if Ben would make his famous spaghetti and meat sauce dinner sometime during the weekend.

Anna told her she had watched Ben several times, and she could make it just like Ben. She said they could do it together.

Cora was now a qualified teacher. She had dreams that she was already teaching. She would wake up disappointed that it was only a dream. She had been told at the college that if she were to volunteer at a school it would be good experience. That is what she planned to do.

Now she must look for a school. She thought about the school on Annette Street, West Toronto. She thought it was called Annette Public School, she had driven by that school several times. She looked in the phone book. She was right. She wrote down the address. She would wear her best dress and walk into Annette Public School tomorrow morning. She was already excited.

In the morning, Cora chose a purse big enough to fit a folder which contained her teachers' certificate. Her Mom wished her luck as she checked herself in the mirror one last time.

She arrived at Annette Public School at ten a.m. She went to the reception area and told the lady her name. She explained to the very friendly lady why she was there. She was a qualified teacher. She had just finished college in London, and was looking for work. She also told her she would volunteer to help in any way she could.

The lady said she would check with the principal to see if he would see her. She came back in a couple minutes and escorted Cora to the principal's office. She told her his name was Mr. Lawrence McLeod.

The lady from reception made the introductions and left. Mr. McLeod asked Cora to take a seat.

Cora said, "Thank you, Mr. McLeod. I do not wish to take up very much of your time."

"So," he said, "you are looking for work, paid or otherwise, I was told."

"Yes, sir, I am," said Cora, "I just finished Teachers' College in London. Teaching has always been my dream." (She reached into her purse and pulled out her certificate and placed it on the desk.)

Mr. McLeod slowly reached and picked it up, looked at it for a few moments, and placed it back on the desk. "Well young lady," he said, "we currently employ a full complement of teaching staff. (Cora expected him to say that.) However, you may be in luck. Mrs. Simmons is retiring in December. I suggest you apply as soon as possible. I cannot promise you will get the job."

"I understand," said Cora, "I will apply immediately. Meanwhile, Sir, I would like to volunteer here at your school in any capacity. I am sure I can be of help and gain valuable experience at the same time."

"I don't see any reason why you can't do that," said Mr. McLeod. "We would love to have such an ambitious young lady helping out. When would you like to start?"

"Monday morning, Sir, and thank you very much. You have been more than kind." Cora picked up her certificate and stood up.

"And you have been a gracious, young lady," he said. "Thank you for your spirit in volunteering. You can pick up an application at the reception desk."

"Thanks again," said Cora, as she turned and headed for the reception area.

Friday evening after dinner, Cora arrived at 46 Robin Hood Road. She parked in the double driveway, a lovely brick driveway. She sat in her car for a few minutes, thinking. Anna has sure come a long way in a short time. From the small apartment they had shared, to this big house. How lucky can one be? She meets a young man, a real hunk, who must have money to buy a house like this. She told herself she was not jealous, she was happy for Anna. Anyway, it was none of her beeswax (a term she used for business), as to where he got the money to buy such a lovely house.

She got out of her car, walked to the door and rang the doorbell.

Anna greeted her with a big hug. They had not seen each other for a few months. She said, "Follow me."

Cora followed her to the kitchen, where Anna opened a bottle of wine. Anna said, "Let's celebrate. One, you have graduated teachers' college, two, you missed our housewarming, and three, this is the first chance we have had in a long time to celebrate anything."

Cora raised her glass and said, "To me, soon to be teaching school. To your beautiful home, and to us." They touched glasses and took a sip of wine.

Cora then told her about her visit to Annette Public School Wednesday morning. Anna was thrilled. They touched glasses once again. (Anna was so happy for Cora. She was a little worried about her after she lost Sammy.)

They each talked about their courses and how much they enjoyed them. Anna would be finished her dental course in just one week.

She told Cora about Peter and how his infatuation with boobs got him fired. (The director of the program replaced him for the last two weeks.)

Cora said if she had been Eva, she would not have used her elbow, she would have used her foot, and kicked him where it hurts most. They both laughed.

She told Anna about the ten thousand dollars that Sammy had left her, and that she would be looking for a house soon.

Anna said, "Wouldn't it be great if you could find one in this area. We should take a drive tomorrow and check out the area."

Cora got a little excited at the thought of looking for a house, and her wine started to disappear a little faster.

The evening had passed quickly. Anna was pouring the last of the bottle of wine into Cora's glass when Ben entered the living room. In an instant Cora was on her feet and moved toward him. They hugged, Ben kissed her cheek. He told her she looked great, and that he was very happy she came to visit.

Anna then informed Ben as to Cora's plans. She was looking for a house in the area. Ben told them there were a couple of houses for sale on Canterbury Road. He had seen them a few days ago. (Canterbury was just north east of Robin Hood Road.)

A short time later, Ben excused himself and went to get ready for work.

At eleven-twenty, he kissed Anna and left for work. Anna made tea and served banana and lemon loaf. They played Scrabble, talked, laughed and headed for bed at one-thirty a.m.

Ben arrived home about eight-thirty a.m. Saturday morning. Anna and Cora were still in their housecoats. They decided on porridge for breakfast. Anna volunteered to do the cooking.

They sat at the kitchen table and chatted. Anna stirred the porridge every now and then.

Ben talked about the graveyard shift he had just completed with his partner Blake. They had issued a few tickets for speeding, running red lights and stop signs. They had given a few drivers the sobriety test, and two young men had failed. They had to park their car and take a taxi. (Blake said they probably had the taxi circle back to their cars and drove them home anyway.)

Ben said Blake told him about the time he was asked to check out a domestic dispute at around eight p.m. one evening, a couple of years ago. He said the call came in from the couple's son, who had gone next door to call the police. The boy said his parents were arguing and he was scared. Blake didn't know the age of the boy, however, the dispatcher said he sounded very young. Blake said domestic disputes can sometimes be a dangerous place for a third party, especially if the third party is a cop. He said he knocked on the door. No answer. He heard loud voices inside. He rapped harder. The door was opened by a tiny woman who looked to be around thirty years old. She had a busted lip, and she looked like she had been crying. A male voice said, "Who is it?" Blake said in a loud voice, "The police. What's going on here?" The man did not say anything. The woman said, "It's okay, we just had a little argument. Everything is fine now." Blake asked her what happened to her lip. She said she fell and hit the coffee table, she was fine now. Blake said he felt she was lying, but there was nothing he could do. The man, who was very young appeared. He said, "We are cool now officer. Like the lady said, we had a disagreement, it's over." Blake said his speech was slurred. The lady then said, "Please leave now, everything is fine." Blake said he left.

Ben said Blake told him one must be very careful when walking into a domestic situation. You never know how drunk, how big, how violent some people might be, and you sure as hell don't know what weapon might be used against you. You should never go alone. I did, but I should not have.

After breakfast, Anna and Cora decided to check out the neighbourhood houses that were for sale.

They drove up Robin Hood Road, turned left onto Wimbleton Road, then right onto Canterbury Road. As they turned they saw a realtor's sign. It was a lovely home with a single car garage. Anna wrote down the realtor's phone number and the house number. A little further down there was another house for sale, same realtor. Anna wrote down the house number. They found two more on Wimbleton Road, but Cora said they were too large. Then they drove down Nottingham Drive. They saw one house for sale, but it did not have a garage. Cora said she wanted a garage.

Back at Anna's place, Cora called the realtor. His name was Tim Wilson. He told her he could show her both houses on Canterbury Road that afternoon if she wanted to see them. He said the occupants of both houses were at their cottages. They agreed to meet at 122 Canterbury at one-thirty p.m.

Ben, Anna and Cora were parked in the driveway when Tim arrived. They walked through the house. Cora really liked it. However, after she was told what the asking price was, she knew she could not afford this house. She kept that thought to herself.

They moved down to the other house. The asking price was even higher than the first one. Cora told Tim it was way out of her price range. She then asked him if there were any others in the neighbourhood. He checked his list. There were two however the asking price was once again much too high for Cora.

Cora thanked him and said she might make an offer on the first house they saw, 122 Canterbury. She thought she should say something positive, although she knew she could not afford the house.

Ben went to bed at three p.m. Saturday afternoon. He was working another graveyard shift.

Anna and Cora went to the Yorkdale Mall and then they went to a restaurant for dinner.

Back at Anna's place they played Scrabble and talked. It was Cora's turn to play. Anna was thinking about the house on Canterbury Road. She knew Cora really liked that house. She would talk to Ben before he went to work. She knew Cora would be very happy if she could buy that house.

Anna told Cora she would be right back. In the bedroom Anna talked to Ben, while he was getting dressed for work. Ben agreed they would help Cora. Anna wrote a cheque for Cora – ten thousand dollars. (Another person was about to learn that Ben Breakwater was a millionaire.)

Cora was waiting for Anna to return. She had placed a Scrabble word worth thirty-seven points. Anna and Ben walked into the living room.

Anna asked Cora if she could afford to buy the house on Canterbury Road, would she buy it. Cora said yes, she would.

Anna said, "Well, now you can". She handed her the cheque.

Cora looked at it. Her mouth came open and for a few moments she didn't say a word. She looked at Anna, she looked at Ben. "Wow," she said, "I don't know what to say. This is a lot of money. How can you afford to do this, it will take me quite a while to pay you back."

"It's not a loan Cora," said Anna, "it's a gift. You don't have to pay us back. Ben will explain."

As he did four times before, Ben told Cora the story explaining how he became a millionaire. He told her not many people know, and he would appreciate if she would keep it that way.

"Of course, I will," said Cora, "however, I would still like to pay it back sometime in the future."

"No," said Ben, "it's our gift to you, to help you buy your first house."

"Thank you very much," said Cora, "this is a little overwhelming."

"You are welcome," said Anna. "Enough said." (The three of them had a group hug.)

Ben left for work. Anna made tea and they enjoyed several pieces of lemon loaf. They did not go to bed until after one a.m.

Sunday afternoon Cora left to go back to her parents' place. She was very happy. Tomorrow, when she deposited the cheque Anna had given her, she would have seventeen thousand dollars in her bank account. She would call Tim Wilson and make an offer on the house on Canterbury Road. She knew that it was available for occupancy on the first of January. She would not have to tell her parents about the money Anna and Ben had given her. They knew that Sammy had left her ten-thousand, which meant she had the money for a down-payment on a house.

One week later, Anna received a call from Cora. Her offer had been accepted, she would be moving into the house number 122 Canterbury Road in the first week of January. Cora told her she had Sammy, her and Ben to thank, otherwise, it would not have happened. She would be forever grateful.

CHAPTER 22

IT WAS FRIDAY NIGHT, AROUND ELEVEN THIRTY. BEN AND Blake were headed west on Dundas Street in an unmarked cruiser. Suddenly, a red car turned right at the intersection ahead. It had not stopped at the red light. Tires squealed as it made the turn and then picked up speed. The car swerved from side to side.

Ben stepped on the gas and quickly gained on the red car. Blake switched on the lights, then, wrote down the licence plate number. Blake said it was a Dodge Coronet. After about twenty seconds the Coronet slowed, pulled onto a side street and stopped. Ben pulled up behind it and stopped. He saw the driver's side window go down. There did not appear to be a passenger in the car. Ben opened the door and stepped out. Just as he closed the door he felt a sharp pain in his side and at the same time he heard a gunshot. The pain became intense and he collapsed on the street. He did not lose consciousness.

Blake saw him go down and he was now firing shots at the red car, as it sped away. He ran to check on Ben. He yelled his name and Ben said, "I'm wounded, my side."

Blake opened the cruiser's door, grabbed the mic, and called dispatch. He said officer shot and bleeding, gave his location and quickly went to attend to Ben. He tried to stop the bleeding as best he could until the ambulance arrived.

Blake led the way to the hospital. He once again called dispatch and gave them Ben's name, and that the ambulance was following him to the hospital. He also gave them the licence plate number of the red Dodge Coronet.

Blake cursed and pounded the steering wheel of the cruiser. He repeated out loud, "Cowardly son of a bitch."

Blake called Anna after he talked to the ambulance attendant, who told him Ben would be fine. He told her where he would be waiting, and that Ben was in good hands and he would be okay.

Meanwhile, an APB (All Points Bulletin) was put out on the red Dodge Coronet.

Anna cried as she drove. She used the Mustang's power as she accelerated from light to light. She hoped she would not be stopped by a policeman.

She met Blake in the waiting area. Her tears rolled down her cheeks once again as Blake held her. Blake once again told her Ben would be fine. They went to the reception area and Blake told them that Anna was the wife of the wounded police officer Ben Breakwater. Anna asked when she could see him. She was told they would check and let her know.

Blake and Anna sat in the waiting area. He explained what had happened. He told her they had the licence plate number and they would track him down.

The lady they had spoken to at the counter came and told them someone would come and speak to them, but she didn't know when.

It seemed like forever before a young doctor came to see them. He said that Ben would be just fine. He said there was an entrance and an exit wound, which meant there was no bullet inside. No main organ had been hit. He was awake and in good spirits. They could go and see him in ten minutes or so.

Blake told Anna to go and see Ben alone. He would be in a little later. Anna thanked him for everything that he had done. Ten minutes later she quickly walked down the hallway to the room number she had been given.

As she entered the room, Ben turned his head and gave her a big smile. Tears once again started to flow as she moved to his bed. This time it was tears of joy. To see Ben smiling was uplifting. They kissed, and Ben wiped away her tears.

He said, "I'll be up and about in a few days. It was just a small bullet that went through a bit of flesh. Lucky me."

"Oh Ben," said Anna, "you could have been killed …"

"Guess I could have," said Ben, "but I wasn't. Here I am in bed, nice clean sheets and my visitor is the most beautiful woman in the world."

"Ben Breakwater," said Anna, "you are making it sound like what happened was trivial. I could have been a widow now, and the child in my womb would have been born fatherless. You are a rich man, you don't have to do this."

"You are right Anna," said Ben. "I don't have to do this, but this is what I've chosen to do. I like being a police officer. I hear your concerns, they are valid. However, not many police officers in Toronto get shot at. I have a better chance to be involved in a car accident than being shot at again."

Before Anna could speak, a voice said, "Hello partner. How are you doing?" It was Blake.

"Fine," said Ben. "I'll be out of here in a few days I hope."

"No need to hurry," said Blake, "take it easy."

They chatted for a while and Blake left.

After about ten minutes Anna noticed Ben's eyes were closing. She kissed him and said she would be back after he got some sleep. She left.

Later that morning, after getting six hours sleep, Blake was at the police station. He checked with the officer that was checking out the licence plate number of the red Dodge Coronet. The news was not good. The licence number was registered to a Mr. Roland Miles, age sixty-seven, who owned a 1958 grey Chevy four-door sedan. He didn't know his plate was stolen until he was called. He said he had parked his car on the street because he had company parked in his driveway.

Blake was very disappointed. The ABP on the Coronet had come up empty. He was thinking of the possibilities – it could be parked in some garage – maybe it was getting a new paint job – or, it could be in some auto wrecker's yard. Even if they were to check out all the red Dodge Coronets in Toronto, the owners would all have an alibi. Blake decided he would never stop looking for the person who shot Ben.

It was noon when Anna arrived at the hospital. Ben said he slept well and he had just finished lunch.

Blake walked into the room at one p.m. He told Ben that the licence plate on the red Coronet had been a stolen one. He said it may take some time to get the individual that shot him.

Ben said he had lots of time and maybe someday they would get him.

THE YOUNG MILLIONAIRE FROM BREAKWATER

Anna said, "Who knows, maybe someday he might talk to the wrong guy and shoot off his big mouth that he got away after taking a shot at a cop."

"Hope you are right," said Ben. "I would like to get him in the right place and rearrange his face."

"I suggest you not do that in uniform," said Blake.

"No," said Ben, "of course not."

Blake left shortly thereafter. Anna stayed until nine p.m.

Five days later Anna drove Ben home from the hospital. The doctor had told Ben he was to stay home and rest for three weeks. He wanted to see him at the end of the three-week period. He told Ben to take short walks each day, and increase the distance when he felt like it.

Ben wondered what he would do for the next three weeks, other than reading and taking walks.

Anna suggested he take guitar lessons since he had talked about learning to play guitar some time ago.

He agreed. Now would be a good time to take guitar lessons. Anna said she would drive him until he could drive himself. He found a couple of places in the Yellow Pages that offered guitar lessons. One was only a fifteen minutes' drive away.

For the next several weeks Ben took guitar lessons every other day. He was a natural. He learned very quickly. His instructor was amazed how little time it took Ben to play the guitar.

Ben told his instructor he would continue to book appointments after he knew his work schedule.

The doctor gave Ben three more weeks before he wanted him to go back to work.

Anna decided she would wait until their baby was at least one year old before she would look for a job. Ben told her she could wait as long as she wanted to. Earning a paycheque wasn't a necessity for either of them. It was a matter of doing something you liked to do. Anna said looking after a baby was a full-time job. She would wait and see how she felt in sixteen months or so.

December, Ben went back to work. He felt one hundred percent. He was back to working days.

Usually Ben and Blake sat in the cruiser and carried on a conversation before they set out on the streets.

Blake told him he would be getting experience directing traffic in the next few weeks. Also, they would be visiting the firing range. He told Ben that the only time he enjoyed holding a gun, was on the practice range. He said he just didn't like having to point a loaded firearm at another human. However, he said he knew it could happen at any time.

Ben said, "It sure can. The criminal target range could be just about anywhere, and we could be the target. Been there, done that."

"I know you have," said Blake. "I guess I am lucky. I have been shot at a couple of times, but never hit. It's mighty scary when someone is shooting at you."

"I didn't have time to be scared when I got shot," said Ben.

"That was a very rare occurrence," said Blake. "It's the first time I saw anyone pull a gun and fire it just because he got pulled over."

"Always a first time for everything," said Ben.

"Let's hope there never is a second," said Blake. (Blake then decided to change the topic.) He turned to Ben, who was sitting in the driver's seat, and said, "I have a couple of one-liners for you: Did you hear about the guy who woke up one morning so horny, even the crack of dawn looked good." (Ben laughed.) Then he said: "Getting old is like a roll of toilet paper, the closer you get to the end, the faster it goes."

"Very funny," said Ben, "but true." He started the cruiser and said, "Let's get visible on some of these busy streets."

Anna made breakfast. They were sitting at the table. She told Ben she would like to invite her parents to come and spend Christmas with them. Ben said it was an excellent idea. She said she would ask them to come a few days before Christmas day and stay until New Year day at least.

Ben suggested they have a Christmas party and invite a few friends. He said they could have a pot luck dinner. It would be more fun than going to a restaurant.

Anna thought it was a great idea. They looked at the calendar and chose the twentieth of December to have the Christmas party. Anna said she would start making phone calls and invite their friends to the party.

Anna was in her housecoat with little on underneath. They kissed as Ben was leaving for work. He placed his hands inside her housecoat. She told him he didn't have much time, he would be late. She walked with him to the door and promised him when he came home she would have nothing on but dinner.

Ben laughed and said, "What time are you serving dinner?"

"That depends," she said, as she closed the door behind her lover boy policeman.

Over the next couple of days, Anna invited nine people to their Christmas party: Her parents, Andrew and Audrey, Leon and Colleen, Cora, Joseph and Angelina, Larry and Cathy. They all had accepted the invite.

Ben later called Larry, his Newfie friend, and asked him to bring a guitar to the party. He did not tell him he was now playing guitar himself. It would be a surprise. However, the biggest surprise for Larry, providing his wife Cathy would go along with the idea, was the game "Under the Blanket".

Getting ready for Christmas was a busy time. The twentieth of December came very quickly. Andrew and Audrey arrived in the early afternoon of the twentieth. Everyone who had been invited showed up. There was lots of food and drink, jokes and laughter.

After dinner everyone sat in the living room and was entertained by Larry.

Larry went to the bathroom and Ben saw his chance to surprise him. He went to the bedroom and came out with his guitar. Everyone cheered. He began strumming his guitar and began singing *Brand on my Heart* (a song written by The Canadian Singing Ranger, Hank Snow, who was born in Liverpool, Nova Scotia).

After leaving the washroom, Larry stopped and listened. He wondered who was singing and playing his guitar. Slowly he walked into the living room. He saw his guitar was sitting where he had left it. Ben could not see Larry from where he was sitting. Larry just stood there in awe. If he had closed his eyes before seeing Ben, he would have wondered where Hank Snow was hiding before he went to the washroom. He had no idea his friend could sing at all, yet there he sat singing like a pro, and playing that guitar like he had been playing for many years. He knew Ben had not. He waited until Ben finished the song. He was the first to applaud as he walked into the room.

Ben smiled and thanked everyone. He said it was his first time singing in front of an audience.

Larry looked at Ben and shook his head. Then he said, "Well done my friend, well done. That was the best rendition of that song I have heard in years. I would like you all to know that Ben was at my place several months ago and he told me he wanted to learn to play guitar. I told him to take lessons from a pro. I guess he did. He didn't tell me he could sing, and I didn't ask him. Now that I have heard him sing, that question would now be redundant." (Everyone applauded.) Larry said, "We would like to hear more, and if you don't mind I will play along with you." (More applause.) He picked up his guitar.

Ben said, "Maybe I'll try one that I wrote some time ago, before I joined the police force. At the time you could have called me a househusband. I cooked, cleaned, and many other chores around the house. I decided to write a song. It's called *Househusband*. He began to sing:

Yes I'm a man secure enough
To do the laundry
Run the vacuum, dust and cook
Change the bedsheets once a week
Clean the bathroom, wash a dish
Sometimes sweep the floor
And lay a lovin' on my wife
When she comes in the door

Chorus:
Househusband, that's what I am
Working like a dog, doing the best I can
I'm a househusband, I have seen the light
I can sleep in in the morning
Watch T.V. sports all night

I just want to tell you, Oh what a deal
I'm a househusband cooking my own meals
And I'd like to say I don't have to fight
All that traffic in the morning
Again coming home at night

Househusband, Oh what a life
I'm a househusband but I didn't make the choice
Househusband and I am my own boss (when she's not home)
Cause the company I worked for
Said here's your severance now get lost.

Repeat verse two.

The song brought laughter and applause. Ben sang a few more
and so did Larry.

Anna saw Cathy (Larry's wife) head to the bathroom. She
waited a minute then followed her to the bathroom. She waited
at the door. When she came out, Anna asked her if she would
like to play a little trick on Larry. She explained what she had
in mind. Cathy thought it was marvelous, and she would do it.
Anna gave her the required clothing and she went back in the
bathroom. Anna waited until Cathy was seated in the living
room before she sat down.

A little while later Anna announced they were going to play
a game called "Under the Blanket". She retrieved the blanket
she had placed behind the chesterfield. She announced that
Cathy, Larry's wife, being the good sport she was, had volunteered to be the one under the blanket. She then asked Cathy
to sit on the floor and spreading out the blanket, covered her.

Anna then explained that Cathy could quit the game any time she wanted. She said the game was played by asking Cathy to take off something she was wearing and place it outside the blanket. She said we would start with Leon and go clockwise. She had calculated that Larry would be the sixth person to ask Cathy to take something off and she would be wearing only bra and panties.

Leon said, "Cathy, take off your earrings."

Cathy complied and placed the earrings outside the blanket.

Colleen was next. She asked her to take off her necklace.

Cathy once again complied.

Cora then asked her to take off her slippers.

She did.

Joseph was next. He asked Cathy to take off her blouse.

Cathy fumbled under the blanket and placed her blouse outside the blanket.

Angelina's turn. She asked her to take off her skirt.

Again, Cathy wiggled and moved around, then pushed her skirt out in view.

Larry was very uncomfortable. He was a good sport however this was going a bit too far. He could now visualize his wife in just bra and panties. He heard Anna say, "Your turn Larry." Then he heard Cathy say, "Top or bottom." Another female voice (that of Angelina) said, "Come on Larry, the game is not over yet. Cathy wants to continue."

Larry very reluctantly said, "Bra."

Cathy's arms moved again. Her bra came slowly out to the edge of the blanket and in view.

Anna quickly said, "Last but not least, take off your panties and let's see them."

Larry sat there shaking his head, as if he couldn't believe what was happening.

Everyone could see by her movements that Cathy was removing her panties. She slowly pushed them to the edge of the blanket. Then she flipped them in the air with a flick of her wrist.

Larry was now stone-faced.

Anna stood and said, "Cathy, you have been a really good sport." She then walked the edge of the blanket and quickly reached down and pulled the blanket completely off Cathy. She looked at Larry as she pulled the blanket. His mouth came open and his eyes grew bigger.

Cathy quickly stood up, in a bathing suit.

She picked up her panties, threw them to Larry and said, "Got ya." (Everyone applauded.)

Larry once again started to shake his head. Then he said, "I guess you did."

Cathy went and sat on his knee and gave him a kiss. (More applause.)

Cathy gathered her clothes and headed for the bathroom.

Larry asked Ben if it was his idea to ask Cathy to be the one under the blanket.

Ben said it was. He then told Larry that a while ago, Anna had been under the blanket. He said that he thought he should pass it on.

Larry said, "I guess people had fun at your expense, and you had fun at my expense. What can I say, your helper was my wife."

"Yes indeed," said Ben, "and she did a really good job." More applause as Cathy came back fully dressed

Joseph said he had been introduced to a real fun game. He said, "Nobody will be taking off any clothes for this one."

He explained that the game involved a dart board. It was called, "Nearest to the bull's eye." He asked Angelina to get the dart board in the trunk of his car. He told everyone to go to the family room. He said, "After you play the game, you then become a spectator." (Everyone except Joseph and Angelina moved to the family room.)

The setting: Joseph held the dart board in front of his chest. He could move it six inches in any direction, so that it would be more of a challenge.

Angelina called Anna to start the game.

Anna stood facing the dart board, about eight feet away. Angelina put a blindfold on her. She then asked Anna to extend her right or left arm out in front of her, and to extend her index finger. She would then move forward toward the dart board. She was told that where her finger touched the dart board would be marked with a tack. Nearest to the bull's eye wins.

Anna walked slowly forward trying to walk in a straight line. What she did not know, was that Angelina was now standing where Joseph had been. She was holding an opened jar of peanut butter.

As Anna approached, Angelina held the jar so that Anna's finger would penetrate the peanut butter.

This caused Anna to scream and quickly draw back her hand. Joseph quickly removed the blindfold as Anna screamed. (Angelina and Joseph were now laughing.) Anna looked at her finger, then she saw the jar of peanut butter and she began laughing. She could not stop. She later told Ben that she had never laughed so much in a very long time. A yellow tack was placed on the dart board.

Ben was called next. Anna gave him a big smile and said, "Bet you can't get closer to the bull's eye than I am. That's my yellow tack."

Ben said, "We will see."

Anna tried hard not to laugh.

Ben received the info on how the game was played.

Ben was blindfolded. Anna held the jar of peanut butter. She had a big smile on her face. As Ben moved slowly toward her she was shaking with silent laughter. When Ben got close enough she pushed the jar into his finger. The sounds Ben made as his finger penetrated the peanut butter caused such laughter it left Anna and Angelina with sore stomachs. Ben of course laughed with them. He congratulated Joseph. He sat down to enjoy the next performance. A blue tack was placed on the board for Ben.

A whole lot of fun was had by all. Each guest went through the same routine.

Leon said it was the best game he had ever taken part in, and the most fun he had ever had with his clothes on. (More laughter)

Larry and Ben sang a few more songs and the party ended around midnight.

Ben and Anna agreed that it was the best house party ever.

CHAPTER 23

CORA MOVED INTO HER HOUSE ON CANTERBURY, NUMBER 122, on the fourth of January. Her parents, Anna and Ben, helped her move. Anna was happy that Cora's house was only a ten-minute walk from her house. They would see each other almost every weekend.

January fourteenth Cora started working full-time at Annette Public School. Most of the teachers there were male. One in particular caught Cora's eye. His name was Roger Rimes. He was tall with an athletic build. As she sat in the lunch room at noon, she wondered if he was married or had a girlfriend. Then she started thinking – was she ready to start dating again – in her heart she knew that Sammy would want her to get on with her life. She was only twenty-two years old. Her best friend, Anna, would be a mother in three months, and she didn't even have a boyfriend. She told herself she was not jealous of Anna, she loved her like a sister. Her and Anna talked children many times. They both wanted a family, a house with a back yard where kids could play. She already had the house and the back yard.

She remembered telling Anna that she wanted to have her children before she reached the age of thirty. She didn't want a teenager around when she was fifty. She wanted to be free to travel or do whatever she could afford to do.

She thought about the night she told Anna that maybe she would look for an older rich man. She would forget about having kids, just go out and see the world. And when he died she would then look for a younger man who would look after her when she grew old.

Anna had said no that was not for her. She said nothing can replace children. She had said she had fallen in love with kids when she started babysitting. Cora remembered her saying, "If I didn't mind changing diapers of someone else's child, I certainly wouldn't mind changing my own child's diapers." She had said babies are the most precious things on earth - more precious than diamonds and gold.

She had agreed with Anna. However, changing diapers was not her favourite thing to do. Many times, when she babysat a small child and changed the diapers, she was tempted to put a clothes pin on her nose. But she never did.

Before leaving the lunch room she checked the bulletin board. At the top right-hand corner there was a notice printed in red. It read: **Birthday party for teachers Paul and Roger at King's restaurant, 1047 Annette Street, Saturday the 19th of January, at six p.m. Spouses, girlfriends and boyfriends are welcome. Hope to see you there.**

Cora decided they would certainly see her there. There was no reason she could not go. She was a new teacher and she did not want to be conspicuous by her absence. She wanted to take part in all the teachers' activities and try to cement her position.

Maybe at the party she would get to talk to Roger. She would definitely find out if he was married or had a girlfriend. Several times they had passed each other in the hallway. Roger had always smiled and said hi. Cora had returned the smile. A few times while in the school café she tried to check his left hand for a ring without success.

Saturday evening Cora waited in her car at the King's Restaurant parking lot. She didn't know how many, if any, of the teachers were already in the restaurant. She decided to wait a little while longer. Then she saw Julie, who was one of the senior teachers, get out of her car. Cora called her name and walked into the restaurant with her. After they were seated, Julie said it looks like the birthday boys will be the last to join us.

Paul and Roger came in together, along with a lady who was holding Paul's hand. Everyone applauded as they approached the table. The lady sat beside Cora, and Paul sat next to her. Roger took the seat opposite Cora. There was only one chair left vacant at the end. He smiled, looked at Cora and said, "Thanks for coming Cora."

Cora said, "You are welcome. Wild horses couldn't keep me away."

Introductions were made around the table. Cora was introduced as the newest member of the teaching staff.

The waiter came to their table. As he started to take drink orders, Roger asked Cora if he could buy her a drink.

She said, "Thank you, yes I would like a glass of white wine. The house wine would be fine."

He said, "How about we share a bottle of my choice of wine. If you would be happy with the house wine, you will really like the one I will choose."

"Okay," said Cora, "you choose, you pay, and I will help you drink. What have I got to lose? (Roger laughed) He ordered his favourite white wine. If Cora knew the price of the bottle of wine that Roger ordered, she would have told him that he had very expensive taste. They chatted until the wine came.

Roger poured the wine. He picked up his glass of wine and leaning toward Cora, in a soft voice, he said, "To the most beautiful woman I've shared wine with." He moved his glass until it touched her glass, took a sip of his wine. Cora didn't know if anyone heard what Roger said, but quickly she said to herself she didn't really care. She sipped her wine. It was very good.

Someone made a toast to recognize the two birthday boys, Paul and Roger.

After everyone ordered food, Roger and Cora continued to talk. Cora saw that there was no ring on his left hand. And she surmised that he didn't have a girlfriend, because he came alone. However, that was not a definite, there could be extenuating circumstances as to why his girlfriend could not be here.

Like her, Roger was an extrovert. They did a few questions and answer sessions, and they each found out that there was no boyfriend or girlfriend in the picture. Roger kept himself busy. He was teaching at a hockey school. However, he would soon have more time for other things because Paul, the other birthday boy, had volunteered to give him a break.

Cora told him that she had just finished Teachers' College in London a while ago, and had just settled down again in Toronto.

After the party was over, Roger walked Cora to her car. He asked her if she would like to have dinner with him tomorrow, which was Sunday. He said they could meet right here in the parking lot.

Cora accepted. They would meet at six thirty.

Driving home Cora once again thought of Sammy. She began to cry. Her feelings were once more mixed. She knew it would be some time before her memories of him would be easier to deal with. She thought maybe she needed more time however it was just a dinner date. She would call and talk to Anna when she arrived home.

She called Anna around nine thirty. They talked for half an hour.

Anna validated Cora's feelings about Sammy. She said if she lost Ben she would feel the same way. She told Cora she should not feel guilty for being alive. What happened was an accident and neither she nor Sammy was to blame. Anna told her to take things slow. She said this man Roger was not a replacement for Sammy. To think so would be most unfair. Anna told her to follow her heart and everything would be fine.

Cora felt much better after talking with Anna.

Roger sat in his car at the parking lot at King's Restaurant, until he saw Cora park her car. He greeted her with a smile and said, "Two nights in a row I have the pleasure of your company. How lucky can a man be?"

"Roger Rimes I do believe you are trying to flatter me," said Cora. "However, I really don't mind."

"You look gorgeous," said Roger. "Let's carry on the conversation at a table for two."

Cora tried to keep the conversation cheerful and light. She talked about her childhood, where she was born and that she was an only child.

Roger told her that he too was an only child. He said he was born in Ottawa, Ontario. His mom had told him when he was about fourteen that his dad was not his biological father. His mom had not married his father. She told him that his father was sent to prison before he was born, and she did not tell him that she was pregnant. She met and married Nelson Rimes. They moved to Toronto when he was one year old. Nelson was the only dad he ever knew.

Cora asked him if he knew his biological father's name. Roger said he did. His name was John, John Dillon. Cora tried very hard not to show her surprise at the mention of John Dillon's name. She asked him if he ever tried to locate his father. He said he had not, so far. But now that he was on his own he had given it some thought. Cora changed the subject. She knew that Ben Breakwater was the one that Roger should talk to about his father. How much Ben was willing to tell him, she did not know. That would be Ben's decision.

Roger told her he and two friends were renting a house on Varsity Road. He said he had been saving for a down-payment on a house of his own. He said he was hoping to have a house in three years. His mom and dad told him for every one-hundred dollars he saved for the down-payment, they would give him thirty.

They talked until nine p.m.

Roger walked Cora to her car. She thanked him for a lovely evening and said she would see him at school tomorrow.

Roger kissed her cheek and said, "Drive carefully." He waited until she drove away, then, walked to his car.

As Cora drove, the one thing foremost in her mind was that Roger Rimes was the son of John Dillon. She now felt she must tell Ben. He was the last person to see John alive. She was confident that Ben would tell Roger the whole story, and in doing so he would feel obligated to share the wealth he had obtained as a gift from Roger's father. She would also tell Ben that she had a dinner date with Roger and that there may be more. She wanted to be truthful so that there would be no regrets later.

Monday morning Roger and Cora were going in opposite directions in the school hallway, when they met. Roger asked her if she would like to go to a movie Friday evening. Cora said she would. He told her to pick the movie and they would talk later. They headed to their respective classrooms.

Light snow was falling as Cora drove home. She wanted to stop at Anna's house on the way home, but decided she would call her after dinner.

At seven thirty she called Anna. She told her she had something very important to tell her and Ben. She told Anna she wanted to tell them in person.

Without hesitation, Anna said, "You can come over now if you want to, we are just watching T.V."

Cora said, "See you in a few minutes."

Anna told Ben that Cora was on her way to see them and she had something important to tell us.

"Hope it's good news," said Ben.

"We will know in a few minutes," said Anna

And it was only a few minutes when the doorbell rang. Anna opened the door. She stepped in, Anna closed and locked the door. They did their usual friendly hug and headed into the living room.

Ben stood up and gave Cora a hug and a kiss on the cheek.

Anna said, "Sit down and give us the news. Hope it is good news."

"Well," said Cora, "it's not bad news. I would call it surprising news."

Cora began to tell them about Roger Rimes. She told them about the birthday party and the dinner date. Anna was all smiles and so was Ben. "So far," said Cora, "I could have told you that over the phone. Now comes the most interesting part. Roger told me that his mother told him when he was fourteen, that his dad Nelson Rimes was not his biological father. I asked him if he knew his biological father's name. He said he did. His mom told him his father's name was John Dillon.

Ben and Anna looked at each other in great surprise. Cora told them that Roger's mom did not marry John, nor did she tell him she was pregnant before he was sent to prison. John Dillon never knew he had a son. Roger said he was born in Ottawa. His mom met Nelson Rimes, married him, and they moved to Toronto when he was one year old.

"Wow," said Ben, "that's quite a story. If I didn't know any of the characters I would have thought you were telling us about a T.V. show you saw. What a twist of fate. If John Dillon knew he had a son, I would still be in the poor house. Well, not really, but I wouldn't be living in this house."

"Well," said Anna, "even if he knew he had a son, he might never have located him."

"That's right," said Cora. "It is possible that the events that took place might not have changed. However, when he gave you that key to his safety deposit box, he probably would have asked you to try to locate his son. Who knows what else he might have said."

Ben said, "I would say that if John knew he had a son, he would have hired a private detective and he just might have found him. Who knows? That's all water under the bridge now."

"What are you going to do Ben?" said Anna. "The man deserves to know what happened to his father."

Cora said, "He told me he was thinking about looking for his father, now that he was on his own."

"That won't be necessary," said Ben. "I have to do what is right. Roger doesn't know his father was a rich man, I do. This reminds me of a little story. There was a man whose mother had dementia and she didn't know who he was, her own son. She lived with her oldest son. But every day he went to see her. One of his friends said, "If she doesn't know who you are, why do you go to see her every day?" The man said, "You are right, she doesn't know me. But, I know her.""

Tears started to appear on Anna's cheeks. She said, "That is very touching. It makes one want to have faith in humanity."

"It sure does," said Ben. "Thank you, Cora, for informing us about Roger."

"How could I not?" said Cora. "I knew you would want to know, and I am sure you will tell Roger the whole story."

"Yes, I will," said Ben. "If Roger and I were to change places, I would want to know the truth, and I would hope he would be willing to share my dad's wealth. I cannot tell Roger a lie. It would be on my mind for the rest of my life. I can live a good life with a lot less money than what I have in the bank. Therefore, I will inform Roger of the exact amount that was in the safety deposit box. Maybe I'll let him decide the amount he would like to have. From what you have told us Cora, he seems like a very decent guy."

"Yes," said Cora, "as far as I can tell, he is a decent guy. I would not have accepted the dinner date if I didn't think so." Ben was now thinking. If Roger becomes Cora's boyfriend that would be good news. Anna and I consider Cora as family. If Cora were to marry Roger, then he would become like family as well. So, all in the family. If not, so be it. Then a little bit of reality came in to his mind.

Ben said, "It may never happen, and I hope it doesn't, but just in case Roger goes rogue on us, I will write a letter and have him sign it. It will state that he is fully satisfied with the amount of money he received from me, and no further claim will be made. I know it's not full-proof, but it will be of some value in a court of law."

"That's a good idea," said Anna. "I do hope we can keep lawyers out of this. Fighting a court battle only makes lawyers rich and others poor, or poorer."

"I'm cool with everything said so far," said Cora. "I will witness the signing of the letter if you want me to Ben."

"Thank you," said Ben. "I want to get this over as soon as possible, like the next couple of days."

"How about tomorrow after school," said Cora. "Roger can follow me here to your place. What would I tell him?"

"Let me think," said Ben. (There was silence for a few moments.) Then he said, "Just tell him that your best friend's husband, who is now a young police officer, has some information about his dad. He wants to talk to you. It's very important. I am sure he will be anxious to see me. I don't see a problem."

"Okay," said Cora, "we should be here between four thirty and five, unless he has another commitment. If so, I will call you as soon as I get home."

The next morning Cora saw Roger in the school hallway before school began. She asked him if he was free after school today. He said he was, "What do you have in mind?"

She then told him the exact words Ben had told her to say. He asked her if she knew what the info might be. She told him she knew some, but Ben knew a lot more than she did, and he wanted to tell him the whole story.

Roger said, "Of course I will follow you to his place, and I won't ask any more questions."

"Thank you," said Cora, "see you later."

"I appreciate what you are doing for me," said Roger, as they moved in different directions." Cora gave him a little wave.

Four thirty Cora left the school parking lot. Roger followed. They arrived at Ben's place twenty minutes later. Cora rang the doorbell. Ben came to the door. Cora introduced them, and they followed Ben into the living room. Cora introduced Roger to Anna. Anna asked them if they would like something to drink. They both said a glass of water. After the water was served, Ben began to tell Roger the same story as he had told a few times before. When he told Roger that he held his dad's hand until he passed, Rogers eyes began to tear up. Then he began to cry. Cora reached out her hand and held his hand. Ben told him that he had cried also on that fateful day.

Roger said, "How can I thank you?" after hearing that Ben carried his dad's body to the edge of town.

Ben said, "I appreciate you saying that, however your dad rewarded me big time before he passed, although I had no idea at the time."

He then told Roger about the trip to Toronto and what he found in the safety deposit box. Roger's eyes grew bigger and he shook his head, when he heard Ben say, "One million dollars". Then he heard Ben say, "When Cora told me you were John Dillon's son, I knew I couldn't live with myself not telling you the whole story."

Roger looked at Ben, then Anna, Cora and back to Ben. He said, "This is almost unbelievable. You didn't have to tell me about the key and the safety deposit box, but you did."

"And I am willing to share with you. Your dad would want me to do just that," said Ben.

"You are a very special person Ben," said Roger. "I can't think of a more deserving young man than you, to receive the key to his savings. And I guess you would consider me a fool to decline your offer, so I will accept your generosity."

"Well," said Ben, "if your dad is looking down upon us, I know he is proud of me and you. I know my dad would be. So what amount did you have in mind?"

"I don't know," said Roger. "The money was given to you, so I will let you determine the figure."

"I've heard it said," said Ben, "that possession is nine tenths of the law. So, I will give you the other tenth – one hundred thousand dollars."

Once again, Roger looked at Anna, Cora and Ben.

"That's a whole lot of money, a whole lot of generosity Ben. I was thinking if you gave me enough to buy a house, I would have been a happy man."

"No Roger, I would not be happy giving you just enough to buy a house. For one hundred thousand dollars you can buy three houses. You could live in one, and rent out the other two. If you invested that rent money, you would have at least a quarter million before you reached fifty. So, Roger I will have a certified cheque for you tomorrow at five p.m., if you would like to drop by and pick it up."

"I think so," said Roger, "I'd be here for a hundred-dollar cheque. That would pay my rent for next month."

"Well I guess that's all for now," said Ben, as he stood up. Roger and Ben shook hands. It was a very firm handshake.

Roger said, "Good evening ladies," as he walked to the door. Then he was gone.

Ben came back to the living room and sat down.

Anna said, "That man is a real gentleman. I'd say his parents did a fine job raising him."

"I agree," said Cora. "I am rather proud of him right now."

"You should be," said Ben. "He could have asked for more. He had the opportunity."

"This morning he asked me to go to a movie with him on Friday evening and I accepted. I think I will let him pay." (Laughter)

"I am so happy to see you dating again," said Anna.

"Yes, I guess I am too," said Cora. "This time I am taking it slow and easy. I promised myself that until I fall in love, my panties stay on." (More laughter)

Anna looked at Ben, she said, "I think the old Cora is back with us."

"Nice to have you back," said Ben.

Cora stayed for dinner.

The following day the doorbell rang at 46 Robin Hood Road. It was five p.m. Ben opened the door and once again he invited Roger Rimes into his house. He said hello to Anna as he entered the living room. Before he sat down, Cora walked into the living room from the other end, carrying four glasses of wine on a tray, as well as the bottle from which she had poured the wine. She said, "Hi Roger, I thought you might like to celebrate your good fortune."

Roger saw the bottle. He said, "You guys are awesome. That is my favourite wine."

"I know," said Cora. "I asked Ben to pick up a bottle for this very occasion."

Cora served the wine, and they sat in the same positions as they did the evening before.

"Let's get right to it," said Ben. "I have your cheque here." He picked up the envelope that was on the end table. He then picked up another envelope and opened it. It contained one sheet of paper. He looked at Roger and said, "Roger we are virtually strangers, would you agree?"

"Yes," said Roger, "but I sure hope we become good friends."

"So do I," said Ben. "However, at the present time I felt the need to write this letter. Please read it if you will." (He handed the letter to Roger.)

The Letter

Toronto, Ontario
Canada
22 January 1965

To whom it may concern:
I, Roger Rimes, on the above date, did hereby receive a cheque from Mr. Ben Breakwater for the sum of two hundred thousand dollars.

By signing this letter, I agree that at no time in the future, and under any circumstances, will I, Roger Rimes, demand or seek any further monies from Mr. Ben Breakwater.

(When Roger read two hundred thousand, he stopped reading and looked at Ben.)

He said, "You doubled the amount we agreed upon."

"Yes," said Ben, "now you can buy six houses, and you will have half a million when you reach fifty."

"You are an amazing young man Ben Breakwater," said Roger. "You have set me up for life. Of course, I will sign this letter." He then signed the letter, witnessed by Cora Roberts.

As he handed the letter back to Ben he said, "If at any time I become half the man you are, Ben, I will consider myself to be a success. I will say right now, that from this moment forward, as far as I am concerned, we will be friends for life. I really mean that."

"I agree," said Ben. "One cannot have too many good friends. Like my police partner said, "You can't have too much fun and you can't have too much money." "I will add, you can't have too many true friends."

"Well said Ben, well said," was Roger's reply.

They exchanged phone numbers.

Before Roger left he told Ben he would have to explain to his mom and dad the circumstances whereby he obtained the cheque he now held in his hand.

Ben just said, "What else can you do. They will be ecstatic."

After Roger left, Ben placed the letter that Roger had signed back in the envelope. He then wrote on the envelope

– Agreement signed by Roger Rimes. He hoped he would never have to look at it ever again.

CHAPTER 24

ANNA GAVE BIRTH TO A SEVEN-POUND BABY BOY ON THE thirtieth of March, 1965. Ben was happier than when he saw what was in John Dillon's safety deposit box. He was less than three months away from his twentieth birthday, yet he had many blessings to count. Thinking back on his young life he remembered his dad telling him that his mom was not coming back to live with them. She had gone to live with the angels. The angels wanted her because she was a special mom. He remembered crying many times, usually alone. Once he had asked his dad why the angels could not find some other mother that didn't have small kids and then he would still have his mom. His dad had told him that maybe the angels knew he would still have his dad to look after him.

School was fun for Ben. He would never forget the good times he spent with his dad. He would never forget the sense of loss and sadness of losing his father, who was the pillar in his life. It was time to count his blessings: He had been blessed with parents that loved him and passed on to him the genes of a good mind and a strong and healthy body - a dad who taught him so much - his good luck in finding John Dillon – meeting Anna, the love of his life – a few really true friends – his acceptance into the police force – meeting John Dillon's son, and how proud he was of himself in sharing his wealth with him. Now he had a son of his own. All these blessings and he was not yet twenty years old. Life was good.

Anna was delighted to be a mother. She was also very happy for her best friend Cora, who had fallen in love. She and Roger had been visiting at least once a week.

Ben and Anna had been discussing a name for their son. They had decided it would be Sandy or Sanford. Ben came up with a second name, Willdrew. Anna said that was a little weird. However, Ben explained how he decided on that name. He told her the name was derived from each of the boy's grandfathers. Will, from his father Willie, and Drew from her father Andrew.

After thinking about it for a while, Anna thought it was kind of neat. However, she said, he would not be called Willdrew, it would be Sandy or Sanford.

Ben decided it was time they choose and told Anna to make the decision. She chose Sanford. Their baby's name would be Sanford Willdrew Breakwater.

Ben said it sounded like a name from long, long ago, but he liked it because it was so different.

One-day Ben looked at his son and said, "I predict one day, son you will be a professor, or a professional athlete, and maybe the Prime Minister of Canada, some day."

Anna said, "These are nice thoughts Ben, but we will let him choose his path in life. We will support him in whatever that may be."

"Course we will," said Ben. "I guess a father usually has big dreams for his son. I read somewhere that a mother wants her son to be successful. A father expects his son to be successful."

"Well," said Anna, "our job is to keep him safe, healthy and give him a good education. The rest will be up him."

Ben said, "I love you Anna, for who you are, and your common-sense approach to things. My grandfather told my dad that common sense is one of the best attributes one can have."

"Thank you, Ben," said Anna, "I think you have told me that before. My dad said that ingenuity is a great attribute. He said he had an uncle who had a very basic education, but he could build or make just about anything he needed. He built a house, a boat, netted his own fishing nets, made his own tent for camping, built a sawmill, and he was also an auto mechanic. My dad said these people are called "Jack of all trades"."

"Some people are amazing," said Ben. "I guess heredity plays a big part. The ability to do things is passed from the parents to their children. If our kids look like you, they will be very good-looking kids that's for sure."

"And I hope they have the intellect of their father," said Anna. (Sanford started to cry.)

"Your turn to change him," said Anna.

Ben was now doing patrols alone.

When Blake Bradley did his assessment of Ben (OJT Assessment) he gave him an excellent report. In his closing remarks in the report, Blake had stated that he would take Ben as his partner in any situation. He recommended that Ben have the opportunity to take detective training, because he was a very intelligent young man, and mature beyond his years.

Ben turned twenty years old on the 24th of June 1965. Anna arranged a surprise birthday party at their house. She had invited everyone that had attended their Christmas party, plus Cora's boyfriend, Roger Rimes.

At this party, Roger became the focus of the party when Cora was "under the blanket". As all men do when their wife or girlfriend is under the blanket, they look very uncomfortable. Roger was no exception. He had a difficult time asking Cora to take off her bra. However, he was a good sport to the end of the game.

Before school started in September, Roger and Cora were engaged, and he had moved in with her. He had bought an acre of land and was planning to build an apartment building, with at least ten apartments. They visited Ben and Anna very often. Their wedding plans were made for the summer of 1966.

When Sanford was one year old, Anna decided she wanted to get out of the house and go to work. Luck was on her side in finding a babysitter. Anna became friends with Sophia who lived across the street. She had employed a babysitter until a year ago when her son started to attend school full-time. Sophia only worked five hours each day and no longer required a babysitter. The lady who babysat for her lived only five houses away. Her name was Tanya Boland. Sophia gave Anna her phone number. Anna called her, and she came to see her within the hour.

Tanya was a lovely lady who was married to a school teacher. She loved children although she did not have any of her own. They had adopted two boys who were now grown and on their own. She would become Anna's babysitter when Anna found a job.

Anna remembered passing the Eglinton Dental Clinic many times. It was not very far from her house.

One morning, she took Sanford with her and drove to the Eglinton clinic. She arrived there at eleven thirty.

She talked to the lady at the front desk and received an application. She had only written her name when she heard a female voice say, "Well look what the cat dragged in." Anna looked up, and standing about five feet away was Eva Bromly. (The lady that had attended the same dental course as Anna had.) She had a big smile on her face.

Anna stood, and they had a friendly hug.

Eva said, "I see you are applying for work here. That your little one? He is adorable."

"Yes, that's my boy. His name is Sanford," said Anna. "Yes, I am applying for work. I wonder what my chances are."

Eva said, "After you complete that form, why don't you join me at the restaurant next door and we can chat. I am on my lunch break."

After completing the application, Anna joined Eva at the restaurant. They chatted about things that happened at the dental school. They had another good laugh when Anna mentioned the incident when Eva elbowed short ass Peter in the face.

Eva told Anna she was working part-time. She said her Uncle Michael was the owner of the clinic, and he had promised her a job when she finished dental school. She would be working full-time in May because Joanne Baker was retiring. She told Anna she would talk to her uncle and recommend that he hire Anna to take her place in May, when she started working full-time.

Two weeks later Anna received a call from the Eglinton Dental Clinic. They wanted her to come in for an interview.

Anna went for the interview, and two weeks later she was working part-time at the clinic.

The department knew that Ben wanted to become a detective. However, he was only twenty-one years old. They decided to assign him to work with their top detective for a few years. His name was Harry King.

They began working on a few cold cases and one new one that was on-going. Ben had to learn to take things slow. At first, he would get a little frustrated with things moving so slow. One day he asked Harry why they were moving so slow on the new case.

Harry said, "Ben, I was built too slow to work fast." (Ben laughed.) Harry said, "In order to do a really good job the first time, one has to be both meticulous and methodical."

Every now and then Harry would quote something that would make Ben laugh. One day they were talking about foresight. Harry said, "You know Ben, there are many more men that have foreskin, than have foresight." (Laughter).

They were on lunch break at a restaurant one day. Harry was talking about some of the characters he had met. He said one day a small time criminal handcuffed, sitting in the back seat of the police car, was whistling and was amazingly jovial. He suddenly went silent for a few moments. Then he said, "You know sir, I know I'm gonna die sometime, and if I go to hell, there is one thing I know, I'll have lots of friends there."

Then he told Ben about the time he had a kidnapper on the phone. The guy was telling him where he wanted the money dropped. Harry said he was trying to keep him on the line long enough to get a trace on where he was calling from. He asked the guy to give himself up. The guy said, "Not today, and tomorrow doesn't look good either." Then he hung up.

Every Friday after work Ben and Harry would stop at one of the bars in downtown Toronto for a couple of beers. Ben had never drunk beer before he met Harry. However, he never did tell him, and he acquired a taste for beer. They never talked shop during these outings, and their limit was two beers. Harry told Ben that he made a promise to himself, seven years ago, that if he was driving, two beers would be the limit. Ben decided that he too would set the limit at two beers.

One Saturday afternoon, Anna took Sanford with her to go and visit Cora. It was the fifteenth of April 1967.

Ben decided to go for a beer. He would do a little thinking and reminiscing about his job. He was enjoying it immensely. Harry was an excellent teacher and one of the best at what he did for a living.

Ben was sitting on a bar stool in Steele's Tavern, sipping a cold beer. It was around two thirty p.m. There was one empty stool on his right. On the next two stools sat two men. Ben noticed as he looked around, that these two men wore their baseball caps on backwards. They were telling jokes and laughing. They were having a good time. Ben could tell by their speech that they had drank a few beers. Ben tried not to pay much attention to them, but they were talking loud, and it was rather difficult to ignore them. He thought about moving to a table, but he didn't. (That decision turned out to be a wise one.)

Suddenly, Ben heard one of them say, "Fucking cops". This piqued his curiosity. He glanced over at the two men. He did not know which one had said that. He went back to drinking his beer. Then music to his ears, he heard, "My brother Ray took a shot at a cop a while back."

Again, Ben didn't know which one said his brother took a shot at a cop. Ben's mind worked fast when he needed it to. He quickly leaned over and in his best drunken voice said, "Did he kill the S.O.B.?"

The man nearest to him looked at Ben and said, "Nah, my brother didn't kill him. The newspaper article said the cop would be just fine." He then looked back at his drinking partner and said, "He had to get rid of his Dodge Coronet though. The bloody cop shot holes in the back of it. It was a wreck anyway. He drove it to an auto junkyard." (More music to Ben's ears.)

Ben didn't say another word to the two men. However, he formulated his plan. He would wait until they left the bar and he would follow them out. He hoped they were both driving cars.

Luck was on his side. Ben had almost finished his second beer, when he heard Ray's brother say, "I gotta go, my wife wants the car. She's going shopping..." Ben didn't hear the rest of what he said. He was headed for the door.

Ben walked slowly at an angle from the door. In his peripheral vision he saw the man walking toward the parked cars. Ben picked up his pace and soon he was near his truck. He could now see the car that the man was getting into. Ben quickly got into his truck, backed it out, and pulled behind the car of interest and noted the licence plate number of the grey Chevy Bel Air.

Ben turned in the opposite direction of the grey Chevy, stopped his truck and wrote down the plate number. He was very pleased with himself. He looked at the number. He thought to himself – this number could lead to the arrest of the man that shot me.

Monday morning Ben told Harry what had happened at Steele's Tavern on Saturday afternoon. (Harry knew that Ben had been shot and that the case was not yet solved.) He told Ben to get the file and they would add the new information.

Ben retrieved the file in question.

Harry said, "First we will check out that licence plate number you obtained at Steele's Tavern parking lot." The plate number was registered to a Mr. Jerry Walling.

They then checked to confirm that there was no other report of a police officer shot from the time Ben was shot and the present.

"So," said Ben, "this guy Ray whose last name must be Walling, if he is Jerry's brother --- just a minute Harry, maybe not. Jerry's brother may have a different name. They could be half-brothers, or one of them could be adopted."

"For a rookie, that's not bad," said Harry, "You are right. Let's take the first step and check to see if we have a Ray or Raymond Walling."

They checked the phone book and found several R. Wallings, several Ray Wallings and a couple of Raymond Wallings.

"Well," said Harry, "this makes things a little more difficult."

Ben said, "Let's add the new info to the file."

Harry took a blank page and after dating it, proceeded to write down all the info that Ben had obtained at the tavern plus the info concerning one Jerry Walling.

Harry said he would have to check with his boss before they could work on the case any further. He said we always inform our boss as to what we are doing. The buck stops with him and therefore he must be in the know. (Harry left to check with his boss.) He returned twenty minutes later with good news: they could work on the case of the shooting of Officer Ben Breakwater.

"The next move," said Harry, "will be to check with the Motor Vehicle Licence Branch and see how many Ray Wallings drove a red Dodge Coronet. (After checking they did not find one.) However, they obtained a list of all the vehicles that were registered in the last eighteen months.

Ben was looking through the list, looking for the name Ray. He was also looking for vehicles that were registered in February and March of 1965. He was thinking that if Ray ditched his Coronet, he might have bought another vehicle. As he scanned the list, he saw the name Ray Morrison had registered a 1957 Pontiac in February of 1965. (That was just a month after Ben was shot.) He pointed it out to Harry and said, "Maybe just a coincidence."

Harry said, "Let's look further back and find out what he was driving, if anything, before February.

This would mean they would have to go back to the Motor Vehicle Licence Branch.

They looked under the name Ray Morrison and found out that in 1954 Ray Morrison had registered a 1953 red Dodge Coronet. Ben and Harry looked at each other. Harry said, "I think we may have our man. What do you say Ben?"

"Well, it looks promising," said Ben. "However, because he once owned a red Dodge Coronet, doesn't mean he is the one that took a shot at me. We need more than this."

"Yes, we do," said Harry, "but I think we are on the right track." Harry knew this was good training for Ben. He knew that Ben had a good brain. Usually, these situations called for a little logic and foresight.

Harry then asked Ben what should be their next move, and told him to think about it for a while.

After thinking about it for a few minutes, Ben outlined what he thought they should do:

Find the red Dodge Coronet. Blake Bradley had fired several bullets into the rear of that car. If they found the car, which Jerry Walling said was driven to an auto junkyard, they may get a description of the man who delivered the car. They had Ray Morrison's address, and if Ray matched the description, then Bob is your uncle, he is our man. Ben then mentioned that they probably would not find fingerprints inside the car, because it had been too long ago.

"Not bad," said Harry. "Let's go and see if we can find a red Dodge Coronet with a few bullet holes in its ass."

They were walking to the unmarked cruiser.

Ben said, "Just thought of something Harry."

"What is it?" asked Harry.

"We should go in disguise, to conceal our identity," said Ben. "What if the auto junkyard guy was paid to keep his mouth shut about the bullet holes in the car. If he knows we are detectives he will lie, and give us a very poor description of the man who drove the car. Hell, he might say the guy who received the car doesn't work there anymore and that would cause us a lot of work."

"I don't know if I like this," said Harry.

"Like what?" asked Ben.

"That my trainee is smarter than the trainer," said Harry.

"I don't think so," said Ben, "however, I am aiming for your job some day."

"I don't doubt that," said Harry. "Let's go to my place and change. Maybe I'll wear by Batman outfit." (They laughed.)

Ben and Harry were nearly the same size. They smeared on a little grease and dirt, as if they were working on an old car. They also drove Harry's old second car that needed a paint job.

They went to the junkyard in West Toronto. No success. Next, they visited the one in East Toronto.

Harry told the man at the counter he was looking for a driver's side window for a Dodge Coronet.

The man said he had a couple of Coronet. He said one was in the front row of cars on the left, and the other one was in the second or third row, he wasn't sure.

Harry asked him if they could take a look.

The man said, "Sure, fill your boots."

After Harry and Ben were a little distance away, Ben said, "I hope one of them is red."

"Me too," said Harry.

They looked in the front row of cars and found the Dodge Coronet. However, it was light green in colour.

"One down, one to go," said Ben.

"Yes, I guess you are right," said Harry. "I don't think that is a fresh coat of paint on the car."

Ben looked at Harry and said, "Right, that possible paint job slipped my mind. To be sure I'll check the rear for bullet holes or body work." (They concluded that it was not the car they were looking for.)

They moved to the second row. No success.

They walked to the third row. As Ben scanned the row of cars he saw red at the end of the row of cars. They walked faster and kept their eyes on the red car. As they got closer, Harry said, "It's a Coronet."

Ben immediately went to the rear of the car. Harry heard him say, "Bingo, bullet hole."

Harry was now looking over the rear of the car. He said, "Not just one line, Ben, I think we have a full card. Jackpot, I see four bullet holes."

"Hot damn," said Ben, "we found it. This was the car that sped away carrying the man that shot me." There were no licence plates on the car.

Harry said, "Let's go see the man at the counter."

As they approached the counter, the man said, "Find what you were looking for, gentleman? Guess you will need tools or did you bring your own?"

"No sir," said Harry. "We don't need any tools, and yes, we did find what we were looking for." He then pulled out his detective badge and showed it to the man behind the counter.

Harry said, "I am Detective Harry King, and my partner here is Officer Ben Breakwater. We are investigating an attempted murder. You are not a suspect sir, and I know you will fully co-operate with us." Harry then asked the man what his name was and if he was the owner. He said he was and his name was Clayton Temple.

Harry then told him about the red Dodge Coronet with the bullet holes that was on his property.

Clayton said he knew nothing about the bullet holes in the car and he didn't know when that car came into his yard. He said if there is no payment made, the vehicle is not recorded in the ledger.

Harry asked him how many people did he employ? He said two men. Harry then asked him how long had these two men been working here at his yard. Clayton told him about two years. Harry asked him if the two men were here at the present time. He said they were.

Harry said he would like to talk to them, one at a time.

1

Clayton said, "Sure." He opened the door to the garage and shouted, "Dale, come here for a minute."

Clayton introduced Harry to Dale Pratt.

Harry asked Dale to come with him to his car. He wanted to ask him a few questions in private. He informed him that he was not a suspect.

Dale said, "Sure, I'd be happy to."

Harry asked Ben to get the police security tape and place it around the Coronet.

Harry and Dale sat in Harry's car. Harry told him he expected him to answer his questions truthfully. Dale said he would, and that he had nothing whatsoever to hide.

After questioning Dale, Harry did not think that he knew or saw the man that drove the red Coronet into the yard.

Harry next questioned a man named Luther Harlow. Luther said yes, he remembered the day the man drove the red Dodge Coronet into the yard. He said it was snowing that day. He was about to walk to his car to clean off the snow, when he saw the red car coming. He said he stopped to see what the man wanted. The car stopped, the man got out, threw him the key, which he said he caught, and the man said, "The wreck is all yours. It burns more oil than gas." He said the man went to the rear of the car and took the licence plate, which must have been taped on, because the man just reached down and ripped it off, and walked away. He said there was no plate on the front.

Harry asked Luther for a description of the man.

Luther said he really couldn't tell how old the man was. He was about five feet nine or ten, slim, long hair, he had a moustache and he walked with a slight limp.

Harry wrote down all the information and thanked Luther for his co-operation.

As they were getting out of the car, Ben was walking toward them. The three of them went back into the building.

Ben thanked Clayton for his co-operation and he told him that the red Coronet in the third row of cars had police security tape around it.

Clayton said, "No one will touch it."

"Thank you," said Ben.

Harry and Ben headed for their car. Suddenly, Ben stopped. He said, "Wait a minute." Harry came to a halt. He looked at Ben. Ben said, "Four bullets went into the back of that car. I am almost certain that Blake fired these bullets. However, if we were to find one in that car, then Ballistics could prove it beyond a shadow of a doubt."

"You are absolutely right Ben," said Harry. "If you had not said anything about finding a bullet in that car by the time we reached my car, I would have asked you if there was anything we missed, like was there anything else we could have looked for. You think like a veteran Ben. Let's go back and see if we can find the Lone Ranger's silver bullet."

They went and saw Clayton once more and told him they were going to check on something that may be in the car.

When they opened the trunk, they could see where two of the bullets entered the back seat. Upon further examination they found that one of the bullets had passed through the seat, but the other one had not.

Harry took out his Boy Scout pocket knife, and after determining where to cut the front of the back seat, he started to cut into the material. He cut out a four-inch square section of the seat. He pulled out the material but did not find anything. He cut a little deeper and his blade hit a piece of metal. Then he started to cut out material below the metal. Suddenly, a bullet fell out onto the seat. "Hello," said Harry, "thanks for sticking around. Nice to see you." He looked at Ben. They both laughed. Harry picked up the bullet. The back half was in good shape. He wrapped it in his spare handkerchief, placed it in his pocket, and said "Let's get out of here before we get charged with vandalism." (Once again laughter.) They stopped in to tell Clayton what they had done. He said, "I would never have sold that back seat anyway."

Ballistics later proved that the bullet found in the red Coronet was fired by Blake Bradley's side arm. Shortly after that confirmation, Ben and Harry went to see Ray Morrison. It was a Friday, there was nobody home.

They decided to go back on Saturday morning.

Parked in the driveway was a grey Chevy Bel Air.

Ben had memorized the licence plate number. As they walked by the car, Ben told Harry that the car was the one registered to Ray Morrison.

Harry said, "Car in the driveway, he must be home."

They proceeded to the front door and rang the doorbell.

A lady opened the door. She said, "Whatever you're selling, we're not buying."

Harry said, "Lady, we are not selling anything." He then introduced himself and Ben, and showed her his badge. He asked her if Ray was home.

She said, "Yes, what has he done? Why are you here?"

Ben said, "We would like to talk to him, it's important."

The lady yelled, "Ray, you are wanted at the door." (Ben did not think that Ray would recognize him.)

Ray appeared and walked slowly towards them.

He said, "How can I help you, gentlemen?"

Harry once again introduced himself. But he did not introduce Ben. He showed Ray his badge, and asked him if he was Ray Morrison.

"Yes, that's my name," he said.

Harry then told the lady that he would like to speak to Ray in private. (The lady left.) He then asked Ray if they could step inside the door.

Ray said, "Sure." Both Harry and Ben realized that Ray Morrison fitted the description given by Luther Harlow and they nodded their heads as they glanced at each other.

Harry then told Ray he was under arrest, for the attempted murder of a police officer. He read him his right to remain silent and his right to a lawyer.

Ray said, "There must be some mistake, sir. I didn't attempt to kill anyone."

"We know, we have proof Ray, that you fired a shot at a police officer from the side window of your red Dodge Coronet. Lies will lead to a longer sentence. You are lucky the police officer survived, otherwise you would be charged with murder one. I guess you are lucky you are a poor shot." (Ray did not say another word.)

"Put handcuffs on Mr. Morrison, Officer Breakwater," said Harry. When Ray heard the name Breakwater, he had a flashback – he remembered that name from the newspaper article that said Officer Breakwater was only wounded and was expected to make a full recovery. He knew he had drank too much that night, and he remembered after reading the article, he looked up and said, "Thank you, God." Then he came back to the present and realized the officer he shot that night was now standing behind him, putting him in handcuffs. He thought, how ironic.

Ray Morrison went to trial. The charge was attempted murder. The evidence was overwhelming.

He pled guilty. He told the judge that he acted in haste and did not intend to kill the police officer. He said he had far too much to drink that night.

Ray Morrison was sentenced to eight years in jail.

CHAPTER 25

CORA AND ROGER WERE MARRIED ON THE 30TH OF JUNE 1967. They left Toronto on the third of July for a two-week honeymoon in New York City.

Ben and Anna made frequent visits to the Riverboat Coffee House on Yorkville Avenue in Toronto. It was a very popular venue for entertainment in the sixties. It helped launch the careers of Gordon Lightfoot, Joni Mitchell and Neil Young. Others that Ben and Anna saw there were John Prine, Doc Watson, Arlo Guthrie, Kris Kristofferson and Bob Dylan.

Sanford was now two years old. Anna and Ben had not changed a diaper in four months. As usual there was still the occasional accident. When he was two and a half, he was taking swimming lessons.

They spent many hours reading stories to him. He loved books, especially ones with pictures of animals. He could recognize many animals.

Shortly after his third birthday, Ben and Anna took Sanford to Marineland in Niagara Falls. They had never seen him so excited. He wore a permanent smile the whole time they were there.

The day he turned four, Ben and Anna took him to see their Newfie friend Larry Whitmore. His golden retriever had a litter of pups that were two months old. When he saw the puppies, Sanford became even more excited than when he was in Marineland. The puppies were all over him and he loved it.

Larry saw how much Sanford loved these puppies. His heart was filled with joy as he watched the little boy interact with the puppies. Without Sanford's knowledge, Larry asked Ben and Anna if it would be okay with them if he gave Sanford a puppy. (How could they refuse?) They told Larry it was very kind of him and it would be the happiest moments in their little boy's life, to own a puppy.

Sanford was on his knees hugging one of the puppies. Larry knelt facing him. The boy looked up and he was wearing a big smile. Larry said, "Would you like to take that puppy home with you, and he would be yours?"

The little boy nodded his head as he looked at his mom and dad. He said, "Can I Dad?"

Ben said, "Sure you can, Son."

He looked back at the puppy he was holding, and tears of joy ran down his little cheeks.

Larry said, "You can choose any one you like."

The little boy said, "This one, thank you."

Larry said, "You are welcome Sanford, and I think he likes you."

Sanford nodded his head as he looked at his mom. Anna saw how much joy that little dog was giving her son, as it wagged its tail and licked its new owner's face. She was nearly as thrilled as Sanford was. She would long remember her son's first puppy.

Larry said, "We better put a collar on him, so you will know which one is yours. They all look the same to me." (He went and found a collar and put it on Sanford's puppy.)

Larry suggested they pick up a book and learn about Golden Retrievers. He also told them to be consistent in their house training. Take him out first thing in the morning and to the same place as before. Dogs know where they went before, and they will do their thing in that same place. He also told them not to feed him between meals.

They had driven Anna's Mustang to see Larry. Ben drove home. Anna watched Sanford in the back seat of the car. At times he was lying down holding the puppy, other times the puppy was on top of him as he lay on his back. Sanford was having the time of his life. Anna also shed a few tears of joy.

Ben said, "Sanford, we have to give him a name." (Silence followed as the three of them thought of a name.)

Ben said, "How about Ruffy?"

Sanford said, "Tuffy, that's a good name." Ben did not bother to correct his son and repeat the name Ruffy, and therefore Sanford had really named his dog. Ben would tell him later.

Ben did purchase a book and read it several times to Sanford. The little boy knew more about his dog than most adults.

The pleasure the little dog gave the boy was unmeasurable. The only time they were separated was at meal time and for training sessions at the training school for dogs. Ben and Sanford took him there several evenings each week.

When Sanford took his afternoon nap, Tuffy slept beside his bed in his doggie bed they had bought at a pet store. Tuffy ran free in their large fenced backyard. He would fetch anything they would throw. They took him for many walks.

Many evenings, Tuffy did not want to come into the house. He would lie on the lawn as if to say, "I want to sleep under the stars tonight."

Ben suggested they build a dog house for Tuffy, and he could sleep in it until the weather turned cold.

As much as Sanford wanted Tuffy to sleep in his room with him, he was in favour of the dog house.

Ben called Larry, who he knew was handy with a saw and hammer.

They went shopping the following Saturday for the material to build a dog house. Six hours later a dog house sat in the backyard.

Ben asked Sanford to get one of Tuffy's blankets from his bedroom and place it in the dog house.

Tuffy immediately went into the dog house and lay on the blanket. With eyes wide open he looked at the four pairs of eyes looking at him - Sanford, Ben, Anna and Larry. They all had a good laugh.

Ben later made Tuffy's bed a little more comfortable by placing one of his old camping blankets under the blanket that Sanford had placed in the dog house.

Tuffy was now six months old. He had known his name for quite a while. He was now one third grown and weighed just over twenty-eight pounds. He seldom barked. Usually he barked when Ben would play a little roughhouse with him in the backyard. At night he never barked.

Ben remarked to Anna that Tuffy would not make a good guard dog. He didn't even bark when someone rang the doorbell. However, he was a lovely pet, obedient, intelligent and friendly.

Many times, Ben, Anna and Sanford would take Tuffy to the Toronto Lake Front to swim in Lake Ontario. He loved the water. Most times Sanford would also swim. Sanford was a good swimmer. Anna once joked with Ben that seeing Sanford in the water, she wondered if he was a kid or a fish.

Ben told her that Sanford was a better swimmer at four years old than he was at seven or eight. He said it just proves that the swimming lessons are the best way to teach a child to swim.

It was mid-summer, and Tuffy spent most nights in his dog house. He could be found every morning waiting on the deck by the door for his breakfast.

It was a Sunday, the fourth of August 1970. Sanford awakened and immediately thought of Tuffy, who he knew would be waiting at the back door. He went to the washroom and then he headed for the back door. He opened the door and looked through the screen of the second door. He could not see Tuffy. He then opened the second door, but did not see Tuffy. He walked out onto the deck and looked at the dog house. He could see inside, but could not see Tuffy. He called his name. The dog did not show. He ran across the lawn and saw that the gate was open. He ran through the gate, and between the houses calling Tuffy's name. When he reached the front lawn, he looked in all directions. Tuffy was nowhere to be seen. He started to cry. He ran back to the back door, into the house, and ran to his parents' bedroom door.

He formed a little fist and rapped on the door. He called out, "Mom, Dad."

The knock on the door woke Anna. Then she heard Sanford call, "Mom, Dad." She quickly slipped out of bed and opened the bedroom door.

Sanford stood there with tears on his cheeks. He looked up at Anna and said, "Tuffy is gone, the gate is open, Tuffy is gone." He once again started to cry.

Anna called Ben as she picked up Sanford and hugged him. She said, "Don't worry son, we will try and find him."

Ben was now on his feet. He said, "Find who?" Then he heard Sanford crying.

Anna said, "Tuffy is missing, the gate is open."

Ben pulled on his jeans and headed for the back door. He thought his son may have been dreaming. He did not see the dog and ran to check the gate. It was open. He ran to the front lawn, looked in all directions. There was no sign of Tuffy. He shook his head, almost in disbelief, that the much-loved dog had disappeared. Sanford had not been dreaming.

Reality began to sink in. To go back in the house and face his broken-hearted son would be the most difficult thing he had faced since he was told his dad had died. But face it he must. He would have to put the most positive spin on this most unfortunate situation. Someone had taken his son's dog. He asked himself the question, who and why?

As he slowly walked back to the backyard, he tried to think of what to say to his son. Could he promise him that they would find his dog? That may be unwise. Maybe he would promise him they would try very hard to find his dog.

As he walked up the steps of the deck, he met Anna, who still had Sanford in her arms. He was still crying. He heard

Anna say, "We are so sorry son, we will try to find Tuffy, I don't know how he got out."

Through his sobs, Sanford said, "Some bad person opened the gate and took him away, and we will never find him. Tuffy is gone forever."

Ben was now standing in front of Anna and Sanford. He said, "Son, we will do our best to try and find Tuffy. Maybe whoever took him may let him go, and he will find his way home. Dogs can do that, you know."

"I know," said the boy. "I remember you read that in the book. Dogs can find their way home."

Anna said, "Maybe the person will feel bad about taking your dog, and he may let him go."

"We hope he does," said Ben, "and before we call the police, let's drive around and try to find him." He looked at his watch. It was six-thirty a.m.

They drove all around the neighbourhood. There was no sign of Tuffy. In his heart Ben did not expect to find him in the area. He knew if the dog was free, he would be back home.

Sanford was a very sad little boy. They did not find his dog. He went to his room, lay on his bed and looked at Tuffy's bed beside his. He cried until he fell to sleep.

Ben called the police to report the dog missing. He explained the circumstances to the officer, the dog's name, type, age and address. He had little hope that the police would ever find the dog. It could be miles away by now, who knows. He hoped not.

After making the phone call, Ben began thinking. He partly blamed himself. He should have put a really good lock on the gate. He knew locks could be cut with large cutters, however, a lock would have prevented easy access. The he started to ask himself questions – How would a stranger know the dog was there in the backyard. Could any of his neighbours have taken the dog? No, why would they, unless they planned to sell the dog. He just couldn't believe that could happen.

Six days later the dog was still missing.

Ben, Anna and Sanford were eating breakfast. The dog had never left Ben's mind. Suddenly, it flashed through his mind – visitors in the neighbourhood – could it be possible that someone visiting a friend or relative near Ben's house could have seen the dog, then came back later and took it. He would have to check out the possibility.

Both neighbours on either side of Ben knew the dog went missing. He would start with them.

He visited Ted and Fran. They had had no visitors.

Next, he went to see Cecil and Marie. They also had no visitors. However, they said they had been away on vacation for ten days in July and their son Rick came to check on their house. They were quite sure that their son would never do such a thing. They told Ben that Rick was a cat person, and not fond of dogs. Ben was now thinking he would have to check out the other neighbours across the street.

Cecil and Marie were walking him to the door. Ben slowed his pace. He had a feeling he had missed something. Suddenly, it came to him. Their son Rick, did he bring any of his friends with him to their house? He then asked Cecil and Marie. They said that Rick had visited them often, but he always came alone. However, they did not know if he had brought anyone with him when they were away, but they would find out.

Ben thanked them and said he was trying to cover all the bases. They said they understood, and they would call Rick right away. It was seven p.m. Cecil called his son Rick and asked him the question. Cecil then listened as Rick told him that yes, he had brought his new friend Troy a couple of times when he came to check on the house. He said he had met Troy in a bar. He said Troy would come over to his place with a few beers in his back pack, occasionally. Rick said Troy lived with his Uncle Rufus, but did not know his last name. Cecil told his son to remain on the phone and that he would be right back to talk to him.

Cecil then relayed to Ben what Rick had told him. Ben asked Cecil to ask Rick to get Uncle Rufus' last name, and to call him when he knew what it was.

Cecil picked-up the phone and asked his son to get Rufus' last name. He told him it was important and that he would explain later. Rick told his dad he would be in touch.

After Cecil hung up the phone, Ben asked him if he thought his son would do as he had requested.

Cecil said, "Of course he will. I told him it was important. I know my son. I have no doubt he will get Rufus' name, I'd bet my house on it." Ben was now convinced.

Ben thanked him and asked him to please let him know as soon as he found out what Rufus' last name was.

"If you are home, you will know within a minute or two," said Cecil.

Ben went home. Sanford was in his room. He told Anna about the conversation he had with Cecil next door. Ben said maybe this guy Troy had nothing to do with Tuffy disappearing, but to satisfy his mind he had to check him out.

Anna said, "At least it's a start."

Ben said, "If this guy Troy is not involved, I guess I will have to check out more of our neighbours."

Two days went by, and there was no word from Cecil. However, on day three, Ben drove his truck into his driveway around five p.m. As he began walking to his door, he heard someone call his name. It was Cecil. He told Ben he had been watching for him for about half an hour. He said Rick had called about an hour ago and informed him that Uncle Rufus' last name was Stilson.

Ben thanked him and told him he would keep him posted. He rushed into his house and immediately picked up the phone book that was on the coffee table.

Anna came from the kitchen and saw Ben looking in the phone book. She said, "You got Rufus' last name." He nodded. Then he said, "Hi honey, I'm home."

Anna then heard him say 22 Ashley Park Road.

Anna said, "Is that where Rufus lives? I know where it is. It's just east and north of here, off Royal York Road."

"Yes," said Ben. "I remember driving down Royal York Road a few times."

"Now what do we do?" asked Anna.

"First, we will have dinner," said Ben. "Then I will call and have an undercover police officer in an unmarked cruiser pick us up tomorrow evening, and we will go see Uncle Rufus Stilson."

While they ate dinner, Ben was thinking about what his approach would be. He would be ringing the doorbell of a stranger, and for what reason and what would he say? He did not want Rufus to ask him any awkward questions that he may have to answer. He would not mention anything about his lost dog. He really only intended to see Troy. He would make up a little story as to why he wanted to see Troy. He then got up from the table and went to the junk drawer where he kept envelopes. He pulled an envelope from the package. He then took out a blank sheet of paper, folded it and placed it in the envelope, and sealed it. He took a pen from his shirt pocket and wrote Troy on the envelope. He explained to Anna why he did it.

At seven p.m. the next day a cruiser pulled into Ben's driveway. Five minutes later it pulled out, carrying Ben, Anna and Sanford. It was headed for 22 Ashley Park Road. Driving the car was Officer Phil Hayden. Ben had known him for several months.

They parked on the street near 22 Ashley Park Road. Ben got out, walked up the driveway, and rang the doorbell. A tall man with an unkept beard opened the door.

Ben said, "Sorry to bother you, sir. Am I speaking to Mr. Rufus Stilson?" The man stepped out and closed the door.

"You are indeed, young man," said Rufus, "and who are you?"

Ben said, "My name is Ben Breakwater. I really came to see your nephew Troy. Is he in?"

"No, he is out walking his dog," said Rufus. "He should be back soon. What business would you be wanting with Troy?"

"Well," said Ben, "I had a flat tire the other day and Troy happened to come along. He helped me change the tire. I was driving by, so I thought I would drop in and thank him again." Ben pulled out the envelope with Troy written on it, showed it to Rufus, winked at him as if to say a little payment for his trouble.

"Oh," said Rufus, "that's very kind of you." Rufus then looked to his right and said, "Here he comes now."

Ben looked and saw a young man holding a leash and beside him walked a Golden Retriever. He was about the same size as Tuffy. Ben held his breath for a few moments. As Troy and the dog got a little closer Ben yelled, "Tuffy". The dog sprang ahead and ripped the leash from Troy's hand and raced toward Ben who was now on his knees. The dog was all over him.

"I'll be damned," said Rufus. "That dog sure knows you."

"He sure does," said Ben. Anna was looking out the car window. She could hardly believe her eyes. Sanford did not see Tuffy and his dad.

The police officer said, "Anna, let your boy out of the car." He stepped out and walked toward Ben's location.

Anna opened the back door and Sanford got out of the car. He then saw the dog licking his dad's face. He was overcome with joy. He also yelled, "Tuffy". The dog immediately looked in the boy's direction, and made three jumps, and as he had done with Ben, he was once again all over the little boy, who was now shedding tears of joy. This all happened very quickly. Troy just stood there and didn't say a word.

Once more, Rufus spoke, "I'll be double damned," as he observed the boy and the dog. He looked at Troy and said, "I think the owners have found their dog."

Troy just nodded his head.

Ben walked to where Troy stood. He said, "Where did you get that dog Troy?"

Troy said, "I found him over in the park. I asked everyone I saw, and I could not find the owner, so I brought him home with me. I took him back to the park every evening. Nobody claimed him."

Officer Hayden was standing about five feet away and heard every word Troy said. He stepped closer to Troy and said, "Why should we believe what you are telling us Troy?"

"Because it's the truth," said Troy. (Rufus was still watching the boy and the dog.)

Officer Hayden walked over to where Rufus was standing. He said, "Tell me sir, how did Troy explain to you where he got that dog?"

Rufus said, "He told me he found him in the park. He said he was a stray, and he could not find the owner."

"Do you believe him?" asked Officer Hayden.

"I see no reason he would lie to me," said Rufus.

"Well sir," said Officer Hayden, "that dog was stolen from that little boy's backyard a week ago, and it broke his little heart. You have witnessed how much that boy loves his dog." Officer Hayden then showed Rufus his badge.

"Yes sir," said Rufus, "I understand what you are saying. I told Troy to call the police and tell them about the dog."

"He didn't call sir," said Officer Hayden. "I guess there are two reasons he didn't. One, he didn't want to involve the police, for reasons only he knows. Two, he really did think the dog was a stray and he wanted to keep him. I will leave these thoughts with you, Mr. Stilson. We will be leaving now. Thank you for your co-operation." He nodded to Ben who was standing beside his son, Anna and Tuffy.

They all got back in the cruiser with an addition they were very happy to reacquire.

Two days later, twenty-two-year-old Troy Stilson called the police. He told them he was the one who stole the Golden Retriever on Robin Hood Road. He said he was very sorry and he was prepared to take his punishment.

The police picked up Troy at his uncle's place. He was charged with the theft of the Breakwater's dog.

He pled guilty. He told the Justice of the Peace that he would not have taken the dog if he had known it belonged to a little boy.

The Justice of the Peace told him he should have known that it was wrong to take the dog under any circumstances. He said he stole someone's property. Because it was his first offence, the Justice of the Peace gave him a suspended sentence and six months' probation.

CHAPTER 26

BEN AND ANNA OFTEN TOOK SHOWERS TOGETHER. BEN TOLD her it would save water. Anna knew it was for a different reason, however, she enjoyed it. Ben had only one regret whenever and wherever he and Anna got naked. He had told Anna even before the first time they made love, that she would be the boss whenever they got naked. Anna held him to his word.

Ben did not like having to interrupt their times of passion to put on a condom. Anna told him that she was the one that had to carry their baby for nine months, therefore, it should be her decision how many times she wanted to get pregnant.

Anna loved working as a dental Assistant, however, she definitely wanted more than one child, and she wanted a daughter. Sanford was now five years old and starting school in September.

As she drove home from work, she decided it was time to try and get pregnant again. She smiled as she thought of a way to let Ben know she wanted another baby.

That night as they cuddled naked in bed (they always slept in the nude), once again their passion grew and as usual, Ben put on a condom. Anna didn't say a word. She reached down and removed the condom. Then she said, "I like it better when there is nothing between us. Give me your best shot. I want a baby girl."

Ben was a happy man. No condoms for months to come. Anna received two shots that night.

Nine months later Anna gave birth to a seven-pound, five ounce baby girl. She was thrilled. They named her Selina Audrey, the names of both her grandmothers.

Time passed quickly for the Breakwater family. Ben gained a lot of experience as a detective. He loved working on difficult cases with Harry King. Ben thought he was the most intelligent man he had ever known. One day, Ben called Harry Mr. Einstein. Harry said, "No, I am not Albert Einstein. He was a very smart man, however, not as smart as Mr. Hindsight". (This brought a chuckle from both.)

Ben would never forget the story that Harry had told him about his first camping trip with his Uncle Gene. Harry said he was about ten years old. His uncle had asked him if he had an air mattress to sleep on in the tent. Harry had told him he didn't need one, he would sleep on the ground. His uncle had said, "Okay little tough guy, you sleep on the ground, I will sleep on my air mattress."

The next morning, as they were eating breakfast, his Uncle Gene asked him if he had slept well. Harry said he had admitted that sleeping on the ground was not a good idea, and he sure would like to have an air mattress. His uncle had said, "I want you to remember what I am going to say, and that is, any fool can be uncomfortable."

Harry said he never forgot that phrase. He said it was a lesson well learned. Gene had been a Royal Canadian Mounted Police Officer for twenty years.

Harry related another little story Gene had told him on the same camping trip.

Gene had been stationed in Regina, Saskatchewan. A bank robber had been apprehended. Gene was transporting him to the local jail house. He asked the man why he had robbed the bank. The man said it was the quickest way to get money. Gene had told him, "Yes it was, however, it's against the law and a sure way to lose your freedom". He then said to the man, "I am going to tell you something, and I want you to listen very carefully. Let it sink into your brain, just seven simple words – long-term pain for short-term gain."

Gene liked to talk to people. He told the man, "There are lots of stupid things people do for short-term gain. The question you have to ask yourself is, Is it worth it? Point in question: You robbed the bank. You didn't even get to spend the money. Now you are going to jail. Like I said, long-term pain for short-term gain."

Gene told Harry that he hoped he planted a positive seed in the man's head.

Harry told Ben that he was only ten years old, but he never forgot about long-term pain. He said it kept him out of trouble, unlike a few of his high school buddies.

It's now the summer of 1971. If one wanted to hear live country music, the Horseshoe Tavern on Queen Street in Toronto was the place to be. It had opened its doors December ninth, 1947. Many country music stars played there in the fifties and sixties.

Ben and Anna decided to check out the Horseshoe Tavern one Saturday night. They did not know who was playing that evening. Before they entered they saw a poster that was displayed. The name of the entertainer was Stompin' Tom Connors.

Ben had heard the name and knew he was from the Maritimes.

The place was full of people. They were lucky to find a seat. They enjoyed the performance very much.

When Stompin' Tom announced his pause for the cause, Ben headed for the washroom. When he came back to his seat, he had a big grin on his face.

Anna asked him what was the big smile all about?

Ben informed her that he was standing at the urinal in the washroom, when a man came in and stood next to him. It was Stompin' Tom. Ben told him he really enjoyed the show. Stompin' Tom said, "Thanks, thanks for coming." Ben and Anna saw him several times at the Horseshoe Tavern.

The summer of 1972, Ben and Anna attended a wedding in Breakwater. Tommy Seal and Suzie Walsh were married. Tommy was doing very well. He was now part owner of the car dealership with his Uncle Gordon.

Ben asked Tommy what was the latest news around Breakwater.

Tommy said he had news, but not many in Breakwater knew of it. He then told Ben that he had found out from a very reliable source that Robert Pebble did in fact commit suicide.

Ben and Anna were driving back to Toronto from Breakwater. They had left Breakwater around nine-thirty on Sunday morning. Ben was driving Anna's Mustang. Twenty minutes later they saw a lady hitchhiking. Ben slowed a little and asked Anna if they should pick her up. (Hitchhiking was very common in the 1960's and 1970's.) Anna said, "Sure, let's give the poor girl a ride."

Ben stopped the car. Anna rolled down the window and asked her where she was headed. She replied, "Toronto."

Anna said, "Your lucky day, that's where we are headed, although we will stop in Belleville for a while."

The Mustang was a two-door coupe. Anna got out and moved the back of the seat forward so that the young lady could get in the back. Suddenly, she felt a hand grab her left arm, and a male voice said, "You get in the back seat." Anna looked and saw a man with long hair, an unshaven face, holding a knife in his left hand. (Ben looked and saw the knife.) Ben said, "Do what the man said."

Anna quickly slipped into the back seat. The man followed her in. The young lady sat in the front passenger seat and closed the door. (It all happened very quickly.)

Ben looked over his shoulder and said, "You don't need that knife. Where do you want to go?"

The man said, "Don't tell me what I need, I am in control. Take us to Toronto, now drive."

Ben pulled back on the road and accelerated to the speed limit. He looked in the rear-view mirror but could not see the knife. He did not want to put Anna in any danger therefore he would have to do whatever the man said. He noticed the man wore an earring in his left ear. He hoped Anna would be able to give a really good description of the man.

Ben was wishing he had his side arm handy. He could surprise the man when they arrived in Toronto, and stopped at a red light. He would have to wait and see what transpired when they arrived at the man's destination.

In his peripheral vision Ben saw the young lady in the front seat open her purse and remove her lipstick and a little mirror. She proceeded to deftly apply the lipstick. She placed both back in her purse. In the rear view mirror, he could see the man but he could not see Anna. He thought she was sitting as far away as possible from him. Ben hoped she would not try anything foolish. He did not think she would. Many thoughts went through his mind as he drove. They guy must have been hiding in the ditch. Was he on drugs? He must want more than a ride to Toronto. He will probably demand cash before he runs away. (Ben had about one hundred dollars in his wallet.) He was tempted to just give him the money at his destination and he might just run.

As Ben once more glanced in the rear-view mirror, he saw that the young lady in the front seat was holding a piece of paper in her right hand, down close to where her belly button was. She was looking straight ahead, but she had turned the paper so that Ben could see it. Ben saw the letters HELP written on the paper.

It was now clearly obvious to Ben that this young lady wanted to get away from the man sitting in the back seat. The situation now became more complex. His biggest concern was Anna. However, he also felt obligated to help this young lady. He thought for a minute. He slowly removed his wallet, which he carried in his left front pocket. Slowly he removed a police business card. He placed the wallet on the floor. He checked the rear-view mirror once again. The man was looking out the side window. He quickly placed the card in the lady's lap. He thought – first phase completed.

He noticed the lady smiled as she placed the card in her purse. He hoped the man sitting in the back seat would not think of the possibility of what had just happened. He just might search her purse and that would cost her a beating. Ben had no doubt she would call him at the first opportunity.

Anna wished her car was a four-door sedan. She was thinking if it was, she could open the door and run, when Ben stopped for a red light. She felt trapped. However, she knew Ben would think of something, he always did. She wondered why the man did not speak to the young lady. It seemed strange to her. The man had not touched her, and she was thankful for that. She tried not to think about the possibilities of what might happen when they finally got to the man's destination. She prayed she would not be taken hostage.

Ben was tempted to put the Mustang to work. He could generally increase speed, maybe the man would not notice, and he could get pulled over for speeding. On second thought, this could put Anna at risk. He wanted to avoid that if possible. He decided to play it cool and wait.

They arrived in Toronto. With the sound of silence, it had been a long trip.

The man spoke. He said, "Drive to Victoria Park subway station and stop as close to the entrance to the subway as possible. The two ladies and I will get out, and you, driver, will drive away. I don't want you following me."

Ben said, "I will not leave my woman and drive away."

Silence followed until Ben drove into Victoria Park subway station.

The man said, "Pull into a parking space."

Ben pulled into the first space he saw.

The man leaned forward and tapped Ben on the shoulder with his knife. He said, "Give me all your cash."

Ben reached down with his left hand and found his wallet. He took out the five twenty-dollar bills and handed them to the man, who then tapped the back of the seat and said, "Out girl and start walking toward the subway entrance."

The young lady opened the door and got out and walked away. The man stepped out quickly and said, "Don't follow me." He closed the door and ran. Ben could not see him because of the other cars that were parked. He locked both doors, and backed out of the parking space. He drove out onto the street and after making a right turn he put the right turn signal on and stopped. He unlocked the doors, got out, went around the back of the car and opened the door. Anna pushed the seat forward and quickly exited the car. They hugged. Anna cried.

Ben said, "Let's go home."

When they got back into the car, Ben asked her if the man had touched her. She said he had not.

Ben then told Anna what had happened between him and the young lady.

Anna said, "That changes what I thought of that young girl. He is probably her pimp."

"I agree," said Ben. "If I could get my hands on him in the right place, he would be a very sad and broken pimp. If he had touched you, he would not only be a very sad pimp, I would re-arrange his face, and his plastic surgeon would say, 'There's so much out of place.'"

Anna said, "You're mean, Ben Breakwater."

"Damn right," said Ben, "for the right reason."

Ben stayed close to his office phone the next day, which was Monday. He examined the file of a cold case he was working on. He was hoping to receive a call from the young lady he had given his business card to yesterday. He wondered if the man had found the card. If he had, there would be no phone call, and therefore, no way to track him down, unless by a chance sighting. He went home disappointed, no phone call.

It was Tuesday morning around ten a.m. He had already received a couple of calls. The phone rang once again. Ben looked at the phone and crossed his fingers, and said to himself, "Let it be her." He picked up the phone and said, "Detective Breakwater." A female voice said, "Hi honey." It was Anna. She told him she was going over to visit Cora for the whole afternoon.

As soon as Ben hung up the phone, it rang again. A soft female voice said, "I want to speak to Ben Breakwater."

Ben said, "Speaking."

The lady said, "My pimp's name is Jig, (she spelled it out JIG) that is what he calls himself. I don't know his real name. You can find him at Steele's Tavern on most Friday nights. Please put him in jail, I don't want to live like this anymore." She hung up the phone.

Ben relayed the story to Harry King. Harry said he would accompany him to Steele's Tavern on Friday night. He said it was time they went for a beer anyway.

Ben decided he would wear his oldest work clothes, baseball cap and a fake mustache.

Friday evening, Ben and Harry sat on bar stools at Steele's Tavern. It was seven thirty when they ordered their first beer.

Ben had looked around as they entered, but did not see Jig. He kept his eye on the entrance door.

Suddenly, there he was. He looked around and went to a table in the far corner and sat with his back to the wall. Ben and Harry left the bar and started walking toward the man who called himself Jig. He didn't seem to notice them, as they chatted to each other. They went just past his table then quickly moved back and sat on the two vacant chairs at his table.

He was very surprised. Before he could say a word, Ben said, "Hello Jig. Remember me?" Ben quickly removed his baseball cap and pulled off his mustache. "I drove you to Toronto last Sunday. Fancy seeing you here."

Jig was stone-faced, and didn't say a word.

Ben and Harry showed him their badges and told him he was under arrest for armed robbery, assault and unlawful confinement. (Ben read him his rights.)

The three of them walked out of the tavern. Harry put handcuffs on Jig and opened the back door of the unmarked cruiser. Jig sat in, and Harry closed the door.

Jig's real name was Jaco Ian Gafney. He had previous convictions for assault and armed robbery. He received five years in prison.

Cora and Roger Rimes were now proud parents of twins - a boy and a girl who were three years old. They raised seven children. Roger was a millionaire at age forty-nine. He had done well with the cheque Ben had given him.

Ben attended the Detective Training Course two months after his 25th birthday. He received the highest marks ever given at the Training School in Toronto.

Ben and Anna remained long-time friends with Larry and Cathy Whitmore. They had many camping trips together, and many people enjoyed their music at the campgrounds.

Ben and Anna raised five children – three boys and two girls. All five received a university education. Their oldest son, Sanford, joined the Canadian Armed Forces. He was promoted to the rank of Major just after his 30th birthday.

Anna retired at age 50.

Ben left the Toronto Police Force after serving 20 years. He then joined Joseph Blackmore and worked part-time as a Private Detective, for 10 years.

After their last child left home, Ben and Anna vacationed all over the world.

In 2011, they moved to Niagara Falls, a place Anna wanted to be for many years.

They rented an apartment overlooking the Horseshoe Falls.

1.

THE SPLENDOR OF MOTHER NATURE

OH NAKED TREE

Oh naked tree where are your clothes
I fear that in the wind it blows
It seems like only yesterday
You flourished in the breeze.
You were a home
But like the birds your leaves have flown
Now you await the ice and snow
That in time will freeze your very soul
You have no fear, you understand
Mother nature keeps you in her plan
Come spring you will again display
A brand new wardrobe.

2.

OUR HOME

EARTH

Can you envision the earth suspended in space
Like the moon and planets and yet not a trace
Of a cable, or chain, to hold them in place
Trillions of tons, and spinning as well
At one thousand miles per hour but one could never tell
And moving through space, yet at the same time
At sixty seven thousand miles per hour and never a sign
Of motion, or speed, as if we were still
The great oceans just sit there, as if trapped in a well
It is with great wonder, this I ponder and tell.

3.

THINKING OF A GREAT GIFT

THE ABILITY TO SEE

THE BLIND LAD

While strolling through the park one day
I met a lad who was blind
He said to me there must be beauty to see
But I never see the sun shine

My Mom she tried to tell me
Just what the sun looked like
But I could never imagine
Cause I never saw the light

You see my world is filled with darkness
And I struggle as each day goes by
For only God up in heaven
Can know the reason why

He said you probably take for granted
The fact that you have your sight
When each day you should thank your Maker
For letting you see the light

As we each said our good-byes
He said I'll pray for you tonight
Unto others be ever so kind
And may you always see the light

4.

MANY LONELY SOULS
LOSE THEIR WAY

LIFE

As I sit here alone, on this old cabin floor
  I wonder how many sat here before,
And as I gaze at the moon through the window pane
  I wonder how many will sit here again.

Yes, I wonder how many will sit here again
  Another lost soul looking out through the pane,
If only I could ask that fly on the wall
  And write down the memories of the things that it saw.

It was only last week, I remember it well
  One lonely man came to sit here a spell,
He talked to himself for he was alone
  He had lost all his family, and now on his own.

Once he was wealthy but now he was broke
  Played poker and lost like many a folk,
When you don't pay up you go on the run
  And with the hounds on your trail, it isn't much fun.

About two days ago, no word of a lie
  A young lad staggered in, he was just a boy,
From his pack-sack he pulled out needles and booze
  And proceeded to OD, his young life to lose.

One could say that life is full of death
  Sometimes a blessing but still hard to forget,
Most times dear friends, you reap what you sow
  Life may be best at a constant, not high, not low.

5.

LIVING IN YOUR OWN WORLD

A DREAM OR REALITY

We all have dreams, so it seems
    We look forward to being inspired,
And I'd live my life to the fullest
    Being younger, rich, and retired!

To be younger, rich and retired
    And forever to be my own boss,
To do what I please when I want to
    With no need to worry 'bout cost!

For the cost of living is death
    Whether you're rich or poor,
Immortality can't be achieved
    No matter how high your score!

Last but not least, one could say
    Live every day as your last
Don't burn your bridges, hold your head high
    And leave boredom, to days in the past.

6.

THERE ARE MANY ROADS
IN LIFE TO CHOOSE

THE ROADS OF LIFE

The roads of life are many
Some made of silver and gold
Be careful of devils who walk them
They will lead you and then take your soul

There are so many roads to be taken
And many are laden with sin
But friends if you walk in good faith
Then Jesus will sure take you in

My intention is not to pass judgment
But one must always analyse
For god gave us power to reason
Let that be a word to the wise

So friends when you chose your road
It's you who will reap or you pay
For living in sin is for sinners
And Satan we must cast away

7.

COUNT YOUR BLESSINGS

MOMENTS OF JOY

The sun set in the west
   The moon rose in the east,
I looked at both in wonder
   How precious was my sight.

Thoughts crossed my mind
   I am a lucky soul,
What if I could not see
   Such things we take for granted.

As I walked the hiking trail
   Birds sang in the trees,
The day was bright, my feet seemed light
   People smiled as they walked by.

Thoughts crossed my mind
   I am a lucky soul,
What if I could not walk
   For a moment I was sad.

From a playground bench
   I watched the children play,
There were no cries of discontent
   As little hearts were gay.

Thoughts crossed my mind
   I am a lucky soul,
I live in a land of peace and plenty
   Where else would I want to go?

8.

REMINISCING A LOST LOVE

LOST LOVE

There was sparkle in her eyes
The day that we met
So much love and beauty
No man could forget

But her eyes now tell me
I am not what they see
Another man stands
Where I used to be

That beautiful woman
Now loves a new man
I cannot deny
I know where I stand

I met her, I loved her
What more can I say
She was the ending
To my every day

9.

THE STRUGGLES AND REWARDS OF FAMILIES

CYCLE OF LIFE

A river was once a small stream
Not a story that starts as a dream
Like an end that's just a beginning
But a beginning that leads to an end

We pass the torch and a name
To carry on to glory if not to fame
For a family tree should be tall and strong
Are reasons for us to carry on

With death comes the celebration of life
Remembering all the struggles and strife
From the cradle all the way to the grave
Nothing left but the memories are saved

10.

LOOKING FOR LOVE

I NEED SOMEONE

I need someone to talk to
To be my turtle dove
I need someone to be there
Just in case I fall in love

I need someone when I'm lonely
I need someone when I'm blue
I need someone to love me
Someone just like you

I'm a lover not a fighter
Pleasure is better than pain
I need someone on a sunny day
Or to walk with in the rain

We all need understanding
We all need space to grow
Feelings must be nurtured
And love can make it so

11.

FROM WALKING TO FLYING

TRAVEL

There was a time not long ago
   Man walked where he wanted to go,
Then he paddled rivers narrow and wide
   Then sailed the seas to the other side.

Camels, horses he did ride
   Traveled far in the country side,
Then horse and carriage came in style
   And one could travel many a mile!

A faster way to get around
   One bright man was soon to find,
A steam engine he did make
   Moved one faster than a horse's gait!

Then along came the automobile
   And man traveled on four faster wheels,
Just step on the gas and the engine would roar
   And man traveled faster than ever before!

At last two brothers' glory bound
   Flew a plane above the ground,
Soon man soared into the sky
   Flying fast, to carry, you and I!

12.

LOVE RECIPROCATED

LIGHT OF MY LIFE

You are the light of my life
    You are the days of my week'
You are the months of my year
    And you are the reason I care.

I was out and I was down
    And you picked me up off the ground,
You gave me hope and happiness
    Yes, you gave me all of your best.

So many times I disappoint you
    Yet you love me more every day,
For you have so much love to give
    And now for your love I live.

You became the light of my life
    You're the one who showed me the way,
For I love you more than you know dear
    And my love I will show every day.

13.

FORGOT TO REMEMBER

SENIOR THOUGHTS

Yes, it's mind over matter
   Now where is my mind
To focus at my age is a chore
   There are times these days I should not care
But I just don't remember any more.

Now it's hard to live in the future
   And you sure can't live in the past
The present is all you can count on
   As long as it will last.

14.

PEOPLE SELDOM SMILE
UNDER THEIR UMBRELLA

WHY CARE ABOUT THE RAIN

If you wake up in the morning not in pain
Who cares if it starts to rain
Rain makes the wild flowers grow
So just take your umbrella and go

The sun is always shining don't you know
But you can't always see it from below
The sun is always shining yes it's true
And the sky above the clouds is always blue

A thought just came my way
And I'm not the first to says
Living what the boy scouts say
Do a good deed every day

Be kind whenever you can
It makes good sense my friend
When you let your kindness show
You may live without a foe

If we smiled more often every day as we journey on
our way
If we just slow down our pace
We could make the world a better place16.

15.

THE PAINS OF GROWING OLD

GROWING OLD

If you ever live to ninety
Oh what a wreck you will be
You will need someone else's eyes
Cause with yours you will never see

You may lose your glasses, misplace your slippers
You can't eat with your teeth in a glass
Your bones start to creak, and you have unsteady feet
Feels good, to reach that sofa at last

And when you reach a ripe old age
You have earned the right to boast
Of all the things that you have lost
You miss your mind the most

16.

CHANGE, THE ONLY CONSTANT WE HAVE

CRAZY OLD WORLD

It's a craze old world that we live in
   We'll be here till the day that we die
It seems we have a few choices
   Laugh, put-up, shut-up, or cry.

The world that we live in is changing
   Much deceit, corruption and lies,
Half of us know the score
   The other half closes their eyes

Must be true God loves stupid people
   Just look at how many he made,
When you see them driving their cars
   You know they're in over their heads.

Oh yes the world is gone crazy
   And the only constant is change
I now have a house in the city
   But I wish it was a home on the range!

17.

FROM AN INNOCENT CHILD
TO A DEFIANT TEEN

GROWING UP

A child so innocent
   A mind void of sin
A body so resilient
   Yet fragile within
Their brain is like a sponge
   In all the early days
They want to know everything
   Just listen to their call,
'Till about the age of sixteen
   By then, they know it all!

18.

DERELICTS LEFT ON MANY SHORES

THE BOAT

Twas on a moonlit shore
    I spotted that old boat,
I knew from just a glance
    That no more would it float

And as I scanned it further
    High and dry there where it lay
I thought of my home town
    Where boats bobbed in the bay

Yes, I can see a boat or two
    Like the one before my eyes
And I am sad for it
    Once if floated on the tides

A boat should never be left to rot
    Upon rocks and sand so dry
It should be scuttled in the deep
    Not left to weather and die

CPSIA information can be obtained
at www.ICGtesting.com
Printed in the USA
LVOW03s0903220318
570731LV00001B/1/P